The Quality of Love

sie Harris was born in Cardiff and grew up
re and in the West Country. After her
rriage she resided for some years on
rseyside before moving to Buckinghamshire
re she still lives. She has three grown-up
ldren, six grandchildren and two great-
ndchildren, and writes full time. *The Quality*
ove is her twentieth novel for Arrow.

Also by Rosie Harris

ROSIE HARRIS

The Quality of Love

arrow books

Published by Arrow Books 2009

2 4 6 8 10 9 7 5 3 1

First published in Great Britain in 2009 by
Arrow Books
Random House, 20 Vauxhall Bridge Road,
London, SW1V 2SA

www.rbooks.co.uk

Addresses for companies within The Random House Group Limited
can be found at: www.randomhouse.co.uk/offices.htm

The Random House Group Limited Reg. No. 954009

A CIP catalogue record for this book
is available from the British Library

ISBN 9780099527381

Typeset in Palatino by Palimpsest Book Production Limited
Grangemouth, Stirlingshire
Printed and bound in Great Britain by
CPI Cox & Wyman, Reading, RG1 8EX

For the Hunt family:
Kathryn, Davin, Marc and Charlotte

Acknowledgements

Behind every book is an editorial team and mine, headed by Georgina Hawtrey-Woore is fabulous. My thanks also to Caroline Sheldon – an essential link.

Chapter One

1920

'Dad, I've been offered a place at Cardiff University and I'll be starting in September,' Sarah Lewis exclaimed triumphantly, passing the letter she'd received that morning across the table to her father as they sat down to their evening meal.

'I'm very pleased to hear that,' Lloyd Lewis stated in a crisp, satisfied voice as he took the letter from her and briefly scanned the contents. 'It's only what I expected with the results you obtained in your Higher School Certificate.'

Sarah bit her lip, trying to hide the tears of disappointment that welled up in her eyes. She'd managed to fulfil their expectations and yet for all that, her father seemed to take almost for granted what she'd had to work so hard to achieve.

A tall, slim seventeen-year-old with shoulder-length thick brown hair and hazel eyes, she was very like her father and sometimes she wondered whether he'd have showered her with praise if she'd been doll-like and petite like her mother.

Although she was nearly forty, Lorna Lewis was still very attractive; she had fair hair, huge grey eyes and a peaches-and-cream complexion. She had an air of serenity about her and her dainty mouth tilted at the corners almost as if she was about to smile at any minute.

Sarah was sure that her mother looked so calm and poised because she led such a charmed life. It was clear to the whole world that her husband adored her and couldn't do enough for her. His attention seemed to be focussed on her and her alone whenever they were together. She usually responded in the same way; it was as if an invisible thread bound them together and they were wrapped in a cocoon which separated them from the rest of the world.

Everything her mother did, whether it was the way she ironed his shirts or how she cooked their evening meal, seemed to bring warm praise from her father. In his eyes she was not only the perfect wife but also exemplary in every way. In her hands he was like putty and she could twist him round her little finger with no effort at all.

Sarah sometimes felt that her mother would drain every drop of love and affection from him and it made her afraid that there might not be any left over for her. There were times when she felt almost an interloper in their lives; an intruder in her own home. It was almost as if they didn't need her, or anyone else, for that matter; all they wanted was each other.

It hadn't always been like that and she wished that she and her mother were still as close as they'd been when she'd been much younger and that Lorna still took her in her arms and hugged her, stroked her hair and kissed her as she used to do.

Although her father was affectionate towards her, always listened to what she had to say and encouraged her, he could be quite strict and he set very high standards, Sarah reflected.

Ever since she could remember he had been urging her to study so that she could make something of herself. She wondered if it was because he would have preferred to have had a son rather than a daughter. A boy who'd grow up to be tall, powerful and as good-looking as he was; someone to fulfil his dreams and ambitions which had been cut short when he'd been called up to serve in the army when war had broken out in 1914.

He'd come through completely unscathed; in fact, it might almost be claimed that he'd had a 'good war' because he'd never left England and had risen from being a private to the important rank of Warrant Officer. She could still remember how excited her mother had been the day he'd come home on leave with a crown above the three stripes on his arm.

It made the coolness of her mother's reaction when she told her parents that she'd been given

3

a place at university all the more disappointing, Sarah thought resentfully. It made her wonder if perhaps her friend Rita was right and it was a waste of time and she'd be better off getting an office job and being independent.

If she went to university then she'd have to rely on her dad for spending money and for an allowance for her clothes for at least the next three years.

More importantly, they'd go on treating her as if she were still a child. The way they frowned in disapproval when she said something frivolous made her feel rebellious. And it made her feel so self-conscious that she turned red in the face, lost the thread of what she was saying, and ended up talking nonsense.

These days her education was the one and only thing that seemed to matter to her parents. Ever since she was about ten they'd expected her to be top of her class. When she'd managed to pass the high school exam there had been expressions of relief from both of them. It was the only time that she could recall that her father had really praised her and said how proud he was of her achievements.

At the time, she'd hoped they would let her have a party and invite all her school friends but no matter how hard she pleaded neither of them would agree.

'That would be boasting,' her father pointed out, 'and think how those who didn't manage to pass the exam would feel.'

She could never remember them having a party, not even when her dad had come home from the war and everybody was celebrating. She was sure that her mam would have loved to have had one; except, of course, that the moment her dad was home again her mam had no time for anyone else.

She and her mother had both enjoyed the war years. She'd just started at the high school and with her father away they'd become quite close. True, there had been a good many shortages and a lot of bad news, but they'd never really had to worry like some of their neighbours who'd had husbands or sons fighting over in France.

Her mother hadn't gone out to work because she'd told everybody that Lloyd strongly disapproved of women going into munitions. He didn't even approve of them doing any work at all; he claimed that a woman's place was at home and her work should be taking care of her family.

He hadn't even liked her having to go down on her hands and knees to scrub the front step and whiten it and willingly would have paid a char woman to do it for her but Lorna had said that other people in the street would probably never have spoken to her again if that had happened.

He always made sure that he was first up in the morning so that he could clean out the ashes from the grate, light the fire and boil the kettle and take her up a cup of tea before she came down to make his breakfast.

He hated washdays; he always insisted on lighting the fire that heated up the huge copper in the scullery so that she could boil the white linen and towels and if he was at home he would always turn the handle of the heavy wooden mangle rather than let her do it.

Lorna's war work, as she liked to call it, had been helping a group of other ladies from the chapel they attended to pack parcels to send to the soldiers who were overseas but she'd only done this a couple of times a week.

It had meant that she was always there when Sarah came home from school and that she was always happy to spend plenty of time with her. They shared so many interests and spent many hours together because Lorna liked to go out and about as much as she possibly could.

In fact, Sarah reflected, they'd enjoyed each other's company and for four years she'd had a wonderful life. Then her father had come home again and all her mother's interest and attention had been diverted away from her and was focussed on him, she thought morosely. It had been almost as if the two of them were on a second honeymoon and she'd cried herself to sleep night after night because she'd felt so utterly alone.

There were times when she'd felt so unhappy that she wished her father had never come back, and that the ground would open and swallow him up, so that she could go on being the centre of her mother's world. She endured a patchwork of frenzied emotions and tasted bitterness and sadness as she struggled to come to terms with the situation.

Perhaps it would have been better if she'd had a brother or sister like her best friend Rita Evans; she had both. Rhys was two years older than Rita and Kelly was three years younger. Although they seemed to squabble a great deal and had their own friends they were always there for each other. You couldn't possibly feel lonely in the Evans household, she thought enviously.

Mr and Mrs Evans didn't seem to take anywhere near such an avid interest in what Rita, her brother and sister achieved although they always praised them. They always had an open house for all their friends and Mrs Evans had hugged Sarah and wished her well when she'd told her she was going in for the School Certificate and patted her on the back and wished her every success when they knew she was sitting her Higher School Certificate exam a year later.

Whenever Sarah brought Rita home her mother always seemed on edge and rarely spoke to her friend, apart from saying hello and goodbye, and she was quick to criticise what they'd being doing or what she'd heard them saying to each other and sometimes she even commented unfavourably on what Rita was wearing.

Once when Rita had turned up wearing

lipstick Lorna had told Sarah that if she ever caught her daubing her face like that she'd ask her father to punish her. When she had pointed out to her mam that she always used lipstick, rouge and face powder, her mam had told her not to be cheeky and sent her up to her room.

When she'd told Rita what had happened Rita had shrugged dismissively and, flicking back her long, fair hair, had said that all parents were the same. 'They don't like to think that you're growing up,' she'd laughed. 'My dad didn't approve the first time I wore some lipstick but if you stand up for yourself, or simply ignore them, they soon get used to it.'

'I don't think my mam and dad would,' Sarah told her despondently. 'They'd most probably send me off to my room for being defiant and audacious like my mam did when I said that she used lipstick so why couldn't I.'

'You want to remind them that you're almost eighteen and that it's the nineteen twenties and women have completely changed since the end of the war.'

'You mean that nowadays women are not content to stay at home leading humdrum lives cooking, cleaning and looking after the children any more.'

'Exactly! Now that I'm earning money I intend to have a good time and after I've given Mam some for my keep I intend to spend the rest on clothes and make-up and anything else I want.'

8

'It's all right for you because you've left school and have started work,' Sarah sighed.

'Then do the same,' Rita told her as they linked arms and began to walk towards the shops.

'I'm going to university because I know it will please my dad,' Sarah sighed. 'It's something he's dreamed about me doing ever since I passed the high school exam, and if I don't then both he and my mam will be terribly upset and I couldn't bear the thought of that because I do want to make them proud of me.'

'You're quite mad,' Rita laughed, tugging on her arm so that they could cross the road and look in the window of a dress shop. 'You could even leave home if you wanted to; if they make a fuss, threaten to do just that.'

'And where would I go and what would I live on? I've no money!'

'You would have if you found yourself a job. You should have taken a shorthand and typing course and then you could have worked in an office like I'm doing. There are plenty of office jobs going in Cardiff.'

'And where would I live? I don't think my dad would let me go on living at home if I disobeyed him like that and if he disapproved I know my mother wouldn't go against his wishes; she never does.'

'You could always come and live with us and share my room,' Rita told her.

'It sounds wonderful but it would break my

dad's heart. He's expecting me not only to go to university and end up with a degree but also to find some really good job afterwards.'

'Like what?'

'I don't know yet. It all depends on what subjects I take. Getting a degree is the important thing in his eyes.'

'Sounds very snobbish to me,' Rita retorted. 'Still,' she sighed, 'if that's what you've set your heart on doing then I suppose it's no good me wasting time talking about it. Maybe one of these days I'll end up as your secretary,' she added with a grin.

'Perhaps, but I would much rather you remained my friend.' Sarah smiled, linking her arm through Rita's and hugging her.

Lloyd Lewis felt a warm glow of satisfaction as he moved away from the table and settled down in his favourite armchair by the fireside and waited for Lorna to bring him a cup of coffee. The knowledge that Sarah had obtained a place at Cardiff University filled him with a tremendous feeling of pride. It was the culmination of one of his dearest dreams.

He looked round the comfortably furnished room with a feeling of satisfaction. Lorna was an excellent homemaker; the furniture was good without being ostentatious and the furnishings had all been chosen with great care. The room was devoid of clutter and yet it had a warmth and homeliness that reflected Lorna's good taste. It was very different from the small hill-side terraced house that had been his childhood home in Pontypridd.

He'd moved on since those days, he thought complacently. Not for him shift work and coal dust in the gruelling darkness of the pits where there was the constant dread of a cave-in and being trapped underground. That had been the lot of his father and of his father before him.

His decision to come to Cardiff after he'd left school had been a good move and it was one he'd never regretted.

His mother had died when he'd been ten and from then on he'd been a latchkey child and had run wild because, being an only child, he'd been left very much to his own devices.

He'd been almost fourteen when his father had been trapped down the pit in an underground explosion. He still sometimes woke in the night, remembering the long hours of waiting at the coal face as they brought up the injured men and hoping that his father wouldn't be too badly hurt when they brought him out. Only his father hadn't been injured; he'd been killed outright.

Neighbours had been kind to him. They'd fed him, let him sleep in their homes, but as soon as he was old enough to do so he'd turned his back on the mining village and struck out on his own.

His first few months in Cardiff had been hard; he'd been destitute and even reduced to begging. After dark he'd often sorted through the bins at the back of cafés and hotels to see if he could find anything in them fit to eat.

He'd slept in doorways and even park benches, often being moved on again by the police in the early hours of the morning and warned that he'd be locked up if they found him there again.

He'd spent hours at the docks desperately trying to get a ship but they'd always turned him away saying that he was too young. He'd thought very seriously about stowing away on one and had even taken to sleeping down on the dockside with every intention of slipping on board one dark night. He didn't care if it was a cargo boat or passenger ship as long as it took him far away to some place where he could start a new life; but the opportunity to do so never arose.

By sheer chance he'd managed to find work in a factory where they made packing cases. At first he'd only been sweeping up and acting as a general labourer. It had provided him with enough money to pay for proper lodgings, and also, by saving every penny, he was able to buy some decent clothes.

His boss had noticed how industrious he was and after a couple of months he'd been promoted to other work including going out in the van with deliveries. It had been back-breaking at times, but he'd refused to give up.

He'd learned everything he could about the

methods they used in manufacturing the cases as well as about all the various sizes they stocked and what they were used for, how everything was labelled, and where it was stored in the warehouse. By the time he was nineteen he had been made foreman.

From that day on he'd made certain that the warehouse was always spick and span and that he could always account for every item in it. He also made sure that orders were completed on schedule and deliveries were made promptly.

Meeting Lorna was his next stroke of luck. She was seventeen and one of the clerks employed in the office. From time to time she came along to the warehouse to ask questions concerning an order or delivery. She was petite and her blond hair framed her round face. She looked like a beautiful doll and was the prettiest girl he'd ever seen.

They'd taken to each other on sight and after a few weeks he'd summoned up all his courage and asked her if she would go for a walk with him.

She'd been rather taken back by his forwardness but she'd agreed she'd do so if her parents gave their approval. It had been the start of their courtship and had turned into a lifelong romance. Three years later, when she was twenty, her parents finally gave their consent for Lorna and Lloyd to be married.

They'd had a white wedding and they'd set

up home in rented rooms in Canton. The moment he was promoted to Factory Manager, and because Lorna was expecting their baby, they moved to a house in Cyfartha Street in Roath; the one they were living in now and where Sarah had been born.

The war had disrupted his secret ambition to become a partner in the business but his background had not been wasted. His skill at organising and keeping records had stood him in good stead. Almost at once he'd been sent to one of the training barracks in the Midlands to work in the stores and in no time at all he'd been put in charge and promoted to Warrant Officer.

After he'd been demobbed from the army, once again he'd been luckier than most and had been offered his job back by his former employers. They'd expanded considerably and now had a thriving transport and haulage side to their business and he rejoined the company as General Manager.

Now older and wiser, he'd decided that with his very limited savings it was probably too great an ambition to hope to become a partner. Instead he concentrated on encouraging Sarah to reach an educational standard that he had never been able to achieve himself.

Lorna Lewis felt very relieved that Sarah would be attending Cardiff University. She knew it was the height of Lloyd's ambition for her and that he was extremely proud of their daughter. Unlike Lorna, he couldn't bring himself to tell Sarah how he felt. Lorna was lavish with her praise and though Sarah knew how delighted both her parents were, Lloyd always gave the impression that it was only what he expected.

There were times when Lorna felt uncomfortable about this because, in contrast, Lloyd was so openly affectionate towards her. The fact that he showed her the same tenderness and devotion as he'd done when they'd first been married and seemed to place her on a pedestal sometimes filled her with a sense of unease because she felt that she had to watch her every step to make sure she didn't fall off and this could be quite onerous. Sometimes she thought she would actually have enjoyed it if they'd had the occasional spat like most married couples did, as long as they could make up afterwards.

Over the years she always tried to fall in with his wishes and do everything to please him but she was no longer as inhibited as she'd been when they'd first married. Nowadays, since the war, she wanted to go out and about more and mix with people and often wished she could invite people to their home but Lloyd liked his privacy and did not welcome visitors.

She'd enjoyed the war years so much because she'd experienced such a feeling of freedom. For the first time in her life she was able to do things her parents had never allowed her to do. Also, knowing that Lloyd was miles and miles away she was at liberty to go out or have friends in whenever she wanted to do so.

It had also given her the opportunity to take Sarah out and about. They'd had a wonderful time together and Lloyd's army allowance, especially after his promotion, was more than adequate for her to be able to do this.

Then Lloyd had been demobbed and, once more, she found herself the centre of his universe. In so many ways he was an extremely good husband because he never begrudged her anything. Lloyd's only failing, as far as she was concerned, was the fact that he seemed to prefer them to live almost in isolation from their neighbours and what few friends she had.

Lloyd was also an outstandingly good father. He worried about Sarah, and he encouraged her in her studies, but his expectations of what he wanted her to achieve were so high that they were almost impossible.

Now, with such a glittering prize as the opportunity to have a university education under her belt, Lorna wondered what the future had to offer; not merely for Sarah but for all of them.

Sarah showed so much promise that undoubtedly she would do well. Lorna wondered what sort of a career Lloyd had in mind for her after she finished university. Perhaps it would have been better if they'd had more children, then all his ambitions wouldn't be concentrated on Sarah's achievements.

She sighed as she spread a thick blanket on the table and covered it with a piece of old sheet in readiness to do the ironing. It was too late to think like that now, she told herself. Nevertheless, she was worried because she was sure that sometimes Lloyd pushed Sarah far too hard.

As she picked up the flat iron from the trivet in front of the fire and held it a couple of inches from her face to test if it was hot enough to begin ironing one of Lloyd's shirts, she wondered if Sarah would ever have a home and family of her own or whether she would make her career her life.

Chapter Two

Sarah found that all the excitement over her going to university was slightly dimmed when it came to leaving High School and saying goodbye to all her teachers and the friends she'd known for the past five years.

Although many of them lived only a few streets away, she knew that once they all started work she wouldn't be seeing very much of any of them. She'd already found that because she had only limited pocket money she was unable to do many of the things her friend Rita did now that she was working.

She also knew that Rita thought she was wasting her time going to university and poring over her books while she was out living it up and having a good time.

She sighed. Probably most of the others did as well because as Rita kept reminding her going to university wasn't a short-term commitment; it would be at least three years if she was to obtain all the qualifications her father had in mind.

The other thing that worried her was that because she was the only one who'd passed to go to university she wouldn't know anyone else there. When she'd moved from elementary school to the high school not only Rita but several other girls, as well as half a dozen boys, had also changed school at the same time.

She could still remember how they'd all huddled together in the playground on that first day. They'd felt small and insignificant because all the others seemed to be so much bigger and far more self-confident than they were and they had wondered if they would ever fit in.

They had soon done so, of course. Once they knew their way around the building, met their teachers and got used to their new routine, all their worries and feelings of shyness had disappeared.

Sarah tried to talk to Rita about all the worries and doubts she was having over what lay ahead but Rita was surprisingly uncooperative.

'It's your own fault; you've only yourself to blame. I've already said that if you don't want to go to university, why did you let your dad think that you did? You should have said that you didn't want to do so,' she stated bluntly.

'I couldn't do that, it would break his heart. He is forever saying how important it is to him; all his plans for the future are built around me going to university.'

'Yes, maybe, but what about your plans? I always thought that, like me, all you've been thinking about for the last year is how soon you can start work and have some money to spend. I know I wouldn't go back to school for anything.'

'It's all right for you,' Sarah argued, 'you talk

about absolutely anything with your parents and say whatever you like to them.'

'You could do the same.'

'No. It's speak when you're spoken to in our house.'

'When you were younger perhaps,' Rita said with raised eyebrows, 'not now when you are almost grown-up.'

'Yes, even now,' Sarah assured her emphatically.

Rita frowned as she concentrated on brushing her long corn-coloured hair. 'If you didn't want to go to university, why did you study so hard and pass all your exams?'

'To please my dad, of course. I wanted him to take notice of me.'

'Perhaps if you hadn't studied so hard and got such good marks he'd have taken even more notice of you,' Rita giggled.

'I couldn't possibly have done anything like that!' Sarah exclaimed aghast. 'I wanted to please him and my mother.'

'And do you think you have?' Rita asked, looking at her curiously.

Sarah shrugged and looked crestfallen. 'I'm not too sure, although I have tried to do what they expected of me.'

'Why on earth bother? I know I wouldn't have done so. You might just as well be out enjoying yourself.'

'You really don't understand, do you?' Sarah sighed. 'It's the way I've been brought up.'

'It's always been the same with your parents,' Rita observed critically. 'When we were little you were never allowed to play out in the street. You were never allowed to join in when we all played hopscotch or skipping or tag. You used to spend hours standing by your front-room window watching us and sucking your thumb.'

'Good heavens, fancy you remembering about that,' Sarah said in astonishment. 'Anyway,' she went on quickly, 'I played out with you all later on.'

'Yes, after your dad went into the army you and your mam used to mix with everyone in the street like normal people and even stand on the doorstep gossiping for hours. Yes, you're right, you played out then and joined in all our games,' she agreed.

'The war years were fun, weren't they?' Sarah smiled.

'Yes, but afterwards, once your dad was demobbed and back home again you were never allowed to come out with any of our crowd, no matter what we were planning to do. Last Christmas when you had a part in the school play, he even objected to that because it meant you staying later at school.'

'No, he didn't,' Sarah defended. 'It was only when we had rehearsals in the evening.'

'Yes, and then he always came to meet you and insisted that you went straight home while we all went off to the milk bar and enjoyed ourselves.'

'It was just his way, it was past my bedtime,' Sarah mumbled, the hot colour rushing to her cheeks.

'Sarah, you were fifteen! You were old enough to decide for yourself what time you went to bed. Does he still expect you to go to bed when he says?'

Sarah bit her lip. 'Does it matter?'

'Not to me it doesn't, but I would have thought it would to you. You'll have to stand up for yourself when you get to university or you'll have no life at all. Perhaps it is just as well that you are not going out to work, you wouldn't do very well; staying on at school is about all you're fit for.'

Sarah looked at her friend open-mouthed. In the past they'd always shared all their problems, especially when they'd felt they were being unfairly treated, whether it was by their teachers or their family. Even so, they'd never been as frank or outspoken as Rita was being now and it left Sarah feeling shocked. She didn't know what to say because she felt that to join in criticising her father like Rita was doing would be disloyal.

Far from persuading her that going to university was wrong for her, Rita's comments were making her all the more determined to go and do her very best. She'd make her father proud of her even if Rita did despise her for doing so.

From now on she wouldn't talk about it.

There would be no more exchanging confidences or soul-searching heart-to-hearts with Rita, she told herself. She took Rita's comments very much to heart. She'd always regarded Rita as being her very best friend and in the past they'd agreed about most things. She'd had no idea that Rita had such strong feelings about what her parents said she could and could not do and she felt quite upset about it.

She'd hoped they would stay friends even though she realised that their interests were no longer the same, but she suspected that they'd never again be as close as they had been while they were growing up. She would be lonely without her company because she was the only really close friend she'd ever had.

There was only one thing she could do and that was to look ahead, make the most of her time at university and hope that at the end of all her studying she would achieve the goal she was setting herself and also be completely independent.

Sarah had been looking forward to spending a great deal of the three months' vacation between the end of the school year and starting at university as a time of relaxation and enjoying herself. There would be days out shopping with her mother and going out with Rita at the weekends. However, it was nothing of the sort. Her father insisted that she should spend at least a portion of each day studying and when he came home at night he questioned her in great detail about what he'd told her to do, so there was no chance to shirk.

It kept her from worrying about the deep chasm growing between herself and Rita and from dwelling on the fact that things would never be the same between them ever again. She tried to console herself that perhaps it was all for the best since from now on they would be leading completely different lives.

There was some respite from studying, however, because her mother insisted that she must have new clothes before she started at university. They spent a good many afternoons looking around the shops in the city centre. The sales were on and Lorna felt that it might be better to wait until the stores had new stock, but it didn't stop them window shopping and browsing before committing themselves as to what they both considered to be suitable.

When the first day of the new term eventually arrived Sarah felt desperately nervous. She and her mother had walked up to Cathays Park on numerous occasions and had sat on one of the benches there, looking across to the other side of Museum Avenue and admiring the university building which was built from the same gleaming Portland stone as the nearby City Hall.

The building was so impressive that Sarah found even the thought of walking through its doors daunting and it made her feel insignificant.

When the actual day arrived, however, she

was so excited that her fears were momentarily quenched. She discovered that on the first day there would be no formal lectures. Instead, they were told where to find the various lecture rooms and were helped to familiarise themselves with the interior of the building so that they could find their way around.

A third-year student was allocated to each small group of three or four newcomers. In charge of the group that Sarah was attached to was Gwyn Roberts. He was about twenty and fairly tall with very broad shoulders and dark brown hair and dark eyes. He seemed to be very sure of himself and slightly supercilious, but when he smiled, his friendly expression compensated for this. Nevertheless, Sarah felt shy of him because he seemed to be so purposeful.

He appeared to be focussing his attention on her and walked alongside her most of the time as if he was anxious to make sure that she personally knew where everything was. He made a point of answering her questions in full while dismissing some of the queries from the others with a few brief words.

By the end of the day she no longer felt a stranger in the vast complex and she also suspected that when Gwyn said he would watch out for her the following day, and that if there was anything she was uncertain about she had only to ask him, she had at least made one friend.

When she'd been at school she'd been used to sitting in class along with thirty others and working to a strict timetable devised by the teacher in charge. Now she found that having selected the subjects she was taking she had to make her own decisions about which lectures she attended.

She often found that the lecture hall was crowded and that boys far outnumbered the girls. It also came as a shock to find that it was left to her own discretion what she did in the way of making notes and preparing for the next lecture.

One-to-one sessions with her tutor were at first terrifying because she was afraid he was going to criticise her for not doing as much preparation as he expected her to, or because she didn't understand something and needed to ask him for a more detailed explanation.

There was so much to learn, so much studying to be done in her own time, that Sarah found she barely noticed the fact that she saw little or nothing of Rita.

'I see you are starting to put your back into things,' her father commented one Sunday when, instead of going to call for Rita and going for a walk as she usually did in the afternoon, she spread out her books on the dining table and sat there busily writing and checking things in her text books.

'She's working far too hard, if you want my opinion.' Lorna sighed as she handed him a cup of tea. 'Every evening and every weekend she's poring over those books. You're only young once and she should be out enjoying herself.'

'There will be plenty of time for her to be doing that sort of thing when she's finished her studies,' Lloyd stated firmly as he took the cup from her and put it down on the little table she'd placed alongside his chair. 'This is a wonderful opportunity for her; a chance to make something of herself.'

'Even so, all work and no play ...' Lorna interceded, then stopped and sighed and said no more.

Sarah knew that in many ways her mother was right. She really was studying far too much; she had no time to try and make any friends. It was almost Christmas and all sorts of extra-curricular activities were coming up at the university and, even though she knew her father wouldn't approve, she fully intended to join in some of them if she was invited to do so.

Most of the other students had far more freedom than she did because very few of them actually lived in Cardiff and so they were either living in one of the halls of residence attached to the university campus or else they were in private lodgings. There were times when she envied them their independence and wished she had been able to choose a university in some other place, perhaps at Lampeter or even further afield.

When she had suggested this to her father

he had been adamant that it must be Cardiff University or nothing and that he wanted her to study law.

'The only way we can afford for you to go to university is if you are living at home,' he'd pointed out. 'Remember, very few girls have such a tremendous opportunity in the first place and most girls of your age have been out to work for a year or more, and are not still being kept by their family.'

He'd been most affronted when she'd told him, 'I know that, Dad, and I'm grateful, but if you are worried about what it is going to cost then I will happily forget all about it and find a job.'

'There's nonsense you talk, girl,' he'd said quickly. 'This is what I've struggled to achieve; what I've scrimped and saved for since the day you were born.'

Knowing how much store he set by her achievements sometimes made her feel rebellious. Was she doing this for herself or simply to please him? Was she the only one there who was trying to fulfil their parents' ambition?

Her friendship with Gwyn had remained fleeting until one afternoon when they both had no lectures; instead of settling down and studying she'd accepted his invitation to go for a coffee at one of the nearby milk bars.

She felt rather nervous about doing so and wished she was dressed in something smarter than the plain grey skirt and white blouse she was wearing that day.

Once away from the confines of the university she felt a wonderful sense of liberation and in no time they were chatting away like old friends. Out of curiosity she even plucked up the courage to ask him if he was there studying because it was what his parents wanted him to do.

'I wouldn't be slogging away like I am just to please them,' he laughed. 'No, I'm doing this for myself. I want to work in journalism and the better my degree, the more opportunity I'll have to get a worthwhile job. What about you?'

'I'm not sure.' Sarah shrugged. 'I sometimes ask myself that question. My dad is very keen for me to do well, to get a good degree in law; one that will enable me to get a top job. I'm finding, though, that there's so much studying involved that sometimes it seems as if my life is slipping by and by the time I've qualified I'll be too old to have fun.'

'You could be right,' he told her in a serious voice. 'The trouble with you is that you are working far too hard. You are only in your first year and most of us only play at learning for the first year, we don't study all the hours there are like you do. I've seen you heading for home at night weighed down like a packhorse with all the text books you are taking home with you.'

'I know, but I feel it's the only possible way I can manage to keep up. There's so much I don't know and unless I study hard all the time I never will.'

'Utter rubbish! Take it more slowly. You'll

find that the lectures will sink in much better if you've a space in your head for them. Cram your brain too full and all the new facts will fall out again because there isn't room for them.' He grinned.

Sarah wasn't sure whether Gwyn was teasing her or not but she thought that perhaps there was something in what he was telling her. She decided that in the New Year she would try taking his advice and start taking things a little bit more slowly and see what happened. If she found she was getting behind then she could always start pushing herself again.

In the last few days before they closed for the Christmas holiday she spent more and more time with Gwyn as they took advantage of the many social activities that were being organised. For the first time since starting university she found herself actually enjoying herself and getting to know some of the other girls.

Christmas at home seemed to be a very subdued affair because she only saw Rita twice and the gulf between them seemed to be greater than ever, but she had plenty of happy memories to dwell on. Even though her books were spread out in front of her more often than not her thoughts were miles away as she looked forward to the new term and to seeing Gwyn Roberts again.

Chapter Three

Sarah had a feeling of panic by the end of the first day of the new term because she couldn't find Gwyn anywhere. She'd been dreaming about their next meeting all through the Christmas vacation and now she was worried. Had she fantasised about him having special feelings for her, she wondered, or had something happened to him?

He might have decided to give up university and start as a junior reporter somewhere and to learn his craft that way and then she might never see him again. Much more likely was that he was ill; he might even have had an accident and be unable to return.

When her classes ended she hung around the campus hoping to catch a glimpse of him but in the end she knew she had better head for home or her own parents would be worrying about her.

By the time she fell asleep that night she'd explored so many scenarios about what might have happened and what she would do if he didn't return that she woke up the next morning feeling so depressed that her father commented on it while they were having breakfast.

'I hope you're not coming down with a cold or the flu just as the new term has started,' he said worriedly. 'You can't afford to take time off and get behind with your studies. Make sure you put a scarf on because it will be bitterly cold outside judging by the frost on the windows.'

It was cold; there was a biting January wind with sleet blowing inland from the Irish Sea. Sarah kept her head down as she made her way up Museum Street and wished she'd said that she was starting a cold and that perhaps a day in bed might nip it in the bud, but it was too late to do that now.

As she joined the throng of other students going into the university she heard someone call her name and to her joy found that Gwyn was pushing his way through the crowd towards her.

'Where were you yesterday?' she gasped in surprise.

'I missed my train back to Cardiff so I thought I'd spend another day at home. Never very much happening on the first day back so I knew I wouldn't be missing very much . . . except seeing you, of course!'

Sarah not only felt her cheeks going red but she also felt quite tongue tied. In her fantasies she had returned his quips with equally smart repartee but now that they were face to face her mind went blank and she felt horrified to discover that she could only blush like a silly schoolgirl.

'I . . . I thought that perhaps you weren't coming back,' Sarah murmured breathlessly, hoping that he wouldn't hear the concern in her voice.

Gwyn frowned and looked puzzled. 'Whatever made you think that?'

Sarah felt so embarrassed that she quickly changed the subject. 'I thought you lived in Cardiff,' she said lamely.

'Heavens no. My family are all miners – we live miles away from Cardiff, at Aberdare up in the Valleys. Have you ever been there?'

'No,' Sarah shook her head, 'I've never been out of Cardiff except to Penarth and Barry Island and those were only day trips.'

'Duw anwyl! You've not lived, cariad, if you haven't been to Aberdare,' Gwyn teased.

Sarah bit her lip, she knew he was laughing at her but she wanted him to take her seriously, to treat her as an equal. She wanted him to talk to her about himself, his background and his home. She wanted him to confide in her and share things with her but she didn't know how to let him know this. Because her father had never allowed her to go out in the evenings with Rita and her crowd she had no idea how to talk to boys. She knew they weren't interested in the same sort of things that girls were and she assumed it was the same when they were older; her dad certainly wasn't interested in many of the things her mother was interested in.

33

'Did you have a nice Christmas?' she asked, her voice shaking. It sounded so crass.

Surely talking about what he did over Christmas and about his family would be a safe subject, though, and far more interesting than their studies, she thought hopefully.

'Look,' Gwyn told her, 'I've got to attend a tutorial in ten minutes and I must sort myself out first. Meet me in the canteen at lunchtime and we'll talk then. Right?'

Sarah nodded. 'Twelve o'clock?'

'Make it half past,' he called over his shoulder as he hurried off.

The rest of the morning flew by and she was late reaching the canteen. Gwyn was already there sitting at a table in the corner in deep conversation with a red-headed girl she'd never seen before. Sarah noticed that there were two cups of tea on the table and a plate of sandwiches and her heart sank. The cosy session she'd been looking forward to so much wasn't going to happen after all.

She was mentally debating whether to try and slip away without Gwyn seeing her, or to brave it out and order a drink and something to eat and carry them over to an adjacent table, when Gwyn looked up and spotted her hovering in the doorway.

To her great surprise he raised his hand and called out her name and waved her over. Her feet feeling like lead she made her way towards his table. Before she reached it the red-headed girl had stood up and moved away and her confusion increased when she realised that Gwyn had ordered the drink and food on the table to share with her.

She wasn't sure what was in the sandwiches, but the novelty of the situation was so over-whelming that she busily concentrated on eating and drinking and left the talking to him. It was a pleasant shock to find he had remem-bered her earlier question and was telling her about what he did over Christmas and about his family. It made her feel that perhaps he had been thinking about her after all.

'Mam always makes a tremendous fuss about Christmas,' he told her. 'All the trimmings, a full-scale Christmas dinner and then presents from under the tree afterwards. We all go along with it, mind, because we all know how much it means to her. Family tradition, see! It's been the same every year for as long as I can remember.'

His voice seemed to grow softer and there was a faraway look in his eyes as he went on talking about his family. Sarah listened entranced as he explained that he had two older brothers as well as a sister. Both his brothers had followed in their father's footsteps and had gone to work down the pit as soon as they were old enough to do so. He was the youngest and when he'd held out about doing the same they'd eventually given in. Even though his dad had declared that it went against the grain, even he could see sense in Gwyn finding a job in newspapers.

'That way, you can tell the world about the struggles and hardships we have to endure. They might listen to your voice, boyo, if you wear a collar and tie and have some learning, whereas they won't listen to a damn word the miners have to say about the terrible conditions they not only work in but also often have to live in as well.'

'And is that what you intend to do, become a voice for the miners and help them right their wrongs?' Sarah breathed, staring at him admiringly, her eyes shining enthusiastically as she hung on to every word he said.

Gwyn shrugged his broad shoulders noncommittaly. 'I'll have to wait and see. They may have managed to solve all their problems by the time I'm qualified and have my own column in one of the top-rated newspapers.'

'I doubt it; there always seems to have been a lot of trouble in the valleys; my dad says they're a discontented lot.'

Even as the words came out, Sarah knew that she had said the wrong thing and that it sounded as though she was being critical. Gwyn's family were all miners so of course he would want to champion their cause.

'I . . . I think you'd do a good job, mind,' she said hastily. 'With your background and so on . . .'

'Will it bring me the sort of notice and fame I'll need to become a real achiever, though?'

he questioned, looking at her thoughtfully. 'Or will it bring me the wrong sort of notoriety? I can't afford to jeopardise my prospects, now can I?' he added with a grin that made her heart beat faster.

Sarah bit her lip, afraid to voice an opinion in case she landed herself in difficulties again.

'Of course,' Gwyn teased, 'if I knew a famous lawyer who'd be willing to take up my case should I land myself in hot water, then I'd have no worries, now would I?'

Sarah felt bemused. She took her studies and the career she was aiming for very seriously but there were times when Gwyn seemed to be so flippant and light-hearted about the future that she wondered if he really cared. Yet at other times he was so enthusiastic about what he wanted to do that she'd thought he was as dedicated as she was.

Seeing the look of bewilderment on her face he laughed. 'You take life far too seriously, you know,' he told her. 'You don't have to be quite so committed as you are. Remember what I told you before Christmas about studying too hard. You need to relax, do other things, go out and about and enjoy yourself occasionally. It won't stop you working; in fact, you will find that a complete break from studying will actually enable you to learn better than ever.'

'I know that's what you told me before and I really am going to try and put it into practice,' Sarah told him seriously.

'Good, well, let's put it to the test right away. What about going to the pictures with me tonight?'

'I can't possibly do that!' Sarah gulped. 'My dad wouldn't allow it, not after all the time we've had off recently.'

'Do you have to tell him?'

'I'd have to explain why I was going out again as soon as I got home instead of settling down to do some work.'

'That's one of the problems of living at home,' Gwyn sighed. 'You could simply say that you are going back to university for an evening session; he's not to know what that involves.'

Sarah shook her head. She felt devastated about having to refuse the invitation because she really did want to go out with Gwyn but she knew the repercussions she'd have to face at home if she told them what she was doing.

'Look, if you feel I've sprung this on you without giving you a chance to prepare some excuse or other for your dad, then let's make it tomorrow night.'

Sarah nodded as if in agreement but her mind was in turmoil. She wanted to go out with him tonight, even though she realised that his suggestion was the most sensible thing to do.

'Simply tell him you are staying late and won't be in for your evening meal. I'll take you for a bite in the canteen or to a milk bar and then we'll go to the pictures. Is there anything special on that you want to see?'

'I don't even know what's on,' Sarah murmured. Her head was spinning at the ideas Gwyn was putting forward. She desperately wanted to fall in with his arrangement but at the same time she didn't want to appear too eager, nor so indifferent that he felt she didn't want to go out with him.

The thought of spending the entire evening in his company was like one of the many fantasies she'd indulged in during the holidays actually coming true.

It also presented numerous other problems, though, because everything was so new to her and so far she hadn't made any other friends she could ask. For one thing, she'd never been out on her own with a boy before and she didn't really know what was expected of her or, for that matter, how to behave.

Although he was inviting her out and she knew that on a date it was usual for the chap to pay she wasn't sure whether he considered it a proper date or not. She wondered whether because they were both students, she was expected to pay for herself. He'd paid for the coffee and sandwiches they were having now but he couldn't be expected to meet the cost for everything if they went to the pictures since, like her, he wasn't earning any money.

'Right, we'll make it tomorrow night, then. I'll be waiting in the main hall at half past five. Don't be late!'

Before she could answer or protest he'd

pushed back his chair, picked up his case full of books, and was walking away, whistling cheerfully as he went out into the corridor.

Sarah stayed at the table for a while longer, going over everything they'd said and debating in her own mind whether or not she was being underhand if she said nothing to her parents about her plans for the following evening.

Throughout the rest of the day thoughts about her forthcoming date kept coming into her mind, making it difficult to concentrate on her lectures. Instead of listening to the lecturer or seeing the printed words on the page in front of her it was Gwyn's deep dark eyes, his thick hair and his strong features that she found herself contemplating.

Several times she thought of searching him out and saying she'd changed her mind but the thought of spending a whole evening in his company was so irresistible that she knew that she couldn't bring herself to do it.

I'll go, just this once, she told herself. I might find that he doesn't ask me again so that will be the end of it and there will never be another time.

In her heart she prayed this wouldn't be the case. She couldn't think of anything she wanted more than for Gwyn to be her steady boyfriend. She knew he was popular with a number of the girls, not only because he was so good-looking but also because he was such good company.

The fact that he had singled her out for special

attention must mean that he was attracted to her and that he wanted to know her better. Unless, of course, she reminded herself, it was simply a matter of making a new conquest. Would it be just one date and then she'd never see anything of him again except by chance when he had another girl on his arm?

She wished Rita was still as close a friend as she'd once been so that she could talk it over with her. Rita had been going out with boys since she was about fourteen and knew so much more of what to do and say to hold their attention. In addition, she not only claimed that she knew how to spot a flirt but also insisted that she knew the right way to deal with that sort of boy.

For all Sarah knew she might be risking heartbreak by going out with Gwyn. She knew she was very attracted to him but did he feel the same way about her?

Although she was debating whether or not to go, Sarah knew in her heart that she had every intention of doing so. How could she turn him down when something that she'd dreamed about for so long was actually about to happen?

She was already planning in her mind's eye which dress she would wear the next day and wondering if either her father or mother would notice. If they did, then how on earth was she going to explain why she had decided to get all dressed up when she was supposed to be attending lectures?

Again, her mind filled with doubts as to whether it was worth all the palaver and intrigue that seemed to be necessary. Perhaps she should tell her parents the truth.

Even as the thought crossed her mind she knew she couldn't. Both of them would say the same thing: that boyfriends were out of the question, that they would distract her from her purpose.

She'd be told very firmly that she must forget all about friendships of that sort until she had achieved a good degree and was holding down a responsible job. Until then, she must keep her mind fixed firmly on her studies and nothing else.

Chapter Four

To Sarah's delight, far from it being the first and only date with Gwyn Roberts, their visit to the pictures resulted in an ongoing friendship that sometimes left her feeling mesmerised by its intensity and confused about his intentions.

She knew so little about what was expected of her. In the darkness of the cinema she was quite prepared to kiss and cuddle because that was so exciting. When his hands began roaming too intimately, however, and her senses started to spin out of control, then she became scared and started pushing him away.

He seemed to understand her reluctance but more often than not found it difficult to control his desire and enthusiasm and that left her feeling more bewitched than ever.

In next to no time it was as if her life centred on being with him. When they weren't together the memory of being in his arms, feeling his lips claiming hers, obscured everything else.

The serious drawback was that although she delighted in their wonderful friendship it took up such a great chunk of her time and filled her thoughts so much that she found focussing on her course work increasingly difficult.

Gwyn didn't seem to have the same problem; when they met for coffee or for a meal he talked enthusiastically about what he'd been doing as if it was the main interest in his life.

To her surprise and relief, Gwyn insisted on paying whether they were eating out, going to the pictures or going dancing but, nevertheless, she felt so concerned, wondering how on earth he could afford to continue doing so, that in the end she mentioned it.

'Don't worry about it, cariad; when I'm broke then I'll ask you for a sub, or else I'll get you to go round with my cap while I sing in the streets,' he joked.

'That's not an answer,' she said stiffly. 'I really am worried, Gwyn. It seems so unfair that you are always the one to foot the bill, but I must admit I wouldn't be able to afford to come out with you so often if I had to pay my way each time.'

'There you are then, my lovely! Stop worrying about it. I've got plenty to spend,' he added, jingling the coins in his trouser pocket as if to prove his point.

'I don't see how you can have,' Sarah persisted. 'Your dad is only a working man the same as mine so he can't give you very much more spending money than mine does, and I find it goes nowhere.'

'I don't have to buy powder and paint and silk stockings to make myself look beautiful,

44

though,' he teased, putting an arm round her waist and burying his face in her hair.

'Seriously, cariad,' he went on when she stiffened and pulled away from him, 'I have plenty to spend. My brothers are working and getting a man's pay so they make me a regular allowance. Our mam used to give them pocket money before they left school and so now they say it's only right that they should give me pocket money, seeing as how I'm still at school.'

Sarah stared at him with raised eyebrows. 'Are you telling me the truth?'

'Of course I am, cariad. What with the pocket money from them and what my mam gives me, I'm rolling in it,' he boasted. 'I sometimes think I'd be just as well off if I stayed a student all my life as long as they kept up the pocket money.'

'I bet they don't know that you spend it taking a girl out, though?' Sarah pointed out.

'Why not? It's probably what they did when they were my age. Anyway, cariad, if they met you, then they'd not only understand but would also be green with envy.'

Although Gwyn treated it all very light-heartedly, there were times when Sarah felt very guilty about all the deception. It worried her so much that in the end she decided that it might be better to be open about it.

'Would you like to come home and meet my parents?' she suggested on Friday evening as they left the pictures.

'Do you mean now?' he asked in surprise. 'Do you think it would be a good idea at this time of night?'

'I didn't mean right now,' she said quickly. 'What about on Sunday? Would you like to come to tea on Sunday afternoon?'

'Well, since the forecast says that this weather is set for the next few days, then it is certainly too wet to sit around in the park, so it might be a better alternative,' he commented as he shivered and pulled his coat collar higher to keep out the driving rain.

'Right, well, I'll tell my mam that I'm inviting you and she can break it gently to my father.'

'You make it sound as though that is going to be a major problem.' Gwyn frowned.

'Not exactly a problem,' Sarah said hastily, 'but I did tell you that my dad is very strict. If he thought that because I was seeing you I was missing any lectures, or not studying as much as I should be, then he'd be very angry.

'Then perhaps it would be better if you didn't take me back to your home. What he doesn't know he can't worry about.'

'That's true enough, but if he found out in some other way, perhaps by someone saying they'd seen me at the pictures, then he'd accuse me of going behind his back and I'd be in even deeper trouble. That's why I think it is better to be open with him.'

'If you take me home then won't he want to know how we come to know each other so well?

Won't he suspect that some of these late evening lectures that you're supposed to be attending might be nights out enjoying yourself?'

They talked about it so much that Sarah felt that it was driving a wedge between them and she wished she'd never thought of the idea, or else that she hadn't told Gwyn what a martinet her dad could be.

'Are you definitely coming on Sunday?' she asked tentatively as they walked home from the pictures on Friday night. 'I need to know so that I can tell my mam and dad.'

'Of course I am. If only because it means that in future I can walk you right to your door instead of having to say goodbye on the corner of the street,' he murmured as he stopped and pulled her into the shelter of a shop doorway and took her in his arms.

As she gave herself up to his passionate embrace Sarah once again felt apprehensive about Sunday but she decided not to voice her thoughts aloud.

On Sunday, Sarah felt so nervous that she couldn't sit still for a moment. Even in chapel she found herself flicking through the pages of her hymn book instead of listening to the service, and when her mother gave her a light nudge with her elbow followed by a warning frown she almost jumped out of her skin.

Back at home she gladly would have foregone their midday meal of cold meat and pickles. It was never her favourite meal but was one which had to be endured because her father would not allow them to do any cooking on a Sunday.

They'd even had to make the Bara Brith – the bread speckled with spices and dried fruit that was one of her mother's specialities – the day before. She would have liked them to have offered Gwyn some bakestones, but she knew it was out of the question because to be at their best they needed to be served freshly made the minute they came off the griddle and even using that on a Sunday was frowned on by her father.

As soon as they'd eaten their midday meal and she'd helped her mother to clear away and wash up, she excused herself saying she was going to her bedroom to study.

'Why can't you do it here on the dining table like you usually do?' her father questioned.

'It's something I need to learn by saying it out aloud over and over again and I don't want to disturb you,' she told him.

'Then bring it down here and I will hear you say it,' he ordered.

'I will when I've learned it,' she murmured evasively.

Upstairs in her bedroom she spent the next hour preparing for Gwyn's visit. She changed her dress twice and each time she messed up her hair so much that she had to do it all over again. She wanted to look her best when he arrived but she had to be careful not to overdo things so she used only a trace of lipstick in case her father commented on it unfavourably.

When she went back downstairs to wait for Gwyn's knock on the door the first thing her father asked her was where was the piece she should be studying as he would listen to her saying it.

'I think I know it well enough now, thank you,' she told him quickly. 'You enjoy your newspaper, it's not often you have the time to sit and read.'

He looked at her questioningly but she avoided his eyes and speedily went out into the kitchen on the pretext of seeing if she could help her mother.

'You're making a lot of extra work, you know, by inviting this chap here,' her father commented when she came back into the room and began laying the table with her mother's best lace tablecloth which was only used on special occasions. 'Was it really necessary to disrupt our Sunday like this, cariad?'

'I thought you would like to meet him since he is a special friend,' Sarah told him.

'I see!' Lloyd Lewis put down his newspaper and stared at her fixedly. 'And just how special is he, then, and why have you never mentioned him before now?'

Sarah felt flummoxed. If she told the truth and said that he was her steady boyfriend it would cause an uproar, yet if she said he was just a casual friend then her dad would want to know why they were making so much fuss about his visit.

'Hang on a minute,' she prevaricated, 'I think Mam is calling me for something.'

Once out in the kitchen she asked her mother what she ought to tell him.

'How do I know, cariad? What is the truth? Is he special, or are you simply saying that to explain why you've asked him here? I'm very surprised at you doing so, I must say, since you know how much your dad dislikes visitors, especially on a Sunday.'

'Well, it's not possible during the week, now is it, because Gwyn is busy studying just as I am,' Sarah argued.

'Oh, I see. He has lectures late at night as well, does he?' her mother asked dryly.

Sarah looked at her quickly, wondering if perhaps she'd guessed the truth but her mother was concentrating on cutting slices of ham off the joint she'd cooked the day before and didn't look up.

For one wild moment Sarah thought of putting on her coat and dashing down to the tram stop to tell Gwyn that one of her parents had such a bad cold that they thought it best to call the whole thing off; only the thought of how stupid that sounded stopped her. She'd asked him, he'd accepted, and therefore she'd have to go through with it and hope for the best.

Everything was ready on the table well before four o'clock. For the umpteenth time Sarah checked, four cups and saucers, four plates, knives, napkins, milk and sugar and a plate of ham sandwiches, a plate of Bara Brith and also a plate of Bara Sinsir, the tasty ginger cake that her father liked so much.

'I'm ready for my tea,' Lloyd pronounced as the grandfather clock in the corner of the room chimed the half-hour. 'What time is this special friend of yours arriving, Sarah?'

'I told him half past four.'

'It's that now, so he's not very punctual, is he?' Even as her father spoke there was a knock on the door and Sarah felt the colour rush to her cheeks as she hurried to answer it.

To her delight, Gwyn had brought flowers for her mother and Lorna was charmed by his thoughtfulness. She welcomed him quite warmly, told Sarah to take his coat and hang it in the hall, and then to bring him through to meet Lloyd.

Sarah felt prickles running down her spine as the two men confronted each other. Gwyn confidently held out his hand to the older man and thanked him for the invitation to visit them. Taken by surprise, Lloyd returned the handshake and motioned him to sit down.

Even though the occasion started off reasonably well it soon became very plain that her father and Gwyn didn't see eye to eye. Lloyd cross-questioned Gwyn in his sergeant-major voice about the course he was studying and what plans he had for his future career.

Sarah hardly said a word, hoping that it would give her father a chance to get to know Gwyn better if they talked man to man, and then regretted her decision the moment Gwyn mentioned that he came from Aberdare and that the men folk in his family were all miners. To make matters worse he went on to say that he hoped that when he became a fully fledged journalist he'd be able to put over their viewpoint and help them fight their corner for better conditions and rates of pay.

The moment she heard him say it she knew he had antagonised her father and she listened in growing dismay as Lloyd held forth on what a discontented lot the miners were and how they were always holding the country to ransom with their demands.

Several times Sarah tried to intervene, to turn the conversation to other topics, but Lloyd silenced her abruptly. 'Quiet, you may be studying law but you know nothing about politics,' he told her in a harsh voice. 'Neither does this young whipper-snapper, but he will know a great deal more after I've pointed out a few home truths to him.'

'He's not come here for a lecture, he's come to enjoy Sunday afternoon tea,' Lorna said mildly as she held out the plate of Bara Sinsir to Gwyn.

'Thank you, Mrs Lewis, and a splendid tea it is.' Gwyn smiled back at her. 'I'd rather have another slice of Bara Brith, though, if I may; I much prefer it to ginger cake.'

'Indeed you may,' she said quickly, holding out the other plate. 'The Bara Sinsir is not to everyone's taste but I always make it because it is my husband's favourite,' Lorna told him.

'Another thing on which we don't agree, then, isn't it?' Lloyd said critically. 'Tell me,' he went on, not waiting for an answer, 'if you are supposed to be studying to be a journalist and my daughter's course is law and commerce, then how is it that the two of you have become so friendly?'

'Well, we are both attending Cardiff University,' Gwyn said with a bland smile.

Lloyd looked thunderous. 'I am well aware of that, but you are not attending the same lectures.'

'No, that's true. I am two years ahead of Sarah, of course, and that makes a considerable difference, doesn't it?' Gwyn told him.

Sarah held her breath. She wasn't sure whether Gwyn was teasing him or challenging him but she could see that her father was riled and she was fearful of what he might say or do next.

As soon as it was possible to do so, Gwyn stood up and said that he must be leaving as he had some studying to do in readiness for the next day's lectures.

With her heart in her mouth, she watched as her father ignored Gwyn's outstretched hand as he took his leave and prayed that he wouldn't kiss her in front of her parents.

'I'll see you tomorrow, then, Sarah,' he said breezily. 'Thank you once again for a lovely meal, Mrs Lewis,' he added as he walked towards the door.

Chapter Five

The moment the door closed behind Gwyn, and Sarah came back into the living room, the row erupted.

'Don't ever bring that chap here again. Furthermore, I want you to stop seeing him altogether. He is not the sort of person I want you associating with; is that understood?'

'Gwyn is my friend, of course I shall go on seeing him,' Sarah said shakily. 'There was no need to be so rude to him; you wouldn't even shake hands with him when he left.'

'He's a troublemaker, mark my words. With his sort of background I suppose it is only to be expected.'

'If you mean that because he comes from the Valleys and his family are miners then you are quite wrong,' Sarah defended. 'They're the salt of the earth. Where would this country be without them? It's coal that powers industry as well as heats our homes.'

'That's the sort of rubbish he's been filling your head with, is it?' her father said scornfully. 'A troublemaker, that's what he is. He's one of those who incite working men to rebel against their lot when they should be thinking themselves lucky to have jobs to go to, not kicking against their fate all the time.'

'Gwyn is not a troublemaker; he's studied and analysed these things in great detail. He's going to be a journalist, remember.'

'Journalist! A rabble-raiser, more likely. No decent newspaper would employ him, not with his radical opinions. He'll use what little talent he has to encourage the miners to go on strike. He'll tell them they are getting a rotten deal from their bosses when in fact they should think themselves lucky to have work, food in their bellies, and a roof over their head.'

'How can you say that, Dad? Gwyn has told me all about what it is like down the pits. The men work in darkness except for the lights on the front of their helmets, the air they breathe is foul, and all the time they are below ground they're dreading there might be an explosion.'

'He'll cause discontent that will put the whole country in jeopardy,' Lloyd went on as if Sarah had never spoken. 'I know his type; I can spot them a mile off. They are theorists, the lot of them, out to stir up trouble. It's happened before and it will happen again and it ends up with the miners out on strike.'

'I don't understand why you have taken such a dislike to him,' Sarah said in bewilderment. 'He's clean and well dressed; he's polite and well mannered . . .'

'Smarmy and smooth-tongued,' her father interrupted. 'I can see he's turned your head.

Bringing flowers for your mother, that's the action of a smart-alec, all right,' Lloyd added caustically.

'I thought it was very nice of him.' Lorna smiled. 'It's been a long time since anyone brought me flowers. I must say I thought he was a very pleasant young chap; I was quite impressed by him.'

'A touch of flattery and all women are taken in as to what the real man is like,' Lloyd said derisively.

'He wasn't trying to flatter you, Mam; it was his way of saying thank you for being invited to tea,' Sarah defended Gwyn. 'It proves how well mannered he is.'

'Well, that's enough about Gwyn Roberts,' her father told her abruptly. 'He won't be invited here again so you can put him out of your mind. I don't want to hear his name mentioned again and I don't want to hear you've been wasting your time talking to him. You are to stop seeing him. Is that understood, Sarah?'

'How can I stop seeing him when we attend the same university?' she muttered rebelliously.

'You don't attend the same lectures, now do you?' he barked as he picked up the newspaper and settled back in his armchair.

'In fact,' he went on, putting the paper to one side, 'exactly how is it that you know him so well? Have you been shirking classes in order to talk to him?'

'Of course I haven't!' Although she said it emphatically the rush of colour to her cheeks immediately roused her father's curiosity.

'So how do you know him well enough to consider him a friend worthy of being brought home to meet us?'

'He was assigned to show me and three other newcomers around on our first day,' she said lamely.

'And have all the others taken him home to meet their families?'

She knew he was being sarcastic but she was determined to stand her ground. 'I very much doubt it because none of them live in Cardiff like I do so they don't have the chance to do so.'

He regarded her speculatively, his eyes hardening. 'Listen to me; watch your step with this Gwyn Roberts. I don't trust him. And he isn't just a casual acquaintance; he's more than that, isn't he? Would he be the reason why you've had to stay late for so many evening lectures lately?'

Sarah looked pleadingly at her mother, hoping she would say something to distract her father's interrogation, but Lorna was also looking at her questioningly.

'Finish with him,' her father said firmly. 'I've already said I don't want you having anything more to do with him, and I mean it. I don't want to hear his name mentioned ever again. That's final. Nor do I want to hear that you are attending evening lectures, not unless you can prove to me in writing that you have to do so. The next time you don't come home at the normal time I'll make it my business to go over to the university and find out why.'

'If you ever come to the university checking up on me like that, then I'll be so ashamed that I'll never be able to go back there again,' Sarah told him, tears glistening in her eyes.

'Then don't give me cause to do so.'

She was about to argue with him, astounded that her father was being so completely unfair, not only in his condemnation of Gwyn but also in treating her as if she was a twelve-year-old, but her mother signalled her not to say any more.

In silence the two of them cleared the tea things from the table and went into the kitchen to wash up. As she filled a bowl with hot water Sarah's thoughts were in turmoil. She felt angry and so bewildered that her father had been even more dictatorial than usual.

'You liked Gwyn, didn't you, Mam?' she asked.

Lorna pushed the kitchen door tightly shut before she answered. 'Yes, I liked him, I thought he was very charming,' she agreed as she began wiping the cups Sarah had washed.

'So you don't want me to stop seeing him?'

'Well,' Lorna hesitated, concentrating on polishing a plate and avoiding Sarah's sideways look, 'he is a very presentable young man but I think your father thinks that you are probably too young to be thinking seriously about boys, you know.'

'He's a friend, that's all,' Sarah muttered belligerently. 'There's no need for Dad to make such a fuss the way he's done.'

'I think your dad is afraid that this boy is going to take your mind off your studies, cariad. You know how important it is to him that you qualify and get yourself a really good job.'

'Gwyn's just as ambitious. He's not going to distract me any more than I will sidetrack him. He helps me in many ways because I can talk about my projects with someone who understands them and he can help answer my queries.'

'I thought that's what your tutor is for, not another student.' Lorna frowned. 'Anyway, you said that Gwyn was aiming to be a journalist, so surely he won't be studying the same courses as you are?'

Sarah threw the dishcloth down into the water, splattering soapsuds everywhere. 'You're as bad as Dad,' she fumed. 'You think you know best, and you seem to want to keep me caged up. Why on earth don't you want me to have any friends of my own?'

'Sarah, listen to me. That's not what I meant...'

Her mother's words followed her as she flounced out of the kitchen and rushed upstairs to her bedroom. She heard her father calling after her, demanding to know what was going on, but she took no notice. Once in her room she flung herself down on the bed and let her tears flow. Why couldn't they try and understand that she was no longer a child, and that she was growing up?

Gwyn Roberts was inwardly fuming as he walked away from the Lewises' house. He knew Sarah had warned him that her father was a difficult man and that he was exceptionally strict, but what he hadn't been prepared for was Lloyd Lewis's frosty rudeness and he regarded that as being not only uncalled for but uncivil. No one treated him so audaciously and got away with it, he decided angrily.

He was puzzled about the reception he'd received because Lloyd Lewis didn't appear to be an ignorant man. In fact, from the way he spoke he was quite well informed, so why had he taken such a violent dislike to him? he wondered.

He'd done his homework well in preparation for meeting him. He'd been taught that to be a good newspaper man you not only had to be tenacious, but you also had to do your research thoroughly and to contemplate the situation logically.

He'd tackled the forthcoming encounter in the same way as he would have done an assignment. He'd spent considerable time checking out Lloyd Lewis's background and finding out what sort of job he was doing, how long he had served in the army and even where he'd been born. He was intrigued to find that Lloyd Lewis was also from the Valleys and that he'd been born not far from Aberdare and that, like him, he came from mining stock. That was why he'd expected him to be supportive when he talked about the miners and their problems instead of which he had taken an opposing viewpoint. Even so, he would have been interested in a discussion about the problems posed by the threatened miners' strike and whether or not he thought that Prime Minister Lloyd George could take steps to alleviate it.

Mrs Lewis had been pleasant enough and obviously had gone out of her way to make him welcome.

Gwyn kicked out idly at a bottle lying on the pavement, sending it spinning into the gutter. If he didn't care so much about Sarah he'd have nothing more to do with her or her family, but she'd really got under his skin.

She was different from any other girl he'd gone out with and there'd been quite a few since he'd been at university. She was passionate, and yet, unlike the others, she'd held out against his advances. The fact that she consistently refused to go all the way not only made her even more desirable but also made him determined to make her his.

A smile twisted Gwyn's firm mouth as he contemplated the situation. That would be one way of getting even with Lloyd Lewis, he thought cynically. He could imagine the look of horror there would be on his face when he found out that he'd had his way with his precious daughter.

His smile faded; that wouldn't be fair on Sarah and it certainly wasn't the way he wanted things between them to go. He'd never felt like this about anyone before and, cynical though he was about such things, he was pretty sure he was in love with her. He knew she cared for him, it showed in her eyes and how she hung on to his every word. He could also sense it in the way she responded to his touch.

Her father was so bigoted that it was probably useless talking to him about this; even a waste of time telling him how much he liked his daughter. That didn't mean that he was prepared to let Lloyd Lewis dismiss him as a nonentity or to simply ignore him. He was determined to retaliate in some way and in doing so prove that he was superior to him. Lloyd was the sort of man whose convictions had to be decried and made to realise that his opinions were outdated.

Once her father accepted that Gwyn was a permanent part of Sarah's life then he'd have to accept him and his views. That would be his target from now on, Gwyn decided. He was quite certain that Sarah would be told to have nothing more to do with him, so reassuring her about his feelings for her would be his first concern.

He was confident, though, that Sarah cared for him so much that she wouldn't be able to stay away from him for very long even if her father told her she must, he thought complacently, and, furthermore, he'd do everything possible to make sure she didn't.

Lorna Lewis finished the washing-up and stacked all the best tea-service away carefully. She'd looked forward to entertaining Sarah's friend but it saddened her that because of Lewis's attitude everything had ended on such a sour note.

There were times when she found it difficult to understand her husband. Surely he didn't expect Sarah to study every minute of the day; she needed to have friends and to go out and enjoy herself occasionally. She didn't even see Rita these days so it was natural that she'd start up a friendship with someone she'd met at university, someone who shared similar interests.

This Gwyn seemed such a nice chap. He was good-looking and polite as well as intelligent. He certainly seemed to be very knowledgeable. She would have thought that would have impressed Lloyd, but he'd seemed to have taken a dislike to him the minute he'd walked into the house.

For a fleeting moment she wondered whether the flowers had anything to do with it; surely Lewis couldn't have been jealous. She almost laughed out loud at the thought; quite sure it couldn't have been that. In fact, the only reason she could see for his outspoken hostility was that he resented or objected to Gwyn's friendship with Sarah. Either he didn't want to recognise the fact that she was growing up and would soon be living a life of her own or else he simply couldn't accept it.

She knew Sarah was very upset so once she'd checked that Lloyd was still engrossed in his newspaper she went upstairs and tapped softly on Sarah's bedroom door.

As she'd expected, Sarah was lying on her bed, her face buried in the pillow, and when she looked up her cheeks were tear stained. Without a word, Lorna sat down on the side of the bed and gathered her daughter in her arms, rocking her backwards and forwards almost as if she was still a small child.

There was no need for words; Lorna sensed that all Sarah wanted was for her to put her arms around her and hold her close; to be comforted and know that her mother understood.

Chapter Six

Sarah found she was no longer enjoying university; she was so smitten with Gwyn that she couldn't concentrate and as a result was getting more and more behind with her work.

She knew Gwyn wasn't altogether happy either although he was doing far more work than she was because it was his final year and he was anxious to achieve a good degree. He was very frustrated, though, because they could spend so little time together.

Much as she wanted to see Gwyn she knew that if her father found out that she was flaunting his ruling then it would only result in trouble at home. That would distress her mother and make her unhappy, so it made Sarah reluctant to defy him.

The excuse that she was staying late into the evening because she was attending special lectures was no longer valid now that her father had discovered the truth. This meant that the only times she and Gwyn could be together now was in odd moments they managed to snatch between lectures during the day.

In recent weeks, since their timetables varied so much and he was not prepared to miss out on any of his tutorials when he was so near his finals, it had meant that she was the one who had to make sacrifices and play truant.

Occasionally she was able to make up the lectures she missed by borrowing someone else's notes but she soon found that doing so was nowhere near as beneficial as actually sitting in on the lecture would have been.

The other thing that troubled her was not only the long summer break that lay ahead but also the fact that Gwyn would be ending his time at university. He would then have to start looking for a job so she would probably see even less of him. This might even mean that she and Gwyn wouldn't see anything at all of each other in the future and she couldn't imagine what life would be like without him.

She also knew her father would expect her to spend most days studying as she'd done between leaving school and starting at university.

She even began to think that perhaps her father was going to get his own way after all and that she and Gwyn would have to stop seeing each other. This might be better than the constant heartache and frustration she was subjected to when they arranged to meet and then one of them found it impossible to do so and had to cancel, she reflected.

When she mentioned this to Gwyn, however, he was so upset that she immediately admitted that it would be impossible and agreed with him wholeheartedly that they couldn't live without each other.

'There is only one thing we can do,' Gwyn told her, taking her in his arms and holding her close. 'We must elope.'

'Elope!' She pulled away and stared at him wide-eyed. 'You're not serious, surely?'

'I've never been more serious in my life,' he told her gravely. 'It's useless asking your parents if we can be married because your father wants nothing at all to do with me, so he's hardly likely to consider me to be a suitable husband for you.'

'Once he realises how much I love you . . .'

'No, cariad, I'm afraid it wouldn't work. I'm surprised you'd even suggest it,' Gwyn told her firmly.

'How can we elope, though,' Sarah frowned, 'I'm still too young to be married without my father's consent and as you've just said, that would be out of the question.'

'Shush!' He pulled her back into his arms and stroked her hair gently. 'Leave it all to me, I'll find a way. Just be patient and don't mention what I've said to anyone. I'll devise a plan for us to be together.'

Sarah found that being patient wasn't easy, but she was determined to try and devote herself to her studies even though a hundred and one questions about what his intentions were remained unanswered.

It was the very end of term before she had

a chance to talk to him and by then she'd almost given up in despair. She was afraid that he might disappear and she would never see him again.

She was packing up her books and papers in readiness to take them home knowing she would be expected to study during the holidays, when he suddenly appeared in the lecture room. He was smiling and brimming with confidence as he quickly outlined his plan, speaking softly so that no one else could overhear what he was saying.

'Tell your parents that you have been invited to spend a few days at the home of one of your classmates,' he told her. 'Make it soon so that we don't have to wait too long to see each other again, perhaps the beginning of August. You can tell them that your friend has invited you to spend the August bank holiday with her—'

'Dad would never agree to me doing that,' she interrupted quickly. 'Anyway, he'll be off work on Bank Holiday Monday and he'll expect me to go out with them, it's a sort of family tradition,' she ended lamely.

'Well,' Gwyn frowned, 'make it later that week, then, perhaps a few days in the middle of the week or the following weekend. It doesn't really matter which as long as I know the exact dates. Do you understand?'

'I think so, but what are you planning we should do?' she asked shyly.

'What do you think I want to do?' He grinned.

'Has this got anything to do with your idea about us eloping?' Sarah persisted.

'No!' He shook his head. 'I simply want us to spend some time alone because we've had so little chance to do so lately.'

'You mean go away together on our own!' For a moment she looked shocked. 'Where are we going?'

'Does it matter as long as we're together?' he teased.

'I'm not sure they'll let me do that. I've never been away on my own before. Who do I say I am going to stay with? I've never mentioned any particular friend except you.'

'Well, you can hardly tell them you are going on holiday with me, now can you!' he laughed. 'Surely you can claim that one of the girls in your year is a special friend. Tell them anything, it doesn't matter. I must know the dates, though, and once you've decided when it is to be then I can go ahead and book somewhere for us to stay and then make all my other arrangements.'

She looked puzzled. 'What do you mean?'

'You'll have to wait and see. I haven't time to tell you all about it right now,' he said impatiently.

Sarah felt really excited at the thought of spending time alone with Gwyn and even though she knew that her parents would be shocked and that she should resist such a temptation she felt she couldn't possibly turn it down.

Even so, she anticipated that there were going to be a great many problems; so many that she wasn't at all confident that it was going to be possible to fall in with his idea. As she'd already told him, she'd never been away on her own before and she wasn't at all sure how her parents would react when she said that was what she wanted to do.

Although it was only a few weeks away from her eighteenth birthday, they'd still probably think she was too young. She might be able to persuade her mother that it would be all right, but her father was so protective that he might object.

'Stop pondering about whether or not it's possible and simply tell them that it's what you are going to do,' Gwyn told her, slightly irritated by her seeming reluctance. 'You do want to be with me and for us to go away together, don't you, Sarah?'

'You know I do,' she said emphatically.

'Then the rest is up to you. I need firm dates, remember, and I need them later today.'

She looked at him puzzled. 'I need time to think about how I am going to ask them at home, so why do you need to have an answer right this minute?'

'Because I go home to Aberdare tonight and after that it's not going to be very easy for us to keep in touch. If I write to you, then your father will probably censure your letter, if I know anything about him.'

'I don't know about that because I never get any letters.' She smiled.

'Exactly; which is all the more reason why he'd be suspicious if you did, especially if he spotted an Aberdare postmark on it.'

'Yes, you're probably right but—'

'Look, if you can't manage the bank holiday, then it had better be later that week. What about meeting me on the Thursday, that will be the fourth of August?'

'Until when?'

'I don't know! Does it matter? Simply say you've been invited for a few days' holiday and leave it at that.'

'My dad will probably say that as we've had a day out on the Monday then I should be content with that,' Sarah murmured rather dubiously.

'It has to be then,' Gwyn told her firmly. 'I'm starting work the following week.'

'You've got a job? Why, that's wonderful.' Sarah beamed. 'Come on, then, tell me all about it,' she enthused.

'Not much to tell, really, because I'm not sure what it entails and it may not be permanent. It's as a reporter on the *Western Mail*.'

Her face lit up. 'So does that mean you will be working here in Cardiff?'

'I think so, initially. I don't really know what the hours or the routine will be until I actually start work.'

'It sounds terribly exciting. It is a good start for what you want to do, isn't it?'

Gwyn shrugged. 'I'm not sure. I'll have to see how it goes. I don't intend to be a run-of-the-mill reporter; I want something more challenging than that. I only had the interview yesterday and they said that my future would depend on what sort of degree I get, but they said they'd give me a month's trial.'

'It sounds promising, though,' Sarah pointed out. 'I do envy you! I wish I was starting work, earning money and about to become independent like you are.'

'Then you'd better put your back into your studies and make sure you do better in your exams so that you are so well qualified you land a top job,' Gwyn told her dryly. 'You also need to learn to stand up for yourself or you'll end up with your dad deciding where you must work.'

'You're being ridiculous.' Sarah frowned, although she knew that was exactly what would probably happen.

'Start the way you intend to go on; tell him that you are going away on holiday for a few days and stick to your decision. It's the only chance we have to see each other over the next couple of months. I'll be waiting for you at Cardiff General railway station at ten o'clock in the morning on the fourth of August, so mind you don't let me down.'

'When did you say you start your new job?'

'The following Monday, on the eighth.'

'So I can tell them that I'll be back home on the Sunday?'

'If you have to; don't be too positive about it, though; you might want to stay another night with me, and we mightn't come back to Cardiff until the Monday morning.'

'You mean the day you start work?'

'That's right; we ought to make the most of it, you never know when we will manage to spend a few days together again after that.'

He pulled her close, oblivious of the other people in the room. 'Don't let me down, Sarah. I've gone to a lot of trouble to make sure we have this very important time together. You do want to be with me, don't you?' he asked urgently.

'More than anything in the world,' she breathed.

'Cardiff General at ten, then,' he confirmed as his mouth sought hers in a brief but passionate kiss.

'Don't let me down,' he warned again as he released her.

Before she could say anything he'd gone, leaving her trembling with a mixture of excitement and anticipation. What on earth was she going to tell her parents, she wondered? Gwyn meant so much to her that she couldn't take the risk of losing him even though it meant defying her parents and going behind their back.

She could think of nothing else for the next few days. Sometimes she felt that time was standing still and she'd never see Gwyn ever again. At other times it seemed to be racing by and she still hadn't plucked up the courage to tell her parents that she was going away for a few days.

She kept going over and over all the things Gwyn had said and wondering if she'd got them right. Had he really meant it when he'd said that he couldn't live without her and had suggested they should elope?

Now he was suggesting spending a few days together. Did that mean he'd changed his mind about them being married? Or was he testing her to see if she really cared enough? Did he assume that if she was prepared to take the risk of spending a few nights away with him, then she would be willing to spend the rest of her life with him as his wife?

She felt more and more confused; she wondered if he was thinking along those lines or whether he was merely out to seduce her. She realised that if she did go away with him as he suggested, then he would be expecting her to sleep with him, not hold him at arm's length as she'd done up until now.

There was so much more to his invitation than merely confronting her parents and asking their permission, she thought worriedly. She hated the idea of having to concoct some sort of story and tell them she would be with a girlfriend, and she still had no idea how she would go about doing that. All she knew was that she must make it clear to them that it was important to her and yet her mind seemed to go blank when she tried to think of what she must say to convince them of that.

Gwyn was asking an awful lot of her, she mused. If her father ever found out he'd probably turn her out and disown her; yet if she didn't go along with Gwyn's suggestion then that really would end things and she would lose him completely, she had no doubts about that.

If only Rita was still living nearby then she could have asked her advice but Rita and her family had moved to Newport and there was no one else she could confide in.

Not for the first time she regretted not having got to know some of the other girls at university. She had been so obsessed with Gwyn, because he was the very first boyfriend she'd ever had, that she'd wanted to be with him and no one else, so she had deliberately avoided them all.

Chapter Seven

Sarah spent hours agonising over when it would be the best time to confront her parents before fate came to her rescue.

A couple of days before the August bank holiday her mother twisted her ankle rather badly and found it painful to walk. Lloyd was extremely concerned. Sarah did all she could to help and her father was full of praise for the way she was waiting on her mother and doing the housework and shopping.

'I'm afraid it means we won't be going out anywhere over the holiday, cariad,' he warned Sarah, 'but perhaps we can go out somewhere special later on.'

'Well, when Mam's ankle is better then perhaps I could go and stay with my friend; she asked me at the end of term if I'd go and stay with her for a few days, but I told her I would have to ask you first,' Sarah gabbled.

'Friend? What friend is this?'

'One of the girls I know at university. We go to the same lectures, because we're studying the same subjects.'

He stared at her challengingly. 'This is the first time you've mentioned this friend. Why haven't you brought her home to meet us?' he asked curtly.

'I don't know,' Sarah said awkwardly, 'except that you don't like visitors very much.'

'I don't like the sort of rabble-raiser you brought home before,' he said sharply.

'So can I go? I said I would let her know. She suggested the Thursday after the bank holiday.'

'I think we'd better see how your mother's ankle is before we make any decision of that sort,' Lloyd said dubiously. 'At the moment she needs you here.'

Although it seemed possible that she would be able to go, Sarah knew he might change his mind, even at the very last minute. As soon as she had the chance she explained the situation to her mother.

'I think that would be a lovely idea and it would make up for your missing out on the bank holiday trip and for the way you've looked after me. Don't you worry, I'll make sure it is quite better well before then,' she promised in a conspiratorial whisper.

'It's only a matter of days away,' Sarah pointed out worriedly.

'Well, if you can't go this week then next week will do just as well, won't it?'

Sarah shook her head. 'She said it had to be this week. They ... they're going away after that, the whole family.'

Even as she said it she hated herself for lying to her mother when she was being so cooperative. She wondered what she would think, or even say, if she knew that she was planning to go away with Gwyn. She'd probably be shocked, she thought miserably.

Things had changed since the end of the war and women were taking liberties in all sorts of ways, but to go on holiday alone with a man when you weren't married to him was still overstepping the mark. She and Gwyn were not even engaged so she had no excuse whatsoever for her brazen behaviour, even though she did love him with every fibre of her being.

By the time Thursday morning arrived, although it had been finally agreed that she could go, Sarah was in such a state of nerves that she was on the point of calling the whole thing off. She'd told so many lies over the last few days that she felt mortified and wondered how she could look either of her parents in the face.

She was wearing a new dress, crisp, pale green cotton, with a matching jacket which had the collar and revers piped in white and a matching pale green cloche hat trimmed with a full-blown white fabric flower. As she kissed her mother goodbye she felt such a wave of guilt that she was shaking; so much so that she could hardly pick up the small brown suitcase she'd packed ready the day before.

'Now don't forget to send us a postcard the moment you get there so that we know you've arrived safely,' her mother told her. 'Remember, letting you go away on your own is almost as big an undertaking for us as it is for you,' she added.

Cardiff General railway station was packed when Sarah arrived and she had a momentary feeling of panic in case she couldn't find Gwyn amongst so many people.

She didn't know where to start looking for him. Her suitcase felt heavy and people kept bumping into her as they rushed for their train so she decided to stand still and hope he would spot her. If he didn't then she'd know that she wasn't meant to go on this illicit holiday, she told herself, though how she would explain her change of plans to her parents she had no idea.

She'd been waiting for almost ten minutes before she felt someone touch her arm and she spun round, almost jumping out of her skin with fright.

It was Gwyn. Somehow he looked even more broad-shouldered and handsome than ever, in his smart grey suit, a raincoat over one arm and a suitcase in the other, and she found it hard to believe that she could possibly be going away on holiday with him.

'Are you all right, Sarah?' He gave a puzzled frown at her startled reaction.

'Yes, yes, of course I am,' she said breathlessly. 'You startled me, that's all.'

'I thought you'd seen me; you were staring over in my direction for long enough. Come on,' he picked up her case, 'our train is in and we'll miss it unless we hurry.'

Sarah followed him, dogging his steps as other passengers barged past them in the opposite direction. She'd dreamed of him sweeping her into his arms, saying how pretty she looked in her new clothes and how wonderful it was that they were going away together, but he hadn't even kissed her, she thought unhappily.

The train was packed; they found two empty seats but they were at opposite sides of the carriage – she had a corner seat and Gwyn was squashed in between a rather large man and a middle-aged lady, so they weren't even able to sit together.

Gwyn had put both their cases up into the luggage rack but even those weren't side by side, Sarah thought forlornly. They'd hardly sat down before a porter came along the platform, slamming shut the carriage doors. The guard blew his whistle and with a noisy belch of steam the train moved out of the station.

She stared across at Gwyn, hoping for a reassuring smile, but he'd pulled a newspaper out of his pocket and all she could see was the top of his thick brown hair as he sat there reading it. He looked more like a businessman or a commercial traveller than someone embarking on the very daring adventure of taking his girlfriend away for the first time, she mused.

Her thoughts were diverted as the ticket collector came along the corridor and into their carriage. She felt his gaze fall on her and for a moment she felt guilty because she hadn't got a ticket and she didn't know if Gwyn had bought tickets for both of them or not; furthermore, she didn't even know where they were going.

As Gwyn held out their tickets to be punched her moment of panic faded. She was being stupid; of course he'd bought both tickets and of course he knew where they were going, so she didn't have to say or do anything.

As he looked in her direction she gave a tremulous smile and her spirits soared as he grinned back at her and winked. Suddenly, knowing how much he cared and how much she figured in his thoughts, all her fears vanished. How could he kiss her or even talk to her when they were surrounded by strangers?

Reassured, she relaxed and settled back more comfortably in her seat, revelling in the thought of how much she meant to him, and she spent the rest of the journey looking out the window enjoying the view of the passing countryside. They'd left Cardiff behind them now. The landscape had changed and they were travelling through places she'd never heard of before; she even caught a glimpse of the sea.

Sarah wasn't sure how long they'd been on the train or where their destination was, but she trusted Gwyn. When he stood up and lifted down their cases she followed him out into the corridor and as the train ground to a halt she let him help her down on to the platform.

Once their tickets had been punched and they were through the barrier, Gwyn paused in a quiet corner of the station entrance and put down their cases.

'You look like a frightened rabbit,' he murmured as he pulled her into his arms. 'I had no idea that everywhere would be so busy or I might have suggested travelling at a different time of day so that at least we could have sat together during the journey.'

'Never mind, we're here now.' She smiled uncertainly. She looked around her questioningly. 'Exactly where are we?'

'We're in Porthcawl, which is about twenty-five miles from Cardiff,' he told her.

'Oh!' She looked slightly crestfallen. 'I thought that perhaps we were going to your home in Aberdare.'

'Are you twp, cariad?' he asked shaking his head. 'That would be a very stupid thing to do, now wouldn't it? We don't want either of our families knowing anything about what we are doing.'

'No, I suppose not.' She looked at him adoringly. 'You do think of everything, don't you?' she breathed.

'Of course I do.' He smiled. 'My mam and dad expect me to establish a worthwhile career before I go gallivanting around with any girls,' he told her solemnly.

'So that's what this is, is it? Gallivanting around doesn't sound very romantic,' she said, pouting.

Gwyn tightened his arms around her. 'Others might think that but then they don't understand our feelings for each other, do they?' he said softly, pulling her closer and running a finger down her cheek.

Sarah breathed a long, happy sigh. It was so wonderful to have someone who understood you so well; someone you could share your thoughts with. She felt convinced that there was the same sort of mutual understanding between herself and Gwyn as there was between her own parents.

To the outside world, and even to her, she knew her father sometimes seemed to be rather strict. Yet with her mother, his every look and touch was full of warmth and understanding. She'd noticed that even the timbre of his voice seemed to change when he spoke to her mother; it became as gentle as a caress.

'Come on, stop day-dreaming,' Gwyn told her. He kissed her so passionately that her cloche hat was pushed so far back on her forehead that it fell off.

'Now look what you've done, and that's my new hat,' she scolded lightly as he bent and picked it up and held it out to her.

'Very pretty it is too.' He smiled as he perched it on top of her head, kissing her again before leaving her to pull it down into place.

'Let's go,' he said, and picked up their cases. As they left Pyle Station he said, 'I've booked a room for us at a boarding house not very far from the sea. It's a fair walk from here – can you manage that, or should we try and find a taxicab?'

'We'll walk,' she said, but once again his thoughtfulness and desire to please her and make things easy for her filled her with warm delight.

'It's quite near the Esplanade. I thought you'd like it there because you might even be able to see the sea from our window.'

Sarah hadn't given any thought to where they would stay and now she felt another surge of appreciation that Gwyn had done all this on his own without a word to her.

As they walked along the busy streets, she felt proud to be with him and wished their time together could last for ever and not merely three days. Still, that was better than nothing, she told herself and it was going to be a wonderful opportunity for them to really get to know each other.

Being so far away from home meant that they were both more relaxed because there was no fear of bumping into anyone they knew either from the university or, in her case, neighbours from around Cyfartha Street.

She'd never been to Porthcawl before so for her it was a great adventure and she was curious to know how Gwyn knew so much about the place; he knew not only where to go but also where to book a room for them.

'Have you been here before?' she asked.

'Once, a long time ago. I came here on a day trip during my last year at school in Aberdare. It was our reward for working hard all year. The headmaster hired a charabanc to bring our class and we were the envy of the whole school.'

'What did you do?'

'Everything we could. We walked along the promenade, explored all the beaches, the sandy ones and the pebbly. We scrambled over rocks and some of us went into the sea. We'd brought our own food so we found a lovely spot at a place called Sandy Bay for a picnic and then to finish off the day we went to Coney Beach. It had only just been turned into a funfair centre and there weren't all that many rides or stalls there but I've heard that it is now quite famous. They named it after Coney Island in New York,' he added knowledgeably, 'so I'll take you there.'

'Where did you say we were staying? Is it very far now? I think I have the wrong shoes on for walking.'

'Oh dear!' He put down the cases and put his arm around her. 'I should have called a taxicab after all,' he said, his voice full of concern. 'Mind, it's not all that far now, only another couple of streets. Do you think you can manage that?'

'I'm sure I can, but you must be feeling worn out carrying both the cases.'

'They do seem to have got heavier, especially yours,' he said grinning.

Sarah felt as if she couldn't walk another step and she was sure she had a blister on her heel when they came to a stop outside a three-storey terraced house in a street where every house was painted white but all the doors and windows of each house were in different colours.

'Here we are!' Gwyn went ahead up the wide stone steps and pulled on the bell. As she joined him and stood by his side waiting for the door to open he said quickly, 'We're booked in as Mr and Mrs Roberts.'

Before Sarah could answer, the door swung open and a buxom woman in her late fifties, with wavy grey hair and wearing a lace-trimmed apron over a dark pink cotton dress, stood looking at them enquiringly.

'Hello, Mrs Williams, I'm Gwyn Roberts and I wrote to you last week and booked a room here for myself and my wife for three nights,' Gwyn announced.

'You'd better come along in, then, hadn't you,' the woman said and turned and walked down the hallway leaving them to follow.

Inside the hall was a long, narrow, polished wooden table with a hand bell on it and beside it was an open book that looked like a register. On the wall above the table was a rack holding six large keys, each with a number on it.

'You're in number five,' Mrs Williams told

him, taking a key from the rack. 'Sign the book first, will you,' she said picking up a pen, dipping it in the inkwell, and then holding it out to him.

Sarah was conscious that Mrs Williams was studying her very keenly as Gwyn bent over the table and she wondered what she was thinking. She felt her colour rising as she wondered if Mrs Williams had noticed she wasn't wearing a wedding ring and knew they weren't married.

'Right.' Mrs Williams scrutinised his signature and then handed him the key. 'Top floor, the door on the right; it has five written on it. Breakfast is between eight and nine o'clock, evening meal at seven, and the front door is locked at eleven o'clock. Until then it is always on the latch. There are clean towels in your bedroom and the bathroom is on the floor below you. Is there anything else you need to know?'

'I don't think so, thank you.' Gwyn smiled as he took the key from her.

'Well, if there is then come down and ring the hand bell. I can hear it and will come out to see what it is you want. Is all that clear?'

'That all sounds fine, thank you,' Gwyn told her in a confident voice. He handed the key to Sarah. 'You take care of that, my dear, and I'll carry the cases.'

Mrs Williams watched them as they made their way up the stairs. As they reached the first landing they heard her walk away and

Gwyn turned and raised his eyebrows at Sarah in such a comical way that she found it hard not to laugh out loud.

'Open the door, then,' he puffed when they reached the top floor and located number five.

Sarah slid the key into the lock, opened the white-painted door and preceded him into the room. The first thing that met her eyes was the big double bed and the enormity of what she was doing came home to her. She was a long way from home, in a strange house, and this was where she would be sleeping that night; not on her own but with Gwyn.

Chapter Eight

Sarah was in such a hurry to get out of the bedroom and away from the sight of the double bed that seemed to dominate the room that the moment Gwyn had put their suitcases down on the floor she asked if they could go out.

'Can we find somewhere to eat? I'm starving hungry,' she said with a shaky smile.

Immediately Gwyn was full of concern. 'You should have said so earlier then we could have had a snack at the railway station. No wonder you felt so tired while we were walking here. Didn't you have any breakfast before you came out?'

'No, I didn't. I was so nervous in case anything went wrong that I couldn't eat anything,' she admitted.

'Cariad!' He put an arm around her shoulder and propelled her towards the bedroom door. 'Come on, the very first thing we'll do now is go and look for a café. Do you want to change into more comfortable shoes first?'

'No, these will be all right now that I've had a short rest,' she told him quickly.

'Well, if you're sure. You can always take them

off when we reach the beach if you want to.'
He smiled.

As they made their way towards the sea-front they found the streets were thronged with holidaymakers all taking advantage of the glorious August sunshine.

Once again Sarah found her new shoes were pinching and rubbing her heel. She tried not to limp in case Gwyn suggested going back to the boarding house so that she could change them and the implication of the double bed still made her feel uncomfortable.

'I like the look of this one,' Gwyn pronounced as he stopped outside a smart little café near the Esplanade. It had a bright-striped awning and little round tables outside, as well as larger ones inside. 'Shall we sit here or would you rather go inside?'

'Inside, please.' The sun was burning down and her feet ached and she longed to be somewhere cool where she could discreetly slip off her shoes and relax.

'Good. We can have an early lunch and then we should be all right until our evening meal at the boarding house,' he suggested as they found a table and he picked up the menu and studied it.

The food was exceptionally good and by the time she'd finished eating Sarah felt much more her old self. The hard knot of unease inside her chest had begun to dissolve.

'You will be having some ice-cream now,

yes?' The waiter smiled as he came to clear away their dishes.

'Would you like some?' Gwyn looked enquiringly at Sarah with raised eyebrows.

She already felt quite full but the temptation was great. 'Well, we are on holiday, so it would be nice.'

'That is good; you make a fine choice.' The waiter beamed. 'My family, the Fulgoni's, we all come from Bardi in the North of Italy and so we are famous for our ice-cream because it is made from a traditional recipe that has been handed down for generations.'

'Shall we start exploring Porthcawl now?' Gwyn suggested after she'd spooned up the last morsel and declared she'd never tasted anything quite so delicious in her life.

They found Porthcawl a pretty and intriguing place. Although Gwyn had been there once before he hadn't realised that as well as the Esplanade and Sandy Bay there was also the Eastern Promenade that extended right the way to Coney Beach.

They decided that for their first day they'd be content to explore the town centre and the streets surrounding the Esplanade. There was certainly plenty to see: the handsome Grand Pavilion, several interesting churches and all the attractive shops in John Street, the main shopping area.

When they finally reached the Esplanade, the splendid promenade with its lovely view of

the sea, and which had been built to commem-
orate Queen Victoria's Jubilee, Sarah's feet
were hurting again. She suggested that she'd
be happy to sit there, watching the throngs of
holidaymakers and enjoying the sparkling view
of the sea, if Gwyn wanted to take a brisk walk
on his own.

He agreed he'd like to do that but not until
she'd taken a short walk with him on the shore
itself. As she experienced the strange, squelchy
feeling as her feet sank into the soft sand, she
grabbed hold of his arm and gave a tiny scream.
Laughingly he steadied her and persuaded her
to remove her stockings so she could feel how
pleasant it was to walk barefoot.

When he led her right down to the water's
edge and the incoming tide lapped at her feet,
she jumped back in shock which again made him
laugh. Together they paddled for about twenty
minutes and then he found her a deckchair and
settled her in it while he went off to try more
adventurous walking and scrambling amongst
the rocks.

She lay back and closed her eyes against the
brilliant light reflected from the sea, wiggling
her bare toes and enjoying the feeling of warmth
from the hot sunshine.

Wonderful though it all was, the image of
the double bed and what it entailed kept
coming back into her mind. She felt excited at
the thought of what lay ahead of her that night,
but also extremely nervous. It would have been

different if they were married or even if Gwyn had made it crystal clear what his intentions were for their future, she thought.

She was positive that he loved her but still she wasn't completely convinced that she was as important to him as her mother seemed to be to her father and she didn't want to settle for anything less.

Ever since she'd been old enough to notice such things she'd always been aware that her father couldn't do enough for her mother. She always seemed to come first in his thoughts and there had been many times, Sarah reflected, when she'd felt jealous of this fact. It was why she was always striving to please him in the hope that one day he would show her as much love and attention as he did her mother. So far she'd never managed to achieve it. There was always a critical gleam in his eyes when he looked at her that made her feel inadequate, or else there was a querulous timbre to his voice when he spoke to her as if somehow he was disappointed because she hadn't quite managed to attain the standard he expected.

This was one of the reasons why she adored Gwyn so much; he didn't criticise her and seemed to consider her the most important aspect of his life and she was sure that meant he was truly in love with her.

Even so, Sarah still felt nervous about being completely alone with him because of what lay ahead. She was not sure what his demands would be and she was worried in case she might disappoint him.

She made sure they were so late returning to their boarding house that there was no time to go up to their bedroom to get changed before going into the dining room for their meal.

The food was mediocre and because every table was occupied the service was slow, but she didn't mind because it meant they spent as long as possible in the dining room.

When it was finally no longer feasible to postpone things any longer she reluctantly preceded Gwyn up the stairs to their room. As he unlocked the door and stood aside to let her pass into the room the first thing that met her eyes was the bed and it seemed to be larger than ever.

She sat down on the side of it wondering what on earth she was going to do. Their suit-cases were still where he'd left them in the middle of the room. When he picked up hers and put it on the stand at the bottom of the bed she busied herself opening it and concentrating on what was inside. She felt awkward and uncomfortable about unpacking her toiletries and underwear in front of him.

'The bathroom is on the floor below if you'd prefer to use it,' he said quietly, breaking the ominous silence.

She looked at the washbasin with its bright pink and white flowers and big matching jug of cold water that was standing on the washstand

94

then picked up the bag containing her flannel and soap and made for the door, preferring to go down there rather than to have a wash in front of him.

'Wait, you'll probably need one of these,' he called after her, handing her one of the pink-and-white striped towels the landlady had left ready for them to use.

The door of the bathroom was locked when she got there so she hung around waiting for whoever was inside to come out. When they did, she rushed in and locked the door behind her then stood with her back against it trying to slow down her rapid breathing.

The room had a bath, a washbasin and a lavatory. As she peeled off her dress she wondered if she dare risk taking a bath. Before she could make up her mind someone rattled the door and a voice called out asking her to hurry up. Hastily she ran some water into the washbasin and had a quick wash. She wished she'd brought a dressing gown; she couldn't run back to their room in her underclothes since there were other people about and so she had to put her dress back on.

'I was coming to look for you, I thought you'd got lost,' Gwyn said worriedly when she returned.

'The bathroom was occupied and I had to wait,' she explained.

'Well, I hope it's free now.' He grinned as he picked up the other towel and headed for the door.

Sarah took advantage of being in the room on her own to undress and put on her new pale blue silk nightgown which was trimmed with ecru lace around the neckline, and which her mother had bought specially for her to bring away with her. The minute she had it on she slipped under the bedcovers, pulling them right up to her chin.

She felt too nervous to lie down and was sitting there, ramrod straight, when Gwyn returned. He'd removed his shirt to have a wash and was carrying it in his hand. Tossing it on to a chair he quickly unbuttoned his trousers, let them fall in a heap at his feet, and was in bed beside her before she had chance to draw a breath.

As his arms went round her, the contact with his bare chest sent a shiver of anticipation through her, then she tensed, not sure what was expected of her.

Very gently he pushed her back against the pillows, his lips nuzzling her neck, then moving slowly down towards her breasts, pushing aside the silky material that was covering them.

With a small murmur of surrender she relaxed and felt a flicker of desire spread through her as they clung to each other. His hands started exploring her body tenderly; it was so different to the furtive fumbles she'd experienced before when they'd said goodnight on the corner of Cyfartha Street.

After that, time had no meaning and the only

sound in the room were his whispered words of endearment followed by her small cries of astonishment as he made known what he wanted of her. Once she overcame her shyness she found herself responding to his quick-breathing eagerness as their love-making became ever more passionate and his ardour astounded her.

Finally, completely exhausted, they slept tangled contentedly in each other's arms until she was wakened by the early morning sun and the scream of seagulls.

For a moment Sarah thought it had all been a dream and she wasn't even sure where she was. Then the heaviness of Gwyn's body against her back brought everything rushing into focus.

Her movement wakened him and he pulled her into his arms, kissing her ardently, rekindling her own desire and passion as once again they made love.

They were almost too late for breakfast and Mrs Williams sniffed in annoyance when they took their place in the dining room.

'There's no porridge left,' she stated, her voice edged with irritation as she brought them a pot of tea. 'So what is it to be?'

'We're sorry about being so late,' Gwyn told her with a slightly apologetic smile. 'Any chance of bacon and eggs and toast and marmalade?' he asked hopefully.

For a moment Sarah thought Mrs Williams

was going to refuse but with a heavy sigh she turned and headed for the kitchen.

'If we have a really good breakfast then we'll be able to manage with just a sandwich at lunchtime,' he whispered quietly to Sarah. 'That will give us more time to explore the seafront and perhaps even go as far as Coney Beach.'

'I think I'll need one of those wonderful ice-creams if we're going to walk that far,' she told him.

'You can only have one of those as a reward if you behave yourself,' he teased. 'I think you deserve one after last night, though,' he added with a devilish smile.

The rest of their short stay in Porthcawl was spent in walking and exploring the coastline during the day and in blissful lovemaking at night. The time passed so quickly that in no time at all it was over and they were cramming their things back into their suitcases and heading back to Pyle Railway Station.

They made the journey home in silence, sitting holding hands, happy and contented with their own thoughts. When they reached Cardiff General, though, the realisation that they would soon be parting and that she had no idea at all when she would see Gwyn again was like a physical blow.

She didn't want to return home or to be parted from him. She was almost in tears as they clung together in a farewell embrace.

'If I'm going to be working in Cardiff, when can I see you?' he asked.

'I don't think it will be possible until the new term starts. My father has forbidden me to have anything more to do with you and if he found out that I was meeting you, he'd be terribly angry.'

'So how can we meet, then?' Gwyn probed with a frown.

'I can always play truant or see you when I haven't any lectures,' she explained. 'If I say I am going out during the holidays they will want to know where I am going. If I say it's to look around the shops, then my mam will probably say she'll come with me.'

'Couldn't you say you were going to the Public Library and I could meet you there?'

'She'd probably come with me.'

'Surely she wouldn't do that if you said you'd be gone a couple of hours because you wanted to read up about something.'

Sarah shook her head. 'You don't understand. She'd say she was coming and that she'd spend an hour looking round Howell's or Morgan's while I was in there.'

'That would be all right, wouldn't it?'

'She might take it into her head to come into the library looking for me and then if I wasn't there she'd know I was cheating on them and I'd be in trouble.'

Gwyn shook his head in disbelief. 'If you are old enough to go to university then surely you are old enough to go out and about on your own when you want to. I'm amazed they let you go away on your own for a few days.'

'So am I, really. I still dread going home and being cross-questioned about where I've been and what I saw and so on. I didn't even send a postcard like they asked me to, and I've already told so many lies that I can hardly remember what I've said.'

'Then the best thing you can do is tell them that you and this girl went to Porthcawl. That way you'll be able to talk about what you've seen and done without any fear of being caught out.'

'Yes,' Sarah brightened, 'you're probably right. That does sound like a good idea.'

'Providing you don't tell them about being with me and everything we've been doing, of course,' Gwyn teased as he gave her a final kiss.

'I certainly won't be doing that!' She smiled.

'You do love me, though, don't you?' he challenged as he handed her suitcase to her.

Chapter Nine

The rest of the summer holiday dragged by so slowly that sometimes Sarah thought she would go mad. She buried herself in her studies but, although she appeared to be working hard, her mind was not really on the books in front of her. She studied as a way of making the days pass more quickly and in order to stop herself dwelling on what had happened between her and Gwyn.

What she really wanted was to see him, to find out if he had enjoyed their time together as much as she had. She wanted to feel his warm breath on her face as he whispered sweet endearments to her and to feel his arms around her, holding her close. More than anything else, though, she wanted to feel their bodies entwined and to relive the blissful feeling of contentment she'd experienced after they'd made love.

She tried to hide her yearning so as not to let her mother know how discontented she felt and she made an effort to be enthusiastic when they got dressed up and went shopping together or went on an occasional trip to one of the parks because she knew it was her mother's way of making sure she took some time off to enjoy herself.

'I'm beginning to think that all this studying is no good for you; it's turning your head, cariad. You need to take some time off, you know. You seem to be in a dream world half the time.' Her mother sighed as they found a shady spot in Cathays Park and sat there waiting for the band to play. 'Twice now I've asked you what you think about that colourful bed of asters over there, and you don't even seem to have heard me.'

'Sorry, Mam. They're lovely. I did hear you, but I was thinking of something else.'

'Your new term will be starting in less than a week and then you really will be hard at it and worrying about exams again.'

'Yes,' Sarah smiled brightly, 'it's not long now and I'm quite looking forward to it.'

'In spite of what your father says and thinks I don't hold with all this studying – well, not for a girl anyway. Anyone would think you are going to have to be the breadwinner for the rest of your life.'

As the band started to play Sarah was glad she didn't need to enter into any further discussion and she merely smiled and patted her mother's arm.

As the music filled the air she gave herself up to remembering Porthcawl and wishing she was back there. Was Gwyn missing her, she wondered, and feeling the same, or was he so caught up in his new job on the *Western Mail* that he'd had no time to think about their holiday together? More to the point, when would she be seeing him? He knew the date she would be back at university, so would he be there waiting for her at the end of the first day?

To Sarah's dismay he wasn't. She hung around for as long as she dared, then reluctantly headed for home hoping she'd manage to get there before her father came home from work and started asking awkward questions about why she was so late.

She was on tenterhooks all evening, wondering if she should find some excuse to go out in case Gwyn had been late and missed her. Common sense told her that it would be a waste of time since he wouldn't still be hanging around the university campus.

The next morning she felt far from well and mentally told herself off for letting the previous evening's disappointment get to her so much. Although she would have liked to have stayed in bed and taken the day off sick she forced herself to get up and behave as normal because Gwyn would be there tonight, she told herself.

The feeling wore off during the day and she was glad that she'd made the effort to attend lectures because at the end of the afternoon Gwyn was waiting outside.

With her heart in her mouth she rushed to greet him; he looked so tall and rugged that she wanted to fling herself into his arms, but she restrained herself because there were so many people about.

He pecked her cheek, squeezed her arm and, taking her bag of books from her, suggested they went to their usual milk bar.

'Come on, I'm going to spoil you; cake and an ice-cream, although I don't suppose either of them will be half as good as the ones we had at the Fulgoni's restaurant in Porthcawl.'

'I expected you to come and meet me yesterday afternoon; I waited around for ages,' she told him as they discreetly held hands under the table while they waited to be served.

'I thought you might, but there was no way of letting you know that I wouldn't be able to manage it because I'd been sent to Bristol to cover a story. Are you quite sure that if I wrote to you your father would open the letter even if it was plainly addressed to you?' he asked, frowning.

'I'm not sure, but he always opens all the letters and if he didn't open mine he would want to know who it was from.'

'Well, what about if I signed it "Ruth" or "Gwyneth"? Couldn't you say it was from a girlfriend? Shall we try it and find out what does happen?' He chuckled.

There were so many things Sarah wanted to ask Gwyn but she wasn't sure how to start, so she ate her chocolate cake and ice-cream in silence. They were delicious but still not quite up to the same standard as the ones she'd had in Porthcawl.

While they were eating Gwyn enthused about his new job and at the same time aired his views about how he would do things differently if he was given a free hand.

'I only go along with the Editor's ideas in order to keep in his good books because I know I am only there on trial,' he told her. 'Once I'm on the permanent staff and able to use my initiative then I'll soon show them what I can do,'

'What do you mean?' She frowned. 'You can't expect promotion right away.'

'Why ever not? I've got a degree, remember. Most of the others have worked their way up from being the copy boy, who's at everybody's beck and call, to the junior reporter who covers council meetings and flower shows and things like that. With my background I should be allowed to specialise in politics; one of these days I might even be Foreign Correspondent or move to London as Parliamentary Correspondent.'

'Well, I hope you don't do that, because then I would never see you,' Sarah reminded him.

'When you get your degree then you could join the paper as one of the legal staff.' He grinned. 'Think about it; we'd probably be able to see each other every day.'

'The way things are going I don't think I will be getting my degree,' she confided worriedly. 'I keep thinking about you when I should be making notes and that always distracts me.'

He pulled a stern face and shook his head disapprovingly. 'You'd better do well or your father will have something to say about it,' he warned.

'I know! As a matter of fact, I think I had better be going because if he gets home from work ahead of me then he'll wonder why I'm late.'

'And the excuse that you've stayed late for a lecture doesn't wash any more as we very well know,' Gwyn said, smiling broadly.

'No,' she shook her head, 'I'm afraid it doesn't.'

'So when am I going to see you again?' he asked as they prepared to leave.

'I don't know, unless you can meet me the same time tomorrow afternoon.'

'I don't think that's going to be possible. I have to do some work, you know. It was quite a wangle getting time off today.' He frowned. 'In fact, in order to do so I have had to agree to do a stint tonight and I won't even have time to walk you home,' he added apologetically as he pushed back his chair and stood up.

Outside he kissed her on the cheek; a parting that was more like brother and sister or good friends, it certainly didn't have the passion she expected him to show towards her after their holiday together.

'Probably the best thing is for me to write and let you know when I can next manage to be here in the afternoon,' he told her.

'Yes,' she agreed reluctantly. 'I suppose that

will be all right. I'll try and make sure I pick up the letters before anyone else does.'

'Don't worry, my letter will be quite safe. I'll sign it "Gwyneth" and then you can tell them that I am a friend and perhaps we can meet more often. Surely you'll be able to get away one evening a week or at the weekend if I let you know in good time?'

He was gone before she could answer and she felt close to tears of disappointment as she watched him disappearing down St Mary Street. Even when he briefly turned and waved to her it did little to quell the feeling of desertion that overwhelmed her.

She turned over in her mind his suggestion of writing to her and wished she'd told him not to do so. If her father did read Gwyn's letter, he was bound to be suspicious because she'd told them that Gwyneth was her friend at university. She'd been so confused after Gwyn had made that suggestion that she hadn't been thinking clearly. What she should have done, of course, was ask him for his address and then she could have been the one to write to him. As it was, she didn't even know where he was living, although she was sure that it must be in Cardiff now that he was working there.

After a restless night she was up early, feeling sick with worry as she listened for the sound of the letter box, even though she realised that Gwyn wouldn't yet have had time to arrange anything or write a letter to her.

The same thing happened the next morning but when her mother placed a plate of sausage and egg on the table for her she had to struggle to eat it and only did so to avoid her mother asking questions. She was sure it was the stress of waiting for a letter that was making her feel unwell, and had no idea how she could explain that to her parents.

The moment she'd finished eating she hurried up to her room on the pretence of getting ready. She felt so bilious that she lay down on her bed for a while and tried to reason with herself that she was being silly and that she was imagining it. She couldn't go on making herself feel ill like this every day. It might be a week before Gwyn wrote to her.

The weekend came and went and no letter arrived and Sarah felt even more tense and unwell.

As soon as they met again she'd have to tell Gwyn that this arrangement was no good at all because all the worry was upsetting her. She not only felt physically sick but also so disorientated until mid-morning that the lectures in the early part of the day simply passed over her head.

A letter arrived on Monday morning and because, once again, Sarah was up so early she was able to retrieve it and secret it away without either of her parents noticing it. She still felt sick but this time she attributed it not to stress but to her tremendous feeling of relief.

The moment she was clear of Cyfartha Street Sarah pulled out the letter that she'd pushed into the pocket of her skirt and eagerly read it. It was so innocuous that she could easily have opened it in front of her parents. All it said was:

Can you come to the cinema with me Wednesday night? Meet me there at 7 p.m.
Gwyneth

She almost laughed out loud with relief. She'd show it to her parents tonight, she decided, and see what they said. Then she realised she could hardly do this because then they'd know she'd collected it in the morning and hidden it away from them.

Why did everything have to be so complicated, she wondered? She thought about it all day, reading the few lines over and over again, deriving comfort from the fact that they'd been written by Gwyn. In the end she thought the best thing to do would be to wait until they were eating their evening meal and then tell them she wanted to go to the pictures with Gwyneth and see how they reacted.

'I think that's a lovely idea,' her mother agreed. 'You've been working so hard lately that you look quite washed out. An evening out will do you good.'

Lloyd was not so certain. 'Is it going to interfere with your studies?' He frowned. 'Those sorts of outings should be undertaken during the holidays, not in term time; I thought I had made that quite clear.'

'One exception isn't going to hurt, surely,' Lorna insisted. 'I think it will do her good to have a night off.'

Sarah stayed silent, concentrating on the food in front of her and letting them argue it out between them. If her mother approved of the idea then she knew that, with a little persuasion, her father would do so as well because he never denied her mother anything. Usually she felt jealous about this but on this occasion she realised that it was going to be to her advantage.

Sarah thought Wednesday would never arrive. When it did she felt so sick that she couldn't touch her breakfast.

'You must eat something,' her mother protested. 'You'll only have a snack in the canteen at midday so if you are meeting your friend and going straight to the pictures, you'll be absolutely starving by the time you get home.'

'We can always have something at a milk bar before the pictures start,' Sarah told her.

'Fair-do's; I suppose you could do that, but it's not the same as sitting down to a proper meal,' her mother protested. 'Still, I don't suppose it will matter for once.'

As she was leaving her mother pressed a half-crown into her hand. 'Now mind you buy yourself a bun and have a milk shake before you go into the pictures. Come straight home afterwards because your dad will have an eye on the clock and if you turn up late he's bound to say you shouldn't have gone out and that you mustn't do it again.'

Sarah nodded, ready to agree to anything now that she knew she would be seeing Gwyn in a few hours' time.

'What did you say was showing?'

'I . . . I don't know. It must be something good because my friend particularly wants to see it.'

'You are a dreamer, cariad; you've always got your head in the clouds. Fancy not knowing,' her mother scolded lightly.

'Sorry, Mam. I never thought you'd be interested.'

'Well, just remember what you see because we'll want to know all about it when you come home,' her mother said, smiling.

Although her visit to the pictures with Gwyn was enjoyable and Sarah found it was wonderful to sit there with his arm round her, cuddling her close after the lights went down, somehow it had none of the magic of Porthcawl.

Afterwards, she was worried about getting back because she knew that if she was late she would have to face questions from her father about why she hadn't come straight home. This annoyed Gwyn because it meant that there was only time for a brief goodnight kiss.

'There's not much point in us going out if

you have to dash home in such a hurry after-wards,' he said irritably.

'If I'm late the first time I'm permitted to go to the pictures with a friend then I won't be allowed to do it again.'

'This is stupid,' he argued. 'You're eighteen now and if you didn't live so near to the university you would have left home ages ago and would be standing on your own two feet. They'd have no idea at all about how you spend your evenings.'

'I know that just as well as you do,' she retorted, her cheeks flaming. 'I don't like all these restrictions either but as long as I have to live at home then I have to do as they ask.'

'I keep telling you, you must stand up for yourself. Tell them you need to have friends of your own and to go out with them occasion-ally. It's not as though you are going to be out every night now, is it?'

'When are we meeting again?' she asked softly, trying to quell his anger.

'If this is how things are going to be then there's not much point in us doing so,' he said churlishly.

'Don't be like that, Gwyn. Like I've already said, if I get home in good time tonight then they might relax. If I don't, then they'll think I'm not to be trusted.'

'Well, you're not, are you? If they knew about where you went and who you were with the other weekend they'd probably throw you out and tell you never to darken their door again. Perhaps I should tell them?'

'You wouldn't!' She stared at him horrified. 'Promise me you will never do anything like that?'

'Why? Don't you trust me?' he questioned.

Her heart was thumping because she wasn't completely sure whether she did or not. Determined not to let their argument develop into a row she put her arms round his neck and pulled his face down so that she could kiss him.

'When are we meeting again?' she asked again. 'Next time I'll tell them in advance that I'll be late home.'

'Make that very late home and I might consider it,' he murmured as he returned her kiss.

'Very well, I'll tell them I will be very late. So when is it to be?'

'I'll write to you. Look out for a letter from Gwyneth,' he told her as they separated and she hurried down Cyfartha Street already later than she'd intended to be.

Chapter Ten

Although Lloyd Lewis looked very pointedly at the clock on the mantelpiece when Sarah arrived home he made no comment. She didn't offer any excuse, although she had already planned what to say if he challenged her on how late she was.

The evening hadn't had the sparkle she'd expected so she said very little to her parents, refused her mother's offer of some supper, and went off to bed right away.

She was late waking next morning and had to rush so much that she had no time to sit down to have what her mother called 'a proper breakfast'. Grabbing a piece of toast and gulping down a cup of tea she promised her mother she'd make up for it with a good meal in the canteen at midday.

'Well, mind you do, cariad,' her mother said worriedly.

About twenty minutes later she was feeling quite sick and wondered whether it was because she'd missed out on breakfast or because of the ice-cream she'd eaten in the pictures the night before when she'd been with Gwyn. As she reached the university building she felt so dizzy that she thought she was going to faint.

The feeling wore off during the morning and she certainly felt better after she'd eaten at lunchtime. The next morning, however, she felt queasy again and this time her mother overheard her being sick and asked her what was the matter.

Although she dismissed it as merely something she'd eaten her mother didn't seem completely satisfied. 'I think you'd better go and see the doctor. I've noticed you've not been looking well for a couple of weeks,' she said worriedly. 'Perhaps the doctor can give you a tonic or something.'

'You're making a fuss about nothing,' Sarah told her. 'I'll be fine in an hour or so, I usually am.'

'Do you mean that you've been sick before and said nothing about it?' Her mother frowned.

'A couple of times. It's nothing. Like you keep saying, I have been working very hard.'

Lorna refused to let the matter drop. That night, when Sarah was going upstairs to bed, her mother followed her saying she wanted a quiet word with her.

'I'm going to make an appointment for you to see the doctor. Now don't worry, I'll come with you,' she added quickly when she saw the look on Sarah's face.

'I can't do that because it means I'll miss out on an important lecture. I tell you what I'll do,' she went on quickly before her mother could start to argue about it, 'I'll report to the sick room and see the matron at the university.'

'When?'

'I'll do it today, I promise.'

'Well, mind you do and when you come home I'll want to know what she said.'

'Probably exactly the same as you; that I've been working too hard.' Sarah smiled as she kissed her mother goodnight.

It was mid-afternoon before Sarah remembered her promise to her mother and dashed along to the sick room. She hoped there would be no one else there and that she could get away again in a matter of minutes so that she wouldn't be late for her next lecture.

Matron was a plump middle-aged woman with grey hair pulled back into a fat bun. She was neatly dressed in a dark blue dress and a white starched apron, and she had a fob watch to which she referred every few minutes as if timing how long her patient had been there.

She took a minute or so to find the card with Sarah's details on it, then she listened in silence as Sarah explained that she didn't really feel ill and that it was only because her mother had insisted she had professional advice that she had come to see her at all.

'She made an appointment for me to see our doctor but it would have meant taking the morning off and I didn't want to do that,' Sarah finished.

Matron nodded understandingly. 'I'll know better if it is anything to worry about after you've told me your symptoms,' she said in a kindly voice.

'I feel sick first thing in the morning. That's all, really.' Sarah smiled. 'It always wears off by mid-morning, though, and then for the rest of the day I feel fine.'

'I see!' Matron picked up her pencil, asked a few pertinent questions, then made some notes on the card in front of her. When she looked up the smile was gone from her face.

'I think that perhaps you will have to go and see your own doctor, my dear,' she said gravely.

'Why?' Sarah looked alarmed. 'Do you really think I've got something wrong with me, then?'

For a moment Matron didn't answer. She looked down at the notes she'd made, tapping her pencil thoughtfully. 'I think you may be pregnant,' she said in an expressionless voice.

'Pregnant?'

Matron was quick to notice the dismay in Sarah's voice and she gave her a piercing look. 'Is there any reason for you to believe that you might be?' she asked in a rather severe voice.

Shaking her head and trying to hold back her tears, Sarah stood up and made for the door, ignoring the order to come back and discuss the matter further.

Once out in the corridor she headed for the cloakroom. All she wanted was to be on her own so that she could think through what she'd been told.

She splashed cold water on her burning face and tried to collect her thoughts. She'd never even thought about such a thing happening. Her parents would be mortified when she told them and what was Gwyn going to say?

Not for the first time she wished there was some way she could get in touch with him. For one wild moment she thought of going to the *Western Mail* offices and asking if she could speak to him, but she didn't think he would like that. Yet it was an emergency, she told herself; she needed him to advise her; to help her sort out the trouble she found herself in.

She walked home in a daze but by the time she reached Cyfartha Street she'd still not decided what to do. As she let herself into the house she resolved she'd wait until she had told Gwyn before she said anything to her mam and dad.

She wondered how he would react. Would he be pleased at the thought of becoming a father or would he be horrified? Perhaps, like her, he'd feel scared by the enormity of what had happened.

'So, what did the matron say, then?' her mother asked almost the minute she walked through the door.

'Not very much, can we talk about it later on, Mam?' Sarah prevaricated.

'Come on, tell me before your dad gets in,' Lorna persisted. 'Is it bad news?'

'I told her you thought I'd been working too hard.'

'Fair-do's, and what did she say to that?'

'Well, what do you think she said?' Sarah smiled.

'She probably agreed with me, if I know anything about it.'

To Sarah's relief there was the sound of the front door opening so she pressed a finger to her lips.

'Yes, all right, then, we'll have a talk about it later on,' her mother whispered.

'There's really not much else to say,' Sarah said hurriedly, hoping that would be the end of the matter.

She knew she was playing for time and the thought that her mother might start questioning her again the moment they were on their own worried her almost as much as the news itself. The last thing that went through her mind as she went to sleep was the hope that there would be a letter from Gwyn on Monday morning.

There wasn't, and, knowing not only how ill she would feel afterwards, but also what the real cause of it was, it took her all her time to sit down and eat the breakfast her mother insisted on her having.

It was Thursday before she received a letter. This time, although she had been determined to be near the hallway when the postman called, it was her mother who picked it up from behind the front door and handed it to her.

'If that's another letter from that friend of yours asking you to go to the pictures again, then you'd better say no. Late nights are the last thing you need at the moment, Sarah, because you are still looking rather washed out.'

'Perhaps it is exactly what I do need,' Sarah argued. 'If I have a night out now and again instead of studying every evening then I'll feel more relaxed, won't I?'

'Having an early night would do you far more good,' her mother told her.

'If I go to bed too early then I wake up in the middle of the night and I can't get back to sleep again.'

'These days you've got an answer for everything, haven't you?' Lorna said rather sharply. 'I'm not sure if all this education is doing you any good. It's certainly making you very difficult to live with, I can tell you that.'

Sarah knew that she ought to apologise to her mother but she couldn't bring herself to do so. She had so many other things to worry about. Even if her parents said she couldn't go out she knew she would have to go and meet Gwyn at all costs so that she could tell him that she was pregnant.

'Well, go on, then, open the damn letter,' her mother said crossly. 'At least let me know what's going on. Why on earth does she have to write to you?' She frowned. 'Why can't she ask you when you meet up at one of the lectures?'

'Gwyneth's no longer at university. She left last July and now she's working,' Sarah muttered tersely.

'Oh! Funny you never mentioned that before. So you went on holiday before she started work, did you?'

'That's right. She started work the following week. I thought I had mentioned it.'

'No, not a word, but then you didn't tell us all that much about your holiday either. Well, go on, then, open that letter and see what it is she has to say.'

Reluctantly Sarah slit open the envelope and pulled out the sheet of writing paper. She'd wanted to be on her own when she read it. The words became blurred in front of her eyes the moment she saw the signature 'Gwyneth'.

'Yes. She does want me to go out again,' she said defiantly. 'Tonight, as a matter of fact, so don't expect me home until about ten o'clock.'

'Ten! Why that late?' her mother queried. 'Surely you'll be going to the first showing so you'll be out by nine and it doesn't take you an hour to walk home.'

'We . . . we might go to a milk bar,' Sarah said shrugging her shoulders nonchalantly.

'Whatever for? Why waste your money like that when there'll be supper waiting here for you when you get in?'

'So that we can have a chat and catch up with what's happening,' Sarah said abruptly.

'The last time you went out together you said you were going to a milk bar before you went to the pictures, so if you do that you'll have plenty of time to talk then.'

'Half past nine, ten o'clock, what does it matter? Why are you making such a fuss, Mam?'

'I'm thinking of you, cariad. I don't want you getting ill.'

'One night out in the week isn't going to do that,' Sarah argued. 'And you keep saying I work too hard. Look, I must go or I'm going to be late.' She grabbed her coat, picked up her bag of books, and headed for the door.

'Hold on, cariad, you haven't had any breakfast again,' her mother remonstrated.

'I know, but because of all this arguing I haven't time now,' Sarah retorted as she banged the front door behind her and hurried down the street ignoring the fact that her mother had come out on to the step and was calling after her.

The day seemed endless and Sarah alternatively longed to see Gwyn and tell him what Matron had said and dreaded the thought of doing so because she wasn't sure what his reaction would be.

He was waiting outside the milk bar as he'd said he would be and as she walked down the street towards him her heart raced. Every time she saw him he seemed to be more handsome than ever.

Since he'd started work he'd become so forceful and even more confident about everything that she sometimes wondered if he still loved her as much as she loved him.

She waited until they were sitting down and she'd listened to all the new developments in his job and how exciting he was finding it before she attempted to tell him her news.

He frowned almost as if he couldn't comprehend what she was telling him.

'So what are we going to do, Gwyn?' she asked meekly.

He sat toying with his knife and avoiding her eyes for several seconds. When he looked up she realised that the news had astounded him and that he was as taken aback as she'd been when Matron had told her.

'You haven't had it confirmed by a doctor yet so you are not a hundred per cent sure,' he pointed out. 'It may not be that at all; it might be something you've been eating that disagrees with you,' he reasoned hopefully. 'Why not leave things as they are for the present?'

'No, I can't. My mother wanted me to go to the doctor but I said I would see Matron instead rather than take a morning off, but she's still insisting that I must do so and I haven't told her yet that Matron believes I am pregnant. If I am, then it will start to show soon and then everyone will know.'

'It's time enough for us to worry when that happens,' he said cheerfully. 'Surely you can tell your mother you're feeling all right again now.'

'You don't understand. Although I am feeling better my mam knows about me being sick and she's bound to notice that I am beginning to find it difficult to fasten my skirt.'

'You're imagining it, cariad, because of what you've been told. Mind you, it could be all the cream cakes and milk shakes you've been having when we go out,' he joked.

Sarah bit her lip and said nothing. She didn't think it was anything to joke about. She'd expected Gwyn to be very surprised, shocked even, but she had been hoping he would understand the predicament she was in and come up with some sort of solution to the problem.

She didn't really want to go to the pictures but she hoped that perhaps it would give Gwyn time to absorb what she had told him and then they could talk about it again afterwards.

She felt upset and worried by his response. Remembering the time when he'd said they should elope she'd thought that he would suggest that it was what they ought to do now. Or, better still, insist that they must get married before her parents discovered her predicament.

Chapter Eleven

It was the last week in February and three weeks since she'd heard from Gwyn when Sarah arrived home to find her mother looking very upset. Even before her mother said a word she knew instantly that she was going to have to tell her the truth.

In one way she felt it would be a great relief. Once her mother knew the truth then they would be able to talk openly about it and she would be able to ask her mother's advice about what she ought to do for the best.

'Don't try giving me any excuses,' Lorna greeted her angrily. 'I know perfectly well what is wrong with you and why you've been sick in the mornings . . .'

'Well, I'm not any more,' Sarah interrupted her quickly. 'That was a long while ago. I'm fine now. It must have been something I ate that disagreed with me. It was probably something I bought from the canteen.'

'Duw anwyl! Stop talking such twaddle, Sarah. I clean your room and I do all your washing, remember, so I know quite well that there is something wrong and has been for some weeks now. What's more, look at the way you're putting on weight. None of your clothes fit you properly any more. You're pregnant, aren't you! Come on now, cariad, admit it!'

They stared at each other in awkward silence. Then Sarah sighed resignedly. 'Since you already seem to have guessed then I suppose there's no point in denying it,' she said reluctantly. 'Yes, Mam, you're quite right, I am pregnant.'

'You're *what*?' The astonished voice of Lloyd broke into their discussion. They'd been so intent on what they were talking about that they hadn't heard him come into the house. Now he stood there in the doorway of the kitchen, his face puce, and his eyes glittering with anger as he stared accusingly at Sarah.

'How dare you bring such disgrace on us,' he stormed. 'Your poor mother was worried to death about you for weeks because you've not been feeling well. *Working* too hard?' he jibed. 'A great excuse! Because we trust you, we were both taken in by it and believed you.'

'Look, Dad, let me explain—'

'You've left it rather too late for explanations. I suppose the father is that boy you brought home to meet us. A rapscallion and a rabble-raiser! I recognised his type the moment he came through the door and from the first words he uttered.'

'Lloyd, let her speak,' Lorna said quietly. 'Let's be fair and hear what she has to say.'

'Go on, then, let's hear what you have to say.

It will be some trumped-up story that you and that fellow have concocted between you no doubt,' he said sardonically.

'I thought you said you wanted me to tell you the truth,' Sarah retorted defiantly.

'That will do, I don't want any of your lip,' her father told her caustically. 'Remember, my girl, you're the one who is in deep trouble; not us.'

'I'm not in trouble, as you put it; I'm pregnant, almost six months pregnant, which means I'm expecting a baby in May. You didn't say Mam was in trouble when she was expecting me, did you?'

'There was no cause to do so. We were a respectable married couple. I don't suppose the boyo who's responsible for your condition even mentioned getting married when you told him?'

Sarah felt the colour rush to her cheeks. 'No, he didn't, but he will do,' she stated confidently.

'Well, I'm pleased to hear it,' Lloyd said with a sarcastic edge to his voice. 'In that case then I suppose we can take it that you have nothing to worry about, which is just as well because you won't be getting any help from us.'

'Lloyd, don't say that,' Lorna protested. 'Of course we'll do all we can to help,' she assured Sarah.

'Help her!' Lloyd's voice rose in anger. 'We've been helping her all these years. We've supported her so that she could go to university and make something of herself, and what has she done? She's thrown it in our face.'

'We'll get through it if we talk about it and all support each other,' Lorna said weakly.

'Talk about it! What the hell are you on about, woman? I wouldn't talk to that reprobate! He's done enough damage to my family already! I wouldn't have him inside my door ever again.'

'Then what are we going to do?' Lorna asked. She looked bewildered as she stared at her husband. 'Since they've no home, perhaps we could let them live here with us until Sarah finishes at university.'

'Out of the question,' Lloyd said scornfully. 'I've already said that I wouldn't have him inside my house ever again.'

'Well, perhaps Sarah could stay here – on her own, I mean, after they're married,' Lorna pleaded. 'Just until they can find a place of their own.'

Lloyd shook his head, his mouth set in a grim line of disapproval. 'She's disgraced us, so there's no place for her here.'

'It's the middle of winter and I've nowhere to go so what do you think I am going to do?' Sarah asked in a frightened voice.

'She's right, Lloyd; we can't turn her out, not in this weather, it would be inhuman to do so.'

'She has to go and go now before anyone realises what has happened; think of the gossip there will be once people do find out,' he interrupted sharply.

'You mean you're more worried about what the neighbours might say than you are about what happens to me?' Sarah challenged. 'So where can I go?'

'That's up to you. You should have thought about that in the first place. Try your friend Gwyneth,' he said sarcastically. 'Or ask that boyfriend of yours to provide for you and his little bastard.'

Anger bubbled up inside Sarah. 'He will, but it all takes time. Surely I can stay here until we have made some arrangements? Remember, Dad, the little bastard, as you call it, will be your grandchild,' she told him boldly.

It was the first time that she'd ever dared to answer her father back and stand up for herself. All her life she'd been meek and obedient, desperately trying to win his love and affection yet never really managing to achieve it. Now, as she saw the look on his face, she felt a strange feeling of freedom because she realised that there was no longer any point in trying.

'Mam,' Sarah looked over at her mother. 'I think Dad is being unreasonable. I know I've let you both down and I'm sorry it has happened, but I've no money and no one else I can ask to help me.'

She waited for her mother to intervene, to take her side or at least suggest again that they should let her stay until after the baby was born, but Lorna gave her a brief, frightened look, and remained silent.

For the first time in her life Sarah no longer felt jealous of the closeness between her mother and father. It wasn't love that united her parents and made them so close; it was power on one side and fear on the other.

'Twenty minutes,' her father said harshly. 'There's the door; you have twenty minutes to collect your belongings together and then I want you gone,' he told her coldly.

As she stared at his grim, unrelenting face Sarah realised that there would be no reprieve for her. She'd expected them both to be angry, to reproach her about what had happened, but she'd never expected them to react like this.

'Think of what the neighbours will say if you throw me out into the street in my condition,' she challenged.

'We've talked long enough. I want you out immediately, with or without your belongings,' her father barked. 'That's my last word. You've already wasted five minutes of your time.'

Putting a hand firmly on Lorna's shoulders he began forcefully propelling her along the hallway towards the living room, ignoring the agonised look on her face.

'Please, Lloyd,' she pleaded. 'Can't we talk about this and think it over?'

Sarah stood where they'd left her; she couldn't hear his reply. Even though she knew that he meant every word he'd said she was still shocked and undecided as to what to do.

She felt both saddened and angry. On

reflection she knew she shouldn't have argued with her father. What she should have done was shown humility and appealed to his honour and his responsibility as her father to take care of her and look after her. He would have probably have liked that because he would have felt confident that from then on she'd do exactly as he told her, she thought bitterly.

She felt disappointed to find that her mother was letting him send her away. She had always turned to her when she was in trouble. Although Lorna always told her that what her dad said was the end of a matter, and that she couldn't intervene, somehow Sarah had expected her mother to do so over this and to be on her side, even though she realised that her mother was hurt and probably felt let down.

A feeling of desolation swept over her. What was she to do? She didn't even know how to contact Gwyn at this time of day. Would he still be at the *Western Mail* offices or would he have gone home? And where was home? She always had to wait for him to contact her. She had no address, so she couldn't even write to him.

She felt despondent and her legs seemed to be as heavy as lead as slowly she made her way upstairs to her bedroom to collect her clothes together.

As she piled everything up on her bed she realised that the small suitcase she'd used when she'd gone to Porthcawl would be nowhere near large enough to take all her clothes and things. Going out on to the landing she called down to her mother to ask if she could use one of their bigger suitcases.

As she waited for her mother to answer she could hear her father voicing his protest and she wondered if he was going to refuse to let her have one.

Her mother came out into the hallway, sniffing back her tears, but before she could speak Lloyd came out and pushed her to one side.

Without a word he came up the stairs, reached down a suitcase that was on top of the landing cupboard, and thrust it towards her. Sarah tried desperately to think of something to say; something that might perhaps make him change his mind about her leaving.

She hesitated to take the case because it made it all seem so final. She truly did feel sorry that she had messed everything up and she was willing to try and put things right if it was possible. There was surely some way she could salvage the mess she was in.

'Can't we talk things over, Dad?' she begged. 'I don't have to leave university, not yet anyway. I could carry on with my studies, get my degree and even—'

'You've three minutes left to pack your bags and leave,' he interrupted coldly looking at his watch and not at her. 'I meant what I said, Sarah; you've brought disgrace on us all. Your mother is as ashamed of you as I am.' And with that he returned to the living room.

As she struggled down the stairs with the suitcases her mother was still standing in the hallway. She looked so forlorn that Sarah felt a lump rise in her throat.

When she went to put her arms round her to kiss her, Lorna stiffened, looking over her shoulder nervously to make sure Lloyd wasn't watching.

As Sarah hugged her and tried to tell her she was sorry about what had happened and for making her so unhappy, her mother pressed a small package into her hand.

'Ssh, say nothing. This will tide you over for a couple of weeks,' she whispered. 'I only wish there was something I could do to make your dad change his mind but you've broken his heart, Sarah.'

'Hurt his pride, more likely,' Sarah said bitterly. 'He's always thought himself better than anyone else.'

'He's a good man, Sarah. He had such high hopes for you,' her mother said sadly, reaching up and stroking Sarah's face. 'I hope this young man of yours is as good to you as Lloyd is to me,' she added tearfully.

'What's going on?' Lloyd had come out into the hall and stood there with his hands in his trouser pockets looking questioningly at his wife. 'I've made my decision and I expect you to uphold it.'

He made no effort to open the door or help Sarah in any way as she picked up the cases and struggled through the door with them.

As she stepped outside on to the pavement she heard her mother pleading with her father to think again and she heard his angry refusal before the door crashed shut behind her.

There was a cold, drizzly rain falling and she had no idea what to do or where to go. She still couldn't believe that it was happening; that her parents would do something like this and actually turn her out. She knew they were close, she had always felt excluded, but she'd hoped that at the last minute her mother would persuade her father to relent and let her stay.

Getting pregnant had been foolish but surely she ought to be able to expect her family to stand by her, she thought angrily. If they wouldn't, then who would?

For a fleeting moment she wondered if she could go and stay with Rita and her family in Newport, even if only for a short while until she had managed to track down Gwyn and let him know what had happened.

Then the thought of having to tell Rita about the disgrace she'd brought down on her own head deterred her. She still had her pride . . . and Gwyn. Gwyn was the only person left who could help her – that was, if she could find him.

Chapter Twelve

Gwyn Roberts gave a sharp tug to the dark blue and grey striped tie that set off his crisp, white shirt and smart dark blue suit and tried to hide his yawn behind the brochure that had been handed to him when he'd arrived at the showroom. He endeavoured to look alert as the press officer began speaking and also to appear interested in what was going on all around him.

Although he tried to concentrate and made notes as they were told factual details about the wonderful new packaging system that the company had developed and which he'd been sent to report on for his paper, a lot of it seemed to wash over his head.

The reason for his lack of attention was that for some time now he'd had some very disturbed nights. Sometimes he hardly slept at all because of the many problems that were churning around all the time in his mind.

The full implication of what Sarah had told him hadn't really hit him for a while. Then it had sunk in that the many problems it raised for both of them were almost insurmountable.

For a start, he was pretty sure that she wouldn't agree to a back-street abortion or to having the baby adopted, so that meant she was going to have to leave university. He could imagine what her father's reaction would be, not to mention how enraged he would be to discover that she was pregnant.

Sarah's mother would be upset, too and he was sorry about that because he'd liked her the one time he had visited and had appreciated the way she'd made him welcome, despite her husband's antagonism.

His own career might also possibly be in jeopardy. He didn't want to remain a run-of-the-mill reporter while waiting to step into a dead man's shoes in the hope of one day becoming Editor; he wanted to aspire to a much more significant role than that. It would mean not only hard work but flair and grasping at every opportunity that came his way.

He had his sights on being a special correspondent or foreign correspondent. That would involve not only travelling widely but also being sent overseas into areas that might be physically dangerous. In order to participate in that sort of life you needed to be free of all encumbrances and most certainly not have the responsibility of a young family dependent on you.

Then there were his personal feelings in the matter to be considered. He'd become extremely fond of Sarah and had even told her he loved her. He'd found the chase both challenging and exciting partly because she was so naïve and also because she was so much under her father's thumb.

Since their brief stay in Porthcawl, when he'd achieved what he was after, his desire had waned somewhat. Their affair had cooled because there were far too many complications. Her father was such a disciplinarian and allowed her so little freedom that even when they did manage to meet she had to be home again at such an early hour that it was very restrictive.

Gwyn had toyed with the idea of writing to Sarah and telling her that they were finished and that he wouldn't be seeing her again. She'd be upset, possibly even heartbroken, and certainly would never want to speak to him again – which, in one way, would suit him fine.

Yet because she was such a sweet girl, he mused, and so very innocent about life, he would feel like a complete heel if he did that.

Then there was the question of the baby. Its future welfare was partly his responsibility. Doubtless she was expecting him to marry her, but so far he had managed to avoid that topic. He was quite sure that sending her a few bob every week to help bring it up wouldn't be acceptable even if it did manage to salve his conscience.

Pushing the problem to the back of his mind, as always, he tried to focus on the job in hand. As he asked what he hoped were intelligent questions, made the relevant notes and then went back to the office to complete his report, he managed to keep his mind on what he was doing.

The moment he'd handed in his copy to the Editor, though, it all came rushing back. Countless hare-brained ideas crowded into his mind, none of them the least bit suitable.

He reached into his pocket for his cigarettes, selected one, lighted it and inhaled deeply, hoping it would steady his nerves and help him to come to a decision about what he ought to do.

He wondered if it was worth asking if he could be sent overseas right now but since he was still not even on the permanent staff he thought that would be highly unlikely. Perhaps he could be transferred to one of their outlying offices, somewhere up in the Valleys where Sarah wouldn't be able to find him.

The trouble was she seemed to have such trust in him that even the thought of running away compounded his feeling of guilt. He couldn't simply desert her; it was his problem as much as hers.

She knew that he came from Aberdare and if she was really desperate she might go looking for him there. Or, worse still, her father might.

He wasn't sure how his own family would react if that happened; not that he cared all that much. Ever since he'd started at university he'd seen very little of them because these days he held such differing views from them that he'd become almost a stranger at home.

Although to the outside world they appeared to be proud of his achievements, he was well aware that deep down they disapproved because he'd refused to become a miner. Even all his talk that he wanted to be well educated so that he could speak up for the miners and ensure they had better conditions had cut little ice with them.

Even so, he knew that his father talked proudly to other people about the fact that a son of his had been to university. His mother simply threw up her arms in resignation and concentrated on making her other sons comfortable at home.

He knew he ought to contact Sarah but he kept putting off writing to her because he couldn't decide what to say. It was about three weeks since he'd seen her but inviting her to the pictures seemed ludicrous when they had such a big problem to face.

No doubt she was expecting him to go along to her home, face her parents and tell them he intended to marry her and provide a home for her and the baby. The trouble was he wasn't ready to take such a momentous step; not yet, at any rate.

At present, because he wasn't on the salaried staff, he earned only a pittance. He'd managed to rent a small room in a lodging house in Canton where the landlady provided a decent evening meal and did his washing. It wasn't a patch on the accommodation he'd had while he'd been living in the university campus but it was all he could afford.

The fine drizzle had turned to heavy rain by the time he'd filed his copy and was ready to leave the office. Turning up the collar of his overcoat and pulling his trilby well down over his eyes, he stepped out into St Mary's Street debating whether to take a tram or walk back to his lodgings in Canton.

He was so engrossed in ducking out of the way of umbrellas, that he pushed aside the young girl who accosted him. It was only when she called out his name that he stopped and spun round.

'Sarah?' He stared in astonishment; she was soaking wet and so bedraggled that for a moment he barely recognised her. Then his heart raced as he saw she had two large suitcases.

'I thought I'd missed you,' she gasped. 'I've been waiting here for ages,' she added forlornly as she gave him a shaky little smile.

He frowned, nodding his head towards the suitcases. 'What's happening? Are you going away somewhere?'

She sniffed back her tears and shook her head. 'I was waiting for you because I don't know what to do; I've nowhere to go. Mam guessed about the baby, I couldn't hide it any longer, and Dad was so cross that he turned me out,' she told him in a doleful voice.

Gwyn guided her into the shelter of a nearby doorway. He'd been worried about her parents' reaction when they discovered she was pregnant but he'd never for one moment thought they would take such a drastic measure as this.

Once they were out of the rain he took her into his arms, holding her close, smoothing back the damp tendrils of hair from her face before he kissed her.

'Can I come and stay with you, Gwyn?' she begged, looking up into his face beseechingly.

'That's not possible, Sarah. I'm living in lodgings and I've only got a very small room; anyway, I don't think for one moment that the landlady would allow it.'

'Oh, Gwyn, I was counting on it. If I can't stay with you then what am I going to do?' she asked in consternation.

For a moment he didn't answer. This was a complete nightmare, something he had never dreamed would happen. It could scotch all his plans and ruin his career prospects.

'Have you any money?' he asked hesitantly. 'Have you enough for a room for tonight? If you have, then that will give us time to make some plans about the future.'

'Only this, and I'm not even sure how much there is.' Sarah reached into her coat pocket and pulled out the small package her mother had secretly pressed into her hand as she was leaving.

'Look, we're both getting wet. Let's go into a milk bar, have a hot drink and find out what's in that envelope. Then we can talk things through and decide what to do for the best,' Gwyn suggested. 'I'll take the big case,' he added, picking it up, 'if you can manage to carry the other one.'

Side by side they struggled through the driving rain, elbowing their way through the hurrying crowds who all seemed to be going in the opposite direction.

They managed to find a table for two tucked away in a quiet corner. Gwyn helped Sarah take off her dripping wet coat and hung it up in the hope that it would dry out a little while they were there. Then he ordered mugs of hot chocolate for them both and a round of buttered toast for her.

Sarah was still shivering, even though it was quite warm in the milk bar, and when he reached out and took her hand it was so cold that he felt concerned.

'You'll soon warm up once you've had a hot drink,' he said giving it an encouraging squeeze.

'I'm not cold, just anxious. I was so scared that I might have missed you. I don't know what I would have done if I had because I don't know where you are living,' she said tremulously.

He stared at her in silence, wondering if there was any way he could unburden himself of his responsibility. He hated being rushed into taking action; he needed time to think about what he must do for the best, but perhaps moving into a couple of rooms somewhere and setting up home with her wouldn't be too bad.

He'd have more space and freedom than he had in his lodgings.

'The first thing we'll do when we leave here is try and find somewhere for you to stay tonight,' he told her reassuringly. 'It will probably have to be a small hotel. Can you afford it, because I only have a couple of bob on me at the moment?'

'I'd better hope that there's enough in here, then,' she said with a rueful smile as she opened the envelope and tipped the contents on to the table.

'That will probably take all the money I have,' she said worriedly after she'd counted it. 'Are you sure I can't stay with you?'

'It's out of the question,' he told her firmly. He looked at his watch. 'Come on, we need to find somewhere right away so that you can get out of your damp clothes and get dry, or else you'll be catching a chill,' he told her.

The rain had stopped and St Mary's Street was much quieter. As he hurried her along side streets where there were several small hotels, he hoped there would be a room available at one of them. Unless he managed to get back to his own room within the next half-hour he would be too late for his own evening meal.

They were lucky; at the second one they tried they were offered a single room but they were told it was very small and at the top of the building.

'I'll have to say goodbye here,' Gwyn

murmured after she'd signed the visitor's book. 'They won't allow me to come up with you.'

'I can't manage to carry my cases up three flights of stairs,' Sarah protested.

'You won't have to. Someone here will carry them up for you.' He gave her a hasty peck on the cheek. 'I'll meet you before I start work tomorrow.'

'You mean you'll come here?'

He frowned. 'No, let's make it the milk bar where we've been tonight. Be there for eight o'clock and we'll have breakfast together. By then I'll have thought about what we are going to do.'

'What about my suitcases, do I have to bring them with me?'

'I would think it would be all right if you left them here. They won't expect you to be out of your room before midday. It might be a good idea to tell whoever is on the desk that you'll pick them up later in the morning, otherwise they might think you're not coming back.'

'Can't we see each other again this evening, Gwyn?' she asked timidly as he gave her a brief kiss and raised his trilby in farewell. 'I feel so frightened,' she whispered.

He shook his head. 'It's impossible; you've sprung this on me without warning so I need to spend the evening planning what I am going to do; we need somewhere to live, remember.'

'You haven't even kissed me properly since we met,' she challenged. 'Are you angry with me, Gwyn, because of what's happened?'

'Of course I'm not angry with you, cariad. I am a little bit taken aback because all this has happened so suddenly. I didn't think we would need to take any positive steps about being together for a while yet.'

'Then why can't you give me a real cuddle and a proper kiss?'

'Sarah! There are too many people watching us,' he said evasively.

'I don't care about them,' she told him defiantly. 'I thought you would be all excited and pleased once you were over the surprise of what has happened. It will be like Porthcawl all over again only we won't have to part at the end of a few days, we'll be together for evermore,' she said, beaming.

'You make it all sound so simple,' he muttered. 'We've got to decide about so many things. There's your education, for a start. When exactly is this baby due?'

Sarah looked at him wide-eyed. 'I don't know for certain. Beginning of May, but it could be born in April.'

'So in that case you will miss sitting your exams.' He frowned.

She shrugged. 'I hadn't really thought that far ahead. Surely all that matters at the moment is that we're together?'

He smiled briefly as he brushed his lips against her cheek. 'Of course. I'll see you tomorrow morning. Don't be late.'

Chapter Thirteen

The following morning Sarah arrived at the milk bar first. To her surprise she'd fallen asleep almost the moment her head had touched the pillow the night before. She'd wakened early, feeling refreshed and much more confident about facing whatever lay ahead of her.

Gwyn was ten minutes late arriving but his smile as he greeted her reassured her that things really were going to be all right. He'd seemed to be so upset by her news the previous evening that there were moments when she wondered if he was going to walk away and she'd never see him again.

Even before he ordered some breakfast for them he told her that he'd already been into the office and that he'd arranged to have the morning off.

'Not only that but I've also made enquiries about where we might find some rooms,' he told her confidently.

'We?' She looked at him with raised eyebrows.

'Yes, Sarah, I did say we,' he confirmed. 'I'll be moving in with you. We can't afford to rent two separate places so we'll be living together from now on.'

'There's nothing I would like more,' she told him, reaching out and taking his hand.

He gave hers a reassuring squeeze. 'That's all right, then. Now,' he drew a piece of paper out of his pocket, 'I've written down a few places we can go and have a look at.'

'Nothing that is too near to Cyfartha Street, I hope,' she said quickly. 'I wouldn't want to run the risk of bumping into my parents when I went out.'

'Nowhere near there at all; we can't afford Cathays.'

'So where are you thinking of?' She frowned. 'I don't fancy Splott or Canton.'

'There's no chance of it being either of them, cariad. It's going to have to be Tiger Bay.'

'Tiger Bay!' Her eyes widened in astonishment. 'We can't live down there.'

'I'm afraid we'll have to; it's the cheapest place in Cardiff.'

'I can understand why,' she said scathingly. 'It's got a terrible reputation.'

'Rubbish, that's all talk. Cardiff's a seaport so there's bound to be a mix of people living near the docks.'

'Yes, sailors from all over the world who've jumped ship and stayed on here.'

'Some of them, yes,' he agreed. 'There're also a great many white people living there as well and some of them are married to the coloured sailors. There are also people who've moved down to Cardiff from the Valleys looking for work there so they can't all be bad.'

Sarah shook her head. 'It's not what I've been used to and I don't like the idea of living down there at all,' she said.

'Think about it while I go and order,' he told her, pushing back his chair and walking over to the counter.

Sarah pondered over the implications, unsure if it was the right thing to do. There was only one good point that she could see and that was that her mam and dad would never think of looking for her in Tiger Bay. From the way her father had spoken and the cowed look on her mother's face, she was pretty sure that neither of them would try and find her anyway.

She looked across at Gwyn as he talked to the woman behind the counter. If he'd decided it was all right for them to live there then she supposed she'd have to go along with it. At least this morning he was offering her a roof over her head whereas last night she'd thought he was going to desert her completely.

When he returned to the table with two steaming cups of hot chocolate and told her they would bring over the rest of their meal in a couple of minutes, she managed to control her dismay at his decision about where they'd be living.

'I suppose it will be fine as long as you are living there with me.' She smiled at him. 'Since it's our first home together it's bound to be special, anyway.'

'It will be two rooms at the most and we'll have to share the kitchen and all the other facilities,' he reminded her grimly. 'It won't be a palace, but at the moment it's all we can afford. We'll only have my wages to pay for everything because you won't be working.'

'If I can find a job then can we live somewhere better?' she asked quickly.

He looked puzzled. 'That would mean you giving up university; you don't want to do that, do you?'

'I don't know.' Sarah shrugged non-committally. 'I've found it so hard to study recently that I've got behind with everything. I'm not even sure if I can catch up.' She stirred her drink thoughtfully. 'Even if I do stay on, what good will it do? I'll have to leave to have the baby before I can take my exams.'

'Don't take too hasty a decision,' Gwyn warned. 'Make some enquiries first and see if, under the circumstances, they will let you sit them later on.'

'Do you think they would let me do that?' she questioned.

'It's just possible, but you'll have to explain why, of course,' he added with a grim smile.

As soon as they'd finished their breakfast they took a tram down to the Pier Head. Sarah studied the shops and buildings on either side of the road as they went down Bute Street with growing dismay. So many of them had strange, foreign signs and names over them; ones that she couldn't even pronounce.

As they left the tram Gwyn pulled the paper out of his pocket again and ran a finger down the addresses listed on it.

'Come on, cheer up; we'll start with the nearest one and that's in Maria Street.'

Even as they approached the terraced house they both knew it was out of the question. Several of the windows were boarded up and the glass in the front door had been smashed and the gaping hole was stuffed with a piece of sacking.

The next two on Gwyn's list were equally depressing. Sarah felt weary and Gwyn was growing increasingly frustrated, knowing that he had to be back at the office before one o'clock, and also that Sarah would have to collect her suitcases.

The last place they looked at was in Louisa Street. It was a three-storey terrace house and although it was almost next door to a pub called the Pembroke Arms it looked quite respectable. The windows were clean, there were net curtains at all of them, and although the front door needed painting the brass knocker and letter box were polished and shining.

The woman who opened the door was middle-aged and plump with dark hair combed back behind her ears. She was wearing a light blue dress with a print pinafore over it. 'Have you come about the rooms?' she asked in a no-nonsense tone of voice.

'We have,' Gwyn said briskly. 'Can we see them, please?'

'Top floor at the back,' she told him, standing aside to let them come in. 'Go on up. Bedroom and living room side by side; the kitchen and a lavatory are on the landing below and you share those with the two families on that floor.'

The rooms were small but clean and the narrow windows looked out on to the backs of the houses in the next street. In the smaller of the rooms there was a bed, a chest of drawers and a built-in cupboard across the alcove.

In the larger of the two rooms, there were cupboards on either side of the very small iron grate that had a tiled surround, a square wooden table with two chairs, and a sofa upholstered in brown Rexene underneath the window. A gas fire had been fitted into the small fireplace. The mottled grey lino was the same in both rooms and so, too, were the floral cretonne curtains that hung at the windows.

Sarah realised that although they were fortunate to have found somewhere that was at least clean it was nowhere near as well furnished or as comfortable as her home in Cyfartha Street had been. She tried to imagine what living here would be like and felt a shudder go through her.

'Let's see what the kitchen is like,' Gwyn

muttered, squeezing her hand as he headed for the door.

It was downstairs on the landing below and so small that Sarah felt an overwhelming sense of dismay. Where would she put everything, she wondered, then realised that, at the moment, she had nothing at all to put anywhere. All she possessed were the clothes she stood up in and the things in her suitcases.

She choked back her tears as they went back up to the two poky little rooms. They were so cold and uninviting that she hoped Gwyn would say no to the idea of living there; if he did, though, then where would they go?

Gwyn looked at her questioningly. 'Have you made up your mind? I've got to get back to work,' he reminded her. 'I think we'd better take it as it's certainly the best we've seen.'

She nodded, afraid to speak in case he heard the fear and disappointment in her voice. She kept remembering the luxury of the hotel room where they had stayed together in Porthcawl; that was the sort of future she had dreamed of having with Gwyn, certainly not living together in a sordid attic in Tiger Bay. It might be only a couple of miles away from her old home and the centre of Cardiff, but it was like another world.

'Come on then.' He took her hand again. 'We'll go and tell the landlady and then you can come back to St Mary Street with me and collect your cases from the hotel. You'd probably better get a taxicab to bring them back here because they'll be too heavy for you to carry from the Pier Head. You won't forget where you're living now, will you?' he teased. 'It's in Louisa Street and it's two doors away from the Pembroke Castle. The landlady's name is Mrs Blackwood and remember you are signed in as Mrs Roberts,' he told her as they walked back to the Pier Head to catch a tram.

'Why have you told her that? We're not married yet.'

He looked at her with raised eyebrows. 'If Mrs Blackwood knew that, then in all probability she wouldn't let us stay here. Even down here in Tiger Bay they set great store by a couple being married, you know,' he said wryly.

Sarah bit her lip and said nothing. Gwyn hadn't even said that he wanted to marry her, she thought miserably. What had suddenly happened to all the romance?

She knew they couldn't have a white wedding and all the celebrations that usually took place but he could have taken her in his arms and asked her if she would marry him. As it was he was taking it for granted that she was prepared to simply move in with him and call herself Mrs Roberts.

'What time will you be coming home?' Sarah asked anxiously as they alighted from the tram in St Mary Street. 'Can't I wait for you so that we can go back together?'

'No, you must go and collect your cases and

it is better if you go straight back with them,' he told her firmly. 'Anyway, I don't know what time I will be finished. It depends what I have to do and where I have to go. I'll be home as soon as I can.'

'So what do I do until then, simply sit and wait for you?' she asked sarcastically.

'I'm afraid so; it's something you are going to have to get used to doing because most of the time I'll be at work and in my job, it's not regular hours. Anyway, it will give you plenty of time to catch up with your studying.'

'You mean I might be there on my own in the evening?' she asked in dismay.

'More than likely. If a story breaks and I am sent to cover it then I have to go, no matter what time of day or night it might be.'

'This will be our first day in Louisa Street, though, so surely you could stay with me, just for once,' she pleaded.

'I was lucky to get the morning off,' he reminded her. 'You take your cases back, unpack them, and then go out and buy some food to last us for a few days. Have you got enough money to do that and to pay for the taxi?'

'I think so, but I don't know where any of the shops are. Anyway, I'll be scared stiff wandering round those streets on my own,' she prevaricated, 'and I don't even know what sort of food to buy because I don't know what you like.'

'What about bread, milk and perhaps some

bacon and eggs or cheese or something like that? Buy whatever you would buy if you were at home.'

'I never had to do any shopping when I lived at home; my mam always did it.'

'Then you'd better start learning,' he told her grimly. 'From now on you'll be doing the shopping, cooking and cleaning like a proper housewife, even if we aren't married.'

As Gwyn hurried off into the offices of the *Western Mail* Sarah stood on the pavement outside debating what to do. On impulse she walked across the road and wandered into the Royal Arcade. She had been able to leave her suitcases at the reception desk in the hotel that morning, and didn't have to be back to collect them just yet. She felt so disheartened by the way things were turning out that she went into a café and ordered a hot drink and a buttered bun in order to give herself time to think about the bleak future that lay ahead of her.

She wasn't sure that her love for Gwyn was strong enough to make such a tremendous sacrifice as all this was going to entail. She was being expected to change her entire way of life and she needed to talk to someone about it; the only person she could think of was her mother.

She was now six months pregnant; her morning sickness seemed to have stopped, and, with her mother's help, she could probably carry on at university right up until the baby was born. Perhaps if they told her father that was what she wanted to do, then he would be more lenient.

Perhaps they could say that she was married. The only trouble was that her father would hate that because he didn't want her to have anything to do with Gwyn, so it might be better to say nothing and let people think whatever they wanted to.

Her father was always so concerned about what the neighbours might say about them that her mother rarely had anything to do with any of them so who was to know, or even to bother to check up?

It was now early afternoon. Her father would be at work and she was tempted to go and see her mother. If they could only talk things over she might be able to reason out what was the best thing to do to placate him so that it was possible for her to go back home again if she found life in Tiger Bay absolutely unbearable.

Chapter Fourteen

As she stood on the doorstep of her home in Cyfartha Street, Sarah felt as if she had been away for months, not merely one night. She slipped her hand through the letter box to find the key that always hung there, and then frowned in bewilderment. It wasn't there. She tried again, feeling carefully all round as far as her hand would stretch, but in vain.

Apprehensively, she raised the knocker and as the sound echoed hollowly, her fears increased: she'd been so sure that her mother would be there, she never went out at this time of the day.

Perhaps she wasn't feeling too well and was lying down resting. She banged again, more loudly this time and then bent down and called out through the letter box, 'Mam, it's me, Sarah', in case her mother was there but had decided not to answer the door to callers.

When nothing happened, when no footsteps came hurrying along the passage, she felt tears pricking at her eyes. This was the last straw; she'd counted on her mam being there for her.

Slowly she retraced her footsteps to the tram stop in Crwys Road. She daren't hang about;

time was passing and she had to collect her cases and take them back to Louisa Street.

She wished she'd had a paper and pencil so that she could have left a note for her mother telling her where she was living. Then the thought that her father might have found it before her mother did made her realise that it was just as well that she hadn't.

It was almost three o'clock by the time she reached the hotel and Sarah worried that Gwyn might arrive back at Louisa Street before she did.

The minute the taxicab drew up in Louisa Street Mrs Blackwood was on the doorstep to see what was happening.

'Oh, it's you is it,' she commented as Sarah stepped out of the cab and stood on the pavement waiting for the driver to hand out her suitcases.

'You'd better carry those suitcases up to her room for her, they're far too heavy for her to carry in her state,' Mrs Blackwood told the driver when he put them down on the pavement and made to get back into the cab.

'It's the top floor, she'll show you. Go on then,' she gave Sarah a prod, 'lead the way; I'll stay here and make sure none of the little tykes round here touch your cab,' she told the driver.

When the cab driver left Sarah hastily began to unpack her clothes and stow them away, hoping to be finished before Gwyn arrived home. It wasn't until she heard him walk in that she realised she'd done no shopping and there was nothing at all to eat. She hadn't even been down into the kitchen and so she had no idea if there was even enough tea to make him a drink.

Guiltily she flung herself into his arms, hugging him and kissing him because she felt so relieved to see him.

'Is this the sort of greeting I can expect every night?' he asked teasingly as he returned her hugs and kisses.

'Only when things go wrong,' she said smiling. 'I don't know where the time has gone but I haven't done any shopping.'

He pulled a face. 'That's too bad because I only had time for a snack at lunchtime and now I'm starving hungry. Perhaps we'd better go and see what we can get before the shops shut.'

There were still shops open in George Street and James Street so they bought enough groceries to last them for several days.

'It's too late to start cooking, so why don't we buy some fish and chips?' he suggested.

Gwyn waited until they had finished their supper before asking Sarah if she had cleaned out the cupboards that were theirs in the kitchen.

She looked at him blankly. 'What cupboards?'

'Well, there must be some place down there that is for our stuff,' he pointed out. 'Come on, let's go and look. There's probably no one there now because it's so late.'

'Then how will we know which is ours?'

'I don't know.' He shrugged. 'If we can't work it out then we'll go down and ask Mrs Blackwood. We should have done so this morning, I suppose.'

The kitchen was so small that Sarah didn't think it was possible for there to be any space for their things but, to her surprise, they found there was a cupboard with 'Top Room' scrawled on it. Inside were cups and saucers, dishes, a couple of jugs, a basin, two saucepans and a frying pan. There was also an open-top wooden box containing an assortment of cutlery.

'Well, there you are,' Gwyn smiled, 'everything you are likely to need and plenty of space for all the things we bought tonight. I'll bring them down and you can put them away.'

'Do you think they will be safe? There are two other families sharing this kitchen, remember.'

'We'll have to wait and see, won't we? Anyway, while you are doing that I'm off back to my lodgings to fetch my things.'

'Oh, Gwyn,' her face fell, 'don't leave me here on my own. Can't I come with you?'

'I think it best if I go on my own. It'll be cheaper, and I won't be all that long. If you've finished unpacking those suitcases then I'll take them with me to bring my stuff back,' he told her as he gave her a brief kiss.

Sarah's first attempts at cooking the following night were a disaster. The potatoes boiled dry, the chops were charcoal-black on the outside but red raw in the middle, and they'd stuck to the bottom of the frying pan so that when she tried to get them out they were in pieces.

Gwyn manfully struggled to eat his then finally pushed his plate to one side. Sarah took one look at it and burst into tears.

'Cariad, there's no need to take on so. Perhaps you should go back to university and finish your course as soon as you've had the baby; you're probably cut out to be a lawyer, not a housewife; even I can cook better than this,' he added dryly.

When he stood up from the table she thought he was coming round to take her in his arms and comfort her, but instead he took down his overcoat from its peg and walked towards the door.

'Don't wait up for me,' he said tersely.

Sarah sat there at the table, staring at the remains of the ruined meal for over an hour. Then, with a sigh, she began to clear everything away. She'd thought Gwyn had simply walked out in anger feeling the need to clear his head. He wasn't home yet, and she wondered what she would do if he didn't come back at all. She had only a few coppers left from the money her mother had given her, not even enough to pay for another week's rent, let alone buy any more food.

As midnight approached she felt so utterly weary that she went and lay down on the bed without troubling to undress. In the last couple of days her size seemed to have ballooned and her feet and legs were swollen by the extra weight.

She'd have to leave university, there was no doubt about that, and to find a job, but who'd employ her now that she was looking so pregnant?

She still hadn't resolved what to do for the best when she drifted off to sleep only to be awakened by the sound of raised voices and some sort of heated argument going on.

For a moment she couldn't even think where she was, then the bedroom door opened and Gwyn stumbled in and flung himself down on the bed beside her. His breath was rank with alcohol and she instinctively pulled away from him with an expression of disgust.

'Don't start; I've already had one bloody mouthing from the landlady about coming in late and waking everybody up,' he hiccuped. 'I don't need another one from you.'

He grabbed her roughly and, ignoring her protest to be gentle with her because of the baby, he attempted to make love to her. When he found he was incapable of doing so he pushed her savagely aside.

Sarah lay perfectly still. She closed her eyes, although she knew that sleep was out of the question, and waited until Gwyn's breathing became steady and rhythmic and she knew he was asleep. Then she crept out of bed to go and make herself a cup of tea.

She paused on the top of the stairs; the whole house was deadly quiet, everyone was in bed and asleep. If she ventured down to the landing below and started moving about in the kitchen there was the chance she might disturb someone so, reluctantly, she abandoned the idea and crept back to bed.

She still found it impossible to sleep. She lay there not moving but revaluing her new life and wondering if she'd made a terrible mistake. Possibly Gwyn thought the same, she decided miserably. Two nights running he'd had no proper meal so it was no wonder that he'd gone out and got drunk. It wouldn't take much drink to make him legless on an empty stomach.

Her mother would be shocked by her inability to look after him properly. She'd always prided herself on providing good nourishing meals and making sure they were always on time.

Lying there in the darkness she made all sorts of resolutions about what she would do in the future. If she couldn't go on studying law then at least she could get herself a basic cookery book and learn how to provide decent meals. It might take a bit of practice but she was determined to succeed.

She wondered whether or not to mention this to Gwyn the next morning but he looked very hung-over and barely said a word, so she decided it might be better to surprise him with a good meal when he came home rather than talk about what she planned to do.

He kissed her briefly before he left for work. He didn't mention the night before so neither did she. There'd been faults on both sides, she decided.

Once he'd gone she cleared up and left for university. She had lectures in the morning and a tutorial immediately after lunch, and needed to make an excuse for her absence over the last few days, but she would be free by mid-afternoon.

On her way home she decided to shop for something simple, like sausages, that she'd have no problem cooking, and resolved to make a tasty onion gravy to go with them.

When she went down to the kitchen to start cooking she was dismayed to find there were two other women already in there preparing their own meals. One was a very large middle-aged woman with crinkly black hair and a shiny dark face. She was stirring something that smelled very spicy in a large saucepan. The other, a tall, angular-looking woman with red hair and green eyes, who looked to be in her late twenties, was standing at the sink peeling potatoes.

They both stared at her as she walked in. 'You from upstairs then, dearie?' the dark woman asked. 'I'm Clara and this is Dilly, we live on this floor. What's your name?'

'Sarah. We've only just moved in.'

'Well, you got to take your turn in the kitchen,' Clara told her. 'Did Mrs Blackwood tell you that?'

'She said we had to share it.'

'That's right and it's first who come here to live who can use it first, so that means you are the one who has to wait.'

Sarah bit her lip. She wanted to bake the sausages in the oven along with some potatoes and unless she got started soon they wouldn't be ready when Gwyn got home.

'How long do you expect to be?' she asked hesitantly.

'As long as it takes!' Clara laughed noisily. 'My three young'uns play out for an hour or so after school until they see their dad come home and then they all like it to be on the table piping hot.'

'What time is that?'

'When he gets here, of course. Sometimes he comes rushing home, other times he stops off for a beer at the Crown and Anchor. He works on the docks and it's the sort of work that gives him a great thirst,' she added with another raucous laugh.

'Dilly has only herself and her two kids to worry about,' she went on. 'Dilly's old man's inside, isn't that right, dearie?' she asked smiling across at the other woman.

Dilly shrugged. 'I suppose he still is. I can't remember when he's due out,' she murmured in a thin, whiny voice.

'Perhaps I could cook my meal in the oven alongside yours,' Sarah suggested.

'Oven!' Both women looked at her in

surprise. 'There ain't no oven here in this kitchen, dearie,' Clara cackled. 'What you can't cook on the gas ring you have to eat raw,' she added, laughing so much that she shook all over.

'What were you thinking of cooking?' Dilly asked, staring pointedly at the package in Sarah's hand.

'I was going to bake some sausages and potatoes. I was also going to make some onion gravy,' she added quickly as she saw Dilly raise her eyebrows.

'Then you'll have to fry the sausages and boil the potatoes. You could always mash them with a knob of margarine.'

'Can I use one of the gas rings now?' Sarah asked.

The two women looked at each other questioningly. 'Well, seeing that it is your first time down here we'll let you, but in future you'll have to wait until we're finished. Can't keep kids waiting, the little blighters are starving hungry when they come home.'

As Sarah took the frying pan out of her cupboard, popped the sausages into it and made to put it on the ring, Clara said, "ain't you going to put a bit of lard or dripping into that pan? If you don't they'll stick like glue to the bottom. Remember to prick them as well, otherwise they'll burst and splatter everywhere.'

'I haven't got any lard,' Sarah muttered.

Clara walked over and opened Sarah's

cupboard. 'You got damn all here apart from a couple of eggs and a drop of milk.' She lifted out the jug and sniffed at it. 'That's on the turn, if you ask me. Take a tip: use condensed milk because fresh milk goes off in a couple of hours in this place. All that's any good for is to be put down outside in the gutter for the cats.'

Sarah felt tears springing to her eyes. All her good intentions to have an appetising meal ready for Gwyn when he came home were vanishing before her eyes.

'Don't worry about it so much, dearie. I have a feeling that you're new to this housekeeping lark and looking after your man. You nip out and fetch some milk while I cook your sausages and Dilly here will give you a couple of spuds out of her pot, won't you, girl?' she asked, smiling across at the other woman.

Dilly shrugged but said nothing.

'Run along, then,' Clara said, giving Sarah a friendly push. 'By the time you get back it will be ready to go on the plates so I just hope that man of yours is home on time.'

Gwyn was home on time and pleasantly surprised when Sarah placed a plate of fried sausages and mashed potato, accompanied by some sort of sauce that smelled of spices, in front of him.

'What's all this?' he exclaimed. 'Have you been taking cookery lessons?'

'Sort of,' Sarah admitted. 'Clara and Dilly, they live on the floor below, helped me out.

I thought there was an oven in the kitchen but there are only a couple of gas rings. We have to take turns.'

'It certainly looks good,' he told her as he picked up his knife and fork.

'Well, don't expect this again in a hurry.' She smiled. 'Tomorrow, Clara is going to show me how to cook chicken but it won't be roasted. I'm not sure how she prepares it but she's going to show me. She says that by the time the baby is born I'll be able to cook anything.'

Chapter Fifteen

Adjusting to her new life was not easy but, to her surprise, Sarah found that her newly formed friendship with Clara and Dilly helped a great deal. They were always ready to assist and rarely criticised; they'd lived in Tiger Bay all their lives and knew a great many people and such a lot about what was going on. They not only told her where to shop but also how to go about getting the best bargains.

They both had children ranging in age from three to fourteen. The older ones were always willing to run messages and when they heard that Sarah was at university they regarded her with awe.

'Are you going to be a school teacher, then?' Cedric, Clara's twelve-year-old asked suspiciously. He breathed a sigh of relief when she assured him she wasn't.

Clara laughed a lot at Sarah's ineffectual skills at cooking but at the same time she was always willing to help and guide her. In no time Sarah found she was not only able to provide appetising meals for Gwyn but also knew how to shop for food economically.

It certainly helped to improve things

domestically although generally she found that life was nowhere near as wonderful with Gwyn nor their lovemaking as romantic as she'd dreamed it would be. They seemed to have settled into a fairly mundane routine, but it wasn't one that she was happy with at all.

She felt it was partly due to the fact that Gwyn was so immersed in his work. His hours were irregular and she could never be quite sure what time he would be home.

When he was late he always claimed that he had been delayed because a story had broken and he'd been sent to cover it. Or else that there was a mad panic in the office over a report or a feature and that entailed working late.

Whenever this happened, she noticed, his breath was redolent of alcohol. Once or twice when she'd commented on it he rounded on her sharply and reminded her that in his job he had to drink occasionally with his colleagues.

'It's their way of unwinding after a gruelling session, and it would look boorish if I didn't join in.'

Apart from the fact that Gwyn had a driving ambition to be promoted, even though he still wasn't yet on the permanent staff, he kept reminding her that his wages had to support them both as well as the baby, which was now due in about two months.

Although she was still attending lectures and tutorials, Sarah knew that her days at university were numbered because it had been so obvious that she was pregnant. The fact was made even more apparent because she couldn't afford to buy the right sort of clothes to disguise her ever-increasing bump.

Dilly had been extremely helpful by letting out both of her skirts at the waistline but there was a limit to how much it was possible to do this and Sarah still felt frumpy.

Although she was now over the initial wrench she'd felt at having to leave Cyfartha Street, she still longed to see her mother. Clara and Dilly were kind and helpful but it wasn't the same as being able to confide in her mother like she'd been able to do in the past.

As the days became weeks and the time for the birth of her baby grew nearer she even wrote a note to her mother, asking if she could come and visit her in Cyfartha Street. She hoped that even if that wasn't feasible, her mother might find it in her heart to come and see her in Louisa Street, since her address was on the note.

When a week passed and there was no response she accepted that her mother wasn't going to get in touch because she never did anything that might upset her father, and that the rift between herself and her parents was permanent.

Sarah knew she could never be like her mother. Even though at present she had to rely on Gwyn to put a roof over her head and pay for food and everything else, she was determined to maintain her independence. She was quite prepared to stand up for herself and argue her corner if she thought that it was necessary.

For all that, she wished her mother would get in touch. Several times she'd been tempted to pay another visit to Cyfartha Street but at the back of her mind was the worry that she might be putting her mother into an awkward situation.

Another thing that made her put off doing so was that she might bump into some of their neighbours.

That was nowhere near as important as seeing her mother again and she kept wondering whether, if she paid them a visit one Sunday, perhaps after the baby was born, and faced them both, they would be so pleased to see their grandchild that it might put matters right.

When she mentioned this to Gwyn he told her she was being silly to even think like that but she remained optimistic. Her mother, at least, would be overjoyed to see the baby and that might soften her father's heart.

When Sarah went into labour on a Tuesday morning in May it was Clara who took charge. Tearfully, Sarah begged them to fetch her mother and then, as the contractions increased and became ever more painful, she pleaded for them to get hold of Gwyn.

Neither Clara nor Dilly knew where to find either of them so they ignored her pleas and carried on regardless. They both told her that they knew what to do and assured her that there was no need to send for a mid-wife or a doctor or anyone else at all.

Fortunately, it was a straightforward birth and by the time Gwyn arrived home late that evening it was all over. Sarah was tucked up in bed and Clara was showing her how to suckle her new daughter.

Gwyn was so absorbed in work problems that he had very little to say about the new arrival and seemed to take it for granted that Clara and Dilly were looking after Sarah and the baby. When they asked him what he wanted to call the baby he merely shrugged and said that it was up to Sarah.

The three women talked about it for a long time but none of the names Clara and Dilly suggested appealed to Sarah. She was so grateful to Clara and Dilly for all they had done for her that she wanted to call her daughter after them so in the end she decided on 'Cladylliss'.

'It's the beginning of your name, Clara, and the ending of Dilly's,' she explained.

Sarah felt weak and inadequate for almost a week after Cladyllis was born. She was tremendously grateful for all the help she received from Clara and Dilly. They not only shopped and cleaned and took care of the washing but also between them provided a cooked meal for her and Gwyn every evening for the next couple of weeks.

When Sarah told Gwyn that Clara was concerned because she thought the baby was underweight, he brushed aside the idea that they ought to see a doctor.

'She looks all right to me and she certainly cries enough,' he said rather irritably. 'She keeps me awake half the night with her whimpering and howling.'

'It's not a healthy cry, though,' Clara insisted. 'She's feeding well enough, so I don't think it is because she's hungry. There is something wrong with her. I think she's probably in some kind of pain, poor little lamb. In fact, she's so frail that I don't think she'll survive unless she has some proper treatment.'

Sarah was distraught when Clara said this and when Gwyn still refused to agree that they should call in a doctor she took matters into her own hands. Cladylliss's future and well-being meant more to her than anything else in the world. She'd never dreamed that she would feel such intense love as she did for her baby. She was determined to do everything in her power to make sure she had a good life, even if it meant defying Gwyn. She decided to swallow her pride and go and visit her mother and ask her advice.

She said nothing to Clara and Dilly except to tell them that since it was such a lovely day and she felt so much stronger she was going to walk as far as the park.

'Wait until this afternoon and we'll come

with you and carry Cladylliss for you,' Dilly suggested.

'No, I want to go now in the morning while it is cool. By this afternoon it may be far too hot.'

'She's too heavy for you to carry; you're not properly over childbirth yet,' Clara pointed out.

'She's three weeks old; a lot of women would be back at work by now,' Sarah told them. 'Let me try. I'll carry her Welsh-fashion in a shawl so that way I won't find her heavy, now will I? If I find it is too much I'll turn back when I get to the end of the road.'

By the time she reached the Pier Head her legs felt quite shaky and she was glad to get on the tram and sit down. As it clanged its way up Bute Road and along St Mary's Street she kept going over in her mind what she would say to her mother, and she wondered what her mother's reaction would be to Cladylliss.

As she left the tram and made her way towards Cyfartha Street she felt nervous in case she saw any of their neighbours. This time she didn't attempt to fish through the letter box for the key but knocked on the door like any other visitor would do.

She was trembling so much that when her mother did open the door she could barely whisper hello.

For a moment they stared at each other almost like strangers. Sarah held her breath. She couldn't believe how much her mother had aged; her face was lined and she'd lost weight.

Then when she saw a look of delight and the smile of welcome that spread across her mother's face she began to breathe easily once more. 'I thought you would like to meet your little granddaughter, Mam,' she said shakily.

As Lorna reached out and helped her into the hallway Sarah was so relieved that she hadn't been turned away that she felt faint and stumbled and almost fell.

'Oh Sarah, Sarah, I was afraid I was never going to see you again. It was so wrong of me to let Lloyd send you away like he did. I've walked the streets looking for you. I've waited for the postman every day hoping there might be a word from you because I knew the baby was due at any time now. Why didn't you write, cariad?'

'I did! I wrote before the baby was born saying how much I wanted to see you. I gave you my address so that if you didn't want me to come here then you could come and see me.'

Lorna shook her head. 'I never received it. I prayed you would get in touch.'

'I thought it might be a waste of time,' Sarah sighed. 'Dad must have picked up the letter and destroyed it. Is he still angry with me?' she asked tentatively.

Lorna didn't answer. She guided Sarah towards an armchair and then began to help unwrap the shawl Sarah had wrapped round herself to support the baby.

'Come and sit down, you must be exhausted in this heat. Here, let me take her while you get settled and then I'll make us a cup of tea and you can tell me everything,' she said taking the baby, cuddling her, and studying her features.

'Oh she's lovely,' she exclaimed. 'She looks like a tiny doll. How old is she?'

'Three weeks.'

'And what have you called her?'

'Cladylliss.'

'Cladylliss? That's an unusual name.' Lorna frowned.

'There's a reason, I'll tell you all about it in a minute. I could do with that cuppa, Mam. Shall I make it?'

'No no, I'll do it.' She handed the baby back to Sarah. 'You sit and nurse her, you must be worn out.'

It wasn't easy revealing to her mother everything that had happened since she'd been thrown out of Cyfartha Street, but as they sat and drank their tea Sarah managed to tell her all she thought she needed to know.

Her mother listened attentively but said very little. When Sarah finally stopped and held out her cup for a refill Lorna remarked quietly, 'You still haven't told me where you and Gwyn are living.'

'We're still in Cardiff, and we're only a tram ride away,' Sarah murmured.

'Yes, but where?' her mother insisted.

'Louisa Street.'

'Where's that?' Lorna looked puzzled. 'I've never heard of it.'

'It's not very far from the Pier Head.'

Lorna looked at her wide-eyed. 'That's Tiger Bay,' she said in a horrified voice. 'Why there, Sarah? Whatever are you doing living in a place like that?'

'It was all we could afford,' Sarah told her with a grim smile. 'I thought you might be shocked; in fact, I wondered if that was why you didn't come and visit me,' she admitted.

Lorna shook her head, 'No, that had nothing to do with it, cariad; I would have come to see you no matter where you were living if I'd known the address.'

'Then make it soon, Mam,' Sarah pleaded as she stood up. 'I'd better get back. I told Clara and Dilly that I was walking as far as the park. They didn't want me to do it on my own and they will be worried out of their minds in case I've come to some harm.'

'Hold on while I get my hat and coat and I'll come with you,' Lorna told her.

'No, Mam, there's no need for you to do that, I'm settled in my own mind now that I've seen you and I know that things are all right between us.'

'I'll come with you,' her mother repeated firmly. 'I can carry little Cladylliss and, what's more, I can find out where it is you live. I've never been down there in my life and I'll never be able to find my way unless you show me.'

Chapter Sixteen

Sarah felt very aware that her mother was becoming more and more nervous as the tram rattled along Bute Street towards the Pier Head. She tried to keep her talking so as to divert her attention from the increasingly dubious characters that boarded the tram and from the fact that the shops and buildings were becoming shabbier all the time.

As they walked from the Pier Head towards Louisa Street she noticed that her mother kept looking nervously back over her shoulder and glancing sideways as coloured people passed them.

Mrs Blackwood came out into the hallway as they went into the house and Sarah introduced them.

'Your first visit,' she said, and it was more a statement than a question. 'I was beginning to think that Sarah didn't have any family, at least not living around here.'

Lorna gave a faint smile but offered no explanation as to why she'd never been there before.

Sarah led the way up to the attic rooms but they were stopped on the second-floor landing by Clara who flung her arms in the air and exclaimed in a loud cross voice, 'So there you are! Dilly has been worrying me silly about where you might have ended up. We both told you not to go out on your own,' she ranted, her bosom heaving and her big dark eyes flashing angrily.

As soon as Clara stopped for breath Sarah introduced her to Lorna and she saw the look of shocked horror on her mother's face. She wasn't sure whether that was because Clara was black or because of the way Clara had been shouting at her.

The atmosphere eased over a cup of tea. Clara chattered at great length about the baby and how anxious she felt because she thought little Cladylliss was delicate. Her concern seemed to greatly impress Lorna and Sarah felt the atmosphere ease. When, a little later, Dilly joined them the three of them went into great details about what the problem might be and what should be done about it.

'I think you should take the baby along to the doctor's, my dear,' Lorna told Sarah. 'I'll come with you, so make the appointment and then let me know when it is.'

'There's no need for you to trail all the way down here, Mrs Lewis,' Clara told her. 'I'll go with Sarah, or if I can't then Dilly will.'

'Gwyn doesn't think it is necessary to see a doctor,' Sarah said hesitantly.

'Don't worry about that, you don't have to say anything to him; I'll pay the fee whatever it is,' her mother told her quickly. 'If there is anything to be concerned about then you can tell Gwyn what you've done afterwards otherwise say nothing about it.'

Sarah thought it over for several days but finally, because the baby's breathing was so shallow and she was so pale and listless, she took her mother's advice.

Clara went with her and they watched in tense silence as the doctor examined the baby and then they listened to his observations with growing concern.

'It's obvious that she is in distress and the cause is a problem with her heart. It's beating irregularly and so I am going to recommend that she goes into hospital where she can be under medical observation,' he told them gravely.

'Will I be able to stay there with her?' Sarah asked anxiously

'You will have to see what the consultant says about that,' he told her. 'I'll give you a note to take to the hospital and I expect they will decide to admit her immediately.'

Sarah was beside herself with worry when they left the surgery and Clara was equally upset.

'Poor little mite,' she kept muttering as they walked home. 'I suppose you'd better take her there right away? Do you want me to come with you?'

'I don't know what to think or do,' Sarah

sniffed, gazing down at Cladylliss and stroking her tiny cheek with her forefinger. 'Poor little love, what a terrible start for her life. I wish my mam was here, I must let her know so perhaps I should go there first.'

'I think the first thing you should do is take little Cladylliss into hospital,' Dilly insisted when they told her what the doctor had said. 'Let Clara go with you and I'll go and let your mother know what has happened and then she can come to the hospital and be with you.'

Sarah nodded in agreement. 'I'd better feed her first,' she said, 'and then I'll do as you say.'

'I'll make you a cup of tea while you are doing that. Would you like something to eat?'

Sarah shook her head. 'I couldn't swallow a thing; I feel as if I'm going to be sick.'

'All the more reason why you should have something to eat before you set off for the hospital. I'll make some sandwiches; it may be hours before any of us can have a proper meal,' Dilly said firmly.

Clara and Sarah had a long wait when they reached Cardiff Infirmary in Newport Road. The waiting room was packed and although Clara emphasised that it was a very young baby when they handed in the note from the doctor, it didn't seem to make any difference.

Dilly had come part of the way on the tram with them and Sarah had told her where to get off and had given her directions so that she could find Cyfartha Street.

They were still in the waiting room when Lorna arrived with Dilly so Clara and Dilly decided that now Lorna was there they would get off home.

Lorna was indignant when she heard how long Sarah had been waiting. 'This isn't right, not when it's a young baby,' she said firmly. Before Sarah could stop her she had gone up to the desk to see if she could hurry things up. Ten minutes later they were being seen by the consultant.

The news was not good. They wanted to keep Cladylliss in for observation. They were not agreeable to Sarah staying with her but since she was breastfeeding they wanted her to come back at four-hourly intervals to feed her.

'You'd better come back home with me,' Lorna told her. 'It's a lot easier to get here from Cyfartha Street than from Louisa Street. As it is, you'll barely have time to have a cup of tea and something to eat before you have to start back again.'

'I'll have to go back to Louisa Street and let Clara and Dilly know what is happening and I'd better leave a note for Gwyn or he'll wonder where I am.'

'While you are there pack a bag with whatever you think you might need and tell Clara and Dilly that you're staying with me so you won't be back there again for a few days.'

'What about Dad; what will he have to say about it when he comes home?'

'Don't you worry about that; leave him to me,' her mother told her, setting her lips in a firm line.

Sarah remained at the hospital, either at the baby's bedside or in the small bare waiting room adjacent to the ward while doctors and nurses ministered to the child. She slept fitfully – dozing, but immediately fully conscious if Cladylliss made the slightest movement.

For most of the time the baby lay impassive, eyes closed, her breathing so light and faint that many times Sarah thought she had stopped breathing altogether.

When the end came it was so peaceful, almost as if Cladylliss was in a deep, untroubled sleep. Even though Sarah had tears streaming down her face she felt a profound relief at knowing that her beautiful baby was at peace and would suffer no more.

Everything seemed to be in a mist for Sarah over the next few days. Lorna took her home and put her to bed in her old room where for two days she drifted in and out of sleep.

Lorna had gone down to Louisa Street to tell Clara and Dilly that the baby had died. She left a note for Gwyn and asked Clara to be sure to tell him what had happened.

Back at Cyfartha Street she looked after Sarah as if she was still a child. Each time she woke, Lorna tempted her with food, but all Sarah wanted to do was go back to sleep.

'You must try to eat and drink,' Lorna insisted. 'You need food as much as you do sleep.'

It was mid-morning four days later before Sarah roused herself sufficiently to help her mother deal with all the details relating to the baby's death and arrange a funeral.

'Does Dad know that I am back here?' she asked worriedly as she struggled to sit up in bed.

'Of course he does!' Lorna assured her.

'Does he know about Cladylliss . . . about what's happened to her?'

'Yes.' Her mother nodded, but said nothing else.

'So what about the funeral,' Sarah persisted. 'Will he come if he knows Gwyn will be there?'

'I don't know.' Lorna looked doubtful. 'Are you sure that Gwyn is going to be there? Clara says that he's out of the country at the moment and he couldn't tell her how long he would be away.'

'So does he know about Cladylliss?' Sarah probed.

'Of course he does. He's very upset but, as he told Clara, work comes first,' Lorna told her as she plumped up the pillows.

'Does it? Did he ask if he could have time off so that he could be with me?'

'Well, I don't know about that of course,' Lorna said hesitantly. 'Gwyn has been abroad a lot lately, hasn't he? He didn't even manage to come to see the baby while she was in hospital, remember.'

'He hasn't been here to see me either,' Sarah said sadly. 'Unless he's been and Dad wouldn't let him in,' she added as an afterthought.

'No, he hasn't come here, but it's not because he and your dad don't see eye to eye. It's because, as I've already told you, he's away. Clara said he was covering a story in Germany or somewhere like that.'

'So how do I get in touch with him to let him know when the funeral is?'

Lorna looked at her in surprise. 'Well, you know where he works so do you know the name of his boss or one of his colleagues?'

Sarah shook her head. 'He's never talked about the people he works with, only about the latest story he was being sent to cover.'

'He works for the *Western Mail*, doesn't he? Then contact William Davis, the Editor, and ask him.'

'However do you know the Editor's name?' Sarah exclaimed in surprise.

'I would have thought most people in Cardiff would know that, especially if they are readers of the *Western Mail*, and your dad has taken it for as long as I can remember.'

'Will Dad mind if Gwyn is there?'

'I'm sure he would expect him to be there – after all, he *is* the baby's father. There won't be many of us, but you will be inviting Clara and Dilly, won't you?'

They arranged for the funeral to take place early in the afternoon on the following Tuesday. Sarah took her mother's advice and went along to the *Western Mail* offices and asked if they could get a message to Gwyn.

The funeral was a very quiet affair and over in less than an hour. Gwyn wasn't there and Clara and Dilly went straight back to Louisa Street because they wanted to be there when the children came home from school.

Sarah felt very distressed that Gwyn didn't come. The deputy editor she'd spoken to had assured her that the paper would not only contact him but also see that he returned in time to be there. The fact that he didn't come meant only one thing; he didn't care enough to do so. It was something she would never forget or forgive.

Looking back, she realised that he had never shown very much interest in their baby. His interest in her had started to wane long before she was born, Sarah thought unhappily. The only thing that he did seem to care about was his job.

When her mother suggested that she should stay with them a little longer, until she knew for certain when Gwyn was coming home, she agreed. Anything was better than the loneliness of being on her own in Louisa Street.

'There were only five people at the funeral,' Sarah sighed as they finished their evening meal. 'No one else knew her.'

Lloyd shook his head but said nothing. He'd said very little to Sarah since she'd come home and she suspected that he was keeping his opinions to himself and tolerating her because it pleased her mother to have her there.

Three days later Sarah went back to Louisa Street. She knew she would have to deal with disposing of all the baby's things and was on the point of asking her mother if she would come with her. Then common sense prevailed. It was time she sorted her own life out, she decided.

Possibly the best thing to do, she resolved, would be to see if she could return to university and finish her course. It was really only a matter of taking her exams, and if she outlined the circumstances that had prevented her coming back earlier, then they might make an exception and still let her sit them.

Once she had a degree under her belt she would be in a position to find a worthwhile job; one where she could earn enough money to be self-supporting and able to build a new future for herself.

As for Gwyn, well, since they weren't married it was only a question of packing her bags and leaving and she could do that right away, she reasoned. Simply walking out on him seemed to be the wrong way to handle the situation, however. It was vital for her own peace of mind to face him and tell him that she was going.

Chapter Seventeen

Sarah looked around the two attic rooms in Louisa Street and shuddered in dismay. After being back living in comfort at Cyfartha Street she wondered how she could ever again live in such a sordid place.

The walls and ceiling were grubby, the lino cracked and in places the mottled pattern had merged into a brown streaky mass where it had been repeatedly walked on and scrubbed. The furniture was so old and dilapidated that it made her cringe to think she had to sit on it.

Her mind was made up; she wouldn't even wait for Gwyn to come back from wherever it was he'd been sent, she'd begin planning her new life right away.

One thing was certain, she didn't intend to go on living in Louisa Street any longer than she had to, whether it was with him or not. She'd miss Clara and Dilly because they'd been really good friends, but they could still visit her – if they wanted to. She'd noticed that when she'd invited them to come back to Cyfartha Street after the funeral they'd seemed uneasy about accepting and they'd looked at each other questioningly before making the excuse that they had to get back home for the children.

Her own career plans were still vague. Completing her education and getting properly qualified was top of her list and so she resolved to find out first if this would be possible.

When she went to see the university officials, they were most understanding and promised her they would take steps to allow her to sit her exams if she was sure she was ready to take them.

Even though she'd now missed out on a lot of tuition she was confident that if she applied herself to studying for the next few weeks she would be able to do so.

Studying would keep her mind off her other major problem of whether or not Gwyn wanted them to remain together, she told herself. Meanwhile, she remained in Louisa Street for a couple of weeks while she resolved what to do, and sorted out everything with the university.

It was the end of the second week, and Sarah had just moved her things back to Cyfartha Street, when Gwyn came home. She expected him to be exhausted but although his kiss was rather brief he seemed to be in very good spirits and she noticed that he was wearing a new light-weight grey suit.

She waited for him to ask about the funeral but he never mentioned it. His immediate demand was that he was hungry and what was there for him to eat.

'Not a lot,' she told him. 'I haven't felt like eating, not since the funeral.'

He frowned, and then put an arm round her shoulder. 'That's all in the past so don't brood over it.'

'You mean I should do like you did and ignore it?' she questioned, shrugging his arm away.

'Come on, Sarah, no need to be like that. I was in Germany and I couldn't get home,' he blustered.

'That's not the way I heard it. Your boss said that he would let you know right away and make sure you came straight home.'

'He did let me know, but it was too late to get back for the funeral,' Gwyn told her evasively. 'Everything went all right, didn't it?'

'Splendidly,' she said in a sarcastic voice. 'Clara and Dilly were there . . . and my dad. He might be a hard-hearted workaholic but he did manage to take the day off even though he'd never seen his granddaughter while she was alive.'

Gwyn chewed on his lower lip and loosened his tie but made no comment. Picking up his suitcase he opened the door of the bedroom and tossed it on to the bed.

'If there's nothing here to eat, why don't I take you out somewhere? It might be easier to talk away from this place,' he suggested as he turned round.

For a moment she thought of refusing, then the sense of what he said registered. He was right. It would be much easier in the anonymity of a café or restaurant than it was in the confines of their two rooms to tell him she intended to get right away from Louisa Street.

To Sarah's surprise he took her to a smart restaurant in St Mary's Street. He seemed on edge and she wondered whether it was because, compared to him, she looked shabby in her black and white cotton dress or whether he was afraid she was going to cause a row about his long absence, so she decided to keep him on tenterhooks a little bit longer.

When they'd selected what they wanted to eat and drink he did start to talk but it was all about his job, the story he'd been covering and how important it had been.

'It was a real step up for me, I can tell you. I knew from the moment they sent me there that if I did a good job it would not only mean a permanent appointment but also be a stepping stone to better things. I came through with flying colours. They even gave me a by-line when they printed the story.'

'So are you on the permanent staff now?'

'It seems that way,' he said confidently. 'In all probability I will be sent abroad again and this time I will be their official Foreign Correspondent . . .'

'Rather a big step for someone who has only just been made an accredited journalist, isn't it?' she interrupted sarcastically.

He reddened. 'I'm afraid you don't understand

the workings of a newspaper office,' he said loftily. 'I would be working with a small team; possibly the same people as I did in Germany.'

'So does that mean you will be going there to live?'

He hesitated again, a dull red creeping up his neck. 'That's one of the things I wanted to talk to you about; something we'll have to discuss.'

'Go on, then, that's why you brought me here, isn't it?'

He waited until their main course was served and the waiter had poured their wine. Raising his glass to her he said, 'Here's to the future.'

'Yes, to the future,' Sarah responded in a studied voice. 'Would that be my future or yours?'

Again Gwyn hesitated, concentrating on loading his fork, and then he laid aside both knife and fork and leaned across the table. 'Let's clear the air. Living together in Louisa Street is not working out, is it?' he declared softly. 'I don't want to spend the rest of my life holed up in two rooms in Tiger Bay and I don't suppose you do either. My mother always used to say "When trouble comes in the door love flies out of the window." It never made sense to me in the past but it does now; but it's more than that. We want different things from life.'

Sarah raised her eyebrows in mock surprise. 'Are you quite sure about that?'

'You moved in with me because you were pregnant and your old man threw you out,' he reminded her.

'And how did I get pregnant? If I remember correctly, you had something to do with that,' she said mildly as she took a sip of her wine.

'Yes, I admit I was responsible and because of that I made sure you had a roof over your head but—'

'Yes,' Sarah said bitterly, 'you provided me with shelter, but you never suggested putting a ring on my finger. You didn't want to be tied down by marriage and you had no time for me when I was pregnant. You weren't at my side when Cladylliss was born and you showed practically no interest in her. You hated all the paraphernalia and responsibility of a baby. You weren't even willing to pay for a doctor when she was ill. You weren't there when she had to go into hospital or even for her funeral.'

She put down her wine glass and sat back, exhausted by her lengthy outburst but glad she had said it. It was all out in the open now. He would know exactly what her feelings were.

He stared at her as if seeing her for the first time. The catalogue of misdeeds seemed to have left him stunned.

'Are you trying to tell me that you want to finish with me?' he demanded, his voice tinged with annoyance.

'Why on earth do you think that?' Sarah asked.

He looked at her in bewilderment. 'After your tirade I thought that would come next,' he admitted.

She smiled coldly. 'Is it what you hoped for?'

He turned back to his meal, eating rapidly, concentrating on what was on the plate, and avoided her questioning stare.

He drained his glass of wine and made to pour himself another, proffering the bottle in her direction. When she placed a hand over the top of her glass he poured some more into his own glass before slamming the bottle back down on the table.

They finished their main course in silence. When he laid down his knife and fork he said, 'Shall we go?'

'Don't they do desserts?' she asked mildly.

He scowled but called the waiter over and asked for the menu.

Sarah studied it. He hadn't said that he wanted to stay with her and she sensed that he had no intention of doing so but wasn't sure how to tell her. Either that or he was hoping that she would be the one to say they were parting, she thought cynically.

After my outburst about the baby he probably thinks it is better to wait until we are outside before talking about it in case I make a scene, she thought wryly.

She waited until the waiter had served them before she said anything, then as she plunged her spoon into the delicious-looking mixture of fruit and ice-cream that was in front of her she asked, 'So are you going to move to Germany, then?'

For a moment she thought he hadn't heard or didn't intend answering. Then he pushed aside his own pudding and, leaning his arms on the table, brought his face as close to hers as he could. 'That's the other thing we haven't discussed,' he said in a controlled voice, 'but I don't think this is the place or the time, do you?'

'I think it is,' she told him. 'You've just treated me to an excellent meal and now I'd like to hear what your plans are for the future.'

His eyes glazed. 'I'm not sure how to tell you this or how you will take it,' he mumbled.

She looked at him expectantly, noticing for the first time the furtive way he avoided her eyes, his weak, slightly receding chin, and the mean tightness of his mouth. He might appear to be handsome but he was weak, she realised. Weak, greedy and self-centred.

A few moments later his words confirmed what she'd expected.

'Look, Sarah, this new job in Germany will depend on team work if I am to make a success of it. That means long hours and no proper home life. I don't think you'd like living in Germany. You're not all that happy in Tiger Bay, so it would be even worse there because you wouldn't be able to see your mother . . .'

'I've only been seeing her in the last couple of weeks, since Cladylliss became so terribly ill, and she was the only one I could turn to,' she said quietly.

He stared at her in silence for a moment, and then he cleared his throat and took a long swig of his wine. 'I think we should call it a day,' he pronounced. 'You're a lovely person and I've enjoyed knowing you, and I hope we can stay friends.'

'So you're walking out on me, are you?' she challenged.

Now that the situation was clear she felt no animosity, only relief and satisfaction that he was the one telling her he was leaving and not the other way round.

'I'll come back to Louisa Street with you and collect all my things and tell Mrs Blackwood that we're giving up the rooms.'

'Right away?'

'I'll pay the rent for next week; that will give you time to make other arrangements, won't it?' he asked awkwardly as they stood up to leave.

Outside the July sun was beating down and it reminded Sarah of their romantic weekend in Porthcawl when she'd thought herself to be madly in love and ready to defy her family and sacrifice her career for Gwyn. So much had happened since then; events that had completely changed not only her life but also her outlook.

As they stepped out on to the pavement Gwyn took her arm to steer her towards the tram stop but she pulled free. 'I'm not coming back with you. I'll leave you to go and collect your things on your own.'

'You mean you want this to be our goodbye?' Surprise mingled with relief in his voice.

'I think it's for the best since your mind is made up,' she told him coolly.

'We . . . we can still be friends?'

She smiled and stepped back out of reach as he made to kiss her. 'As you said, there's nothing at all binding us together. We're just ships that passed in the night, that sort of thing,' she said stiffly.

She walked away quickly, determined not to let him see her tears. Although the outcome was what she wanted she still felt desolate that it was all over between them. It seemed so foolish now that she'd truly believed herself to be in love with Gwyn and that they'd be together for ever.

Automatically she made her way to Cyfartha Street to seek solace in her mother's company. She wasn't sure that her dad would welcome her with open arms, but she knew her mother would. She hoped he would tolerate her being there when she told him that she intended to complete her studies and get her degree.

Even if he didn't say so in as many words she was pretty sure that the very fact that she had separated from Gwyn Roberts and was determined to salvage her career would please him.

Chapter Eighteen

Sarah breathed a deep sigh of relief. At long last her studies were finally over, and fervently she hoped that this would mean that the new year would be a new beginning for her and that all the troubles and frustration she'd had to face were now over.

She had needed to resit one of her final exams, and it wasn't until a few days before Christmas that she'd heard that she had passed and that it was confirmed that she really was qualified to be considered for the job she'd applied for in the Housing Department at Cardiff City Hall.

She still didn't know if she'd got it, of course, but they had promised to let her know immediately after Christmas so the letter should arrive within the next few days.

That in itself would be the start of a new life. For the first time ever she would be earning money and no longer be dependent on her parents to provide for her, and it gave her a tremendous feeling of freedom.

She still grieved for Cladylliss and knew she could never forgive Gwyn for his callousness over her death – or, for that matter, how little interest he'd shown in her from the day she'd been born. It had brought her to her senses though, and now that she'd seen him in his true colours she no longer had any feelings for him.

It had been a hard lesson but she felt she'd come out of it so much stronger. She no longer worried about what other people said or thought. She was determined that in future she would concentrate on her career to the exclusion of all else.

When the letter came a couple of days later telling her that her application had been successful, it was an added incentive.

For once her father showed real pleasure in her achievement. Although he'd not raised any objection to her coming back home he had remained tight-lipped and, she suspected, unforgiving over her misdemeanour and in going to live with Gwyn when she wasn't even married to him. That was all in the past, however, and possibly because she had applied herself so wholeheartedly to studying and had achieved the sort of success he expected, he was slowly becoming reconciled.

The fact that as soon as she was earning money she would be able to start repaying her parents for their support and generosity was uppermost in Sarah's mind. When she asked her mother to agree a figure for her keep, so that she could work out a budget, Lorna demurred.

'I have no idea about that sort of thing; you'll have to talk to your dad about it.'

'Couldn't you discuss it with him?' Sarah begged.

Lorna hesitated then shook her head. 'No, cariad; I think it would be a good way for the two of you to overcome any hard feelings. He will be proud of the fact that you can pay your way, so let him be the one to decide.'

Lloyd took her offer very seriously. When she stipulated that she also wanted to start repaying the money he had invested in her all those years he looked both surprised and pleased.

She waited while he did some elaborate figuring and wondered if she had done the wisest thing or whether it would have been better if she'd been the one to make an offer. Arguing about it would be both difficult and humiliating.

To her surprise the amount he asked for was considerably less than she would have suggested. When she said she felt she ought to pay more he shook his head.

'You have never been in the business world before so you have no idea of what other expenses will be incurred. You'll probably find that you have to subscribe to some sort of trade union and then there will be your morning breaks, lunches and fares, not to mention the fact that you are probably going to need a great many new clothes. I doubt if very many of the ones you have will be suitable for that sort of business environment and dressing correctly can be almost as important as your qualifications.'

She quickly discovered that he was right. Her colleagues, both men and women, all wore smart suits. As well as union dues, there always seemed to be collections of one sort or another going on. As a newcomer she had no idea which to refuse and which to support and although she kept her contributions within reasonable limits she was surprised to discover how much she spent on such things.

Buying new clothes was a top priority and it would have been impossible if her mother had not come to her aid.

'You can pay me back week by week,' her mother told her. 'It's a pleasure for me to go shopping like this and to see you looking so smart.'

Sarah also found that she needed money for socialising. At first she tended to avoid invitations to group outings but then she realised that if she continued to do so she would never really get to know her colleagues so she started going to the occasional event when it was something that interested her.

From the very first she was determined to be friendly with everyone but not to single out any one person as a special friend or to allow anyone to dominate her life. After a while, however, Sarah found herself more and more in the company of Stefan Vaughan. He was in his mid-thirties, thin, of a medium build, and was so well groomed that with his well-oiled black hair, green eyes, pencil-thin moustache and trim goatee beard, he looked like a sleek cat. His walk also had a feline grace to it. His position in the Educational Offices was one of importance and most people seemed to be wary of him and to treat him with deference.

Sarah felt no such compunction; her own position was sufficiently important that she felt she could meet him on an equal level. This seemed to impress him and after they'd met on one or two occasions he suggested they went out one night on their own.

'I'd like the chance to get to know you better,' he told her, expecting her to be overwhelmed by such flattery.

Her cool acceptance surprised him; it also astonished her. In the past she would have felt intimidated but not now. She accepted and had every intention of enjoying herself; but she didn't intend to let him overstep the mark in the slightest.

It was the start of a whole new episode in her life. In no time at all she was marked down as a 'good-time girl' by many of her colleagues; envied by the women, and a challenge to the men.

Until she'd met Gwyn Sarah had never gone dancing or to the pictures but now, because she was able to pay her own way, she resolved to do these things whenever she wished.

Stefan introduced her to jazz which was becoming all the rage and in next to no time, with her bobbed hair cut even shorter, she stood out in the crowd he mixed with as being very modern. She only demurred about having a shingle or an Eton crop because she thought that her superiors at the City Hall might consider that to be too revolutionary.

Outside working hours she began using heavy make-up; kohl to outline her eyes and vivid kiss-proof lipstick to define the shape of her mouth. Stefan had given her one of the new-style powder compacts and a lipstick that was neatly packaged in a shiny metal case.

Her figure was still slim and very trim, so when she went out dancing she discarded her corset. She wore a bust bodice for decorum's sake and used pretty garters to hold up her rayon stockings.

When she had had her hair cut into a smart, boyish style and had begun using make-up, her mother had been quick to warn her to be careful not to overdo things.

'You've made one mistake that cost you dearly so you don't want to make any more,' she warned. 'I don't think that your dad altogether approves of this eat-drink-and be-merry attitude that you're adopting.'

'He's not said anything to me,' Sarah told her.

'Perhaps not, but he's noticed all the same. He's very concerned that you seem to be behaving rather wild and that you seem to be becoming a flapper.'

'I'm only catching up with what I should have been doing years ago,' Sarah told her. 'Perhaps if I'd been allowed more freedom when I was growing up, instead of being made to study all the time, then I wouldn't be so eager to do these sorts of things now.'

Lorna sighed but made no comment, other than to reiterate that Sarah should take care not to land herself in any more trouble.

'I've grown up and now I'm as hard as nails; no man is ever going to break my heart ever again,' Sarah told her with a brittle laugh. Nevertheless, she modified her hairstyle so that although it was still very short it had finger waves in it and at one side a single, big flat curl that rested prettily on her cheek.

She was also very circumspect about what she wore to work and kept the knee-high flimsy floaty dresses for when she went dancing. By day she wore plain colours, demure necklines and long sleeves. Mostly she favoured black skirts that reached to mid-calf and white blouses. In winter she wore black stockings, in summer the new flesh-coloured ones and strap shoes.

She enjoyed her work and the responsibility her position carried but nevertheless she was determined to make the most of her leisure time and Stefan was certainly the perfect companion when it came to flirting. What was more, like her he was sedate and conventional during working hours.

In the office he was high-powered, efficient and respected, but his leisure hours were spent in pursuit of enjoyment and the friends he mixed with in the evenings and at weekends were not in any way connected with the City Hall.

Even though Sarah refused to partake in any of their drug sessions, he encouraged her to smoke ordinary cigarettes and presented her with an elegant ivory cigarette holder that was elaborately carved with flowers.

She'd known him for almost six months before she summoned up the courage to take him home. She warned him in advance that her parents were easily shocked and he promised to be on his best behaviour.

The occasion went far better than she could have hoped; her father treated him very civilly and was impressed by his business acumen and his knowledge of world affairs. Her mother was charmed by his saturnine good looks and his impeccable manners.

Their friendship had reached a new plateau and when a week later he invited her to a party at his flat in Tydfil Place she felt that it was time to make the situation between them crystal clear.

'I love the excitement of flirting with you but I don't want things to become serious between us,' she told him. 'I'm enjoying my life as it is,' she added by way of explanation.

He smiled sardonically and raised his eyebrows. 'Who says it has to change? Getting to know each other better could improve it.'

'What's that supposed to mean?'

'Do you think I haven't noticed how reluctant you are to take part in petting parties? If you want to enjoy life to the full perhaps now that you know there is no commitment on either side you will relax and indulge. Believe me, you don't know what you are missing out on,' he told her with a lecherous smile.

Sarah felt the colour rushing to her cheeks. She'd told no one that she had been living with Gwyn or that she'd already had a child and she wasn't sure whether she ought to tell Stefan or not.

He took her hesitation and reluctance for shyness and, taking her in his arms, whispered that he was an experienced lover so she had nothing to worry about.

'Spend the night with me, there's nothing at all to be scared about,' he urged. 'I'll be so gentle, so tender that you'll be transported into a trance of heavenly bliss,' he promised her. 'I'll make sure that it is highly romantic,' he assured her.

'For us, maybe, but how will our families feel about us sleeping together if they ever find out?'

'I have no family to consider and yours need never know unless you tell them.'

For the first time since she'd met him Sarah

was acutely aware that she knew nothing at all about his background. He'd never mentioned his parents or even if they were still alive; she didn't know if he had any brothers or sisters, or even if he had lived in Cardiff all his life.

She now felt that she needed to know these things; he was in his thirties so he might have been married and even have children.

The thought not only alarmed her but also made her realise that she had told him nothing at all about her own background. If she probed too deeply into his then in fairness she would have to recount details about her own past life and tell him things that she'd sooner keep quiet about. Perhaps his idea of secrecy was a good one after all.

'I don't think we should make our affair public,' he went on, cutting across her thoughts. 'It's not the policy of Cardiff City Corporation to encourage liaisons between members of staff. If it was all out in the open then you might be expected to resign and where would you find a job as lucrative as the one you are doing now?'

She felt a secret admiration for his forethought. She was enjoying her present lifestyle and she knew she wouldn't be able to afford to continue doing so if she didn't have such a high-paid job. She also suspected that Stefan was thinking of his own position as Head of Department because she was quite sure that his salary was considerably more than her own.

He was far too clever to rush her, and he

waited until the end of one of the Jazz parties staged in his flat. They'd been dancing with wild abandonment late into the evening and she'd had far more to drink than usual and her head was reeling. She felt so woozy that when it was time to go home she was unsteady on her feet.

'Go and lie down on my bed for a few minutes and as soon as everyone has gone I'll make you a strong coffee and that will put things right,' he told her.

When he brought in the coffee she was still in a daze and she made no protest when he sat down on the side of the bed and began to gently smooth her hair back from her forehead.

She barely touched the coffee because her senses were so aroused and after a few minutes, when he started kissing her, Sarah found she was responding and she made no resistance at all when he began making love to her.

Chapter Nineteen

In the months that followed, Sarah revelled in her double life. By day she was a well-paid, highly respected member of the Housing Department; by night she was a fast-living, crazy flapper partaking in petting sessions where there were drink, drugs and abandoned dancing.

Sometimes their wild capers reached the headlines of the gossip pages of the *Western Mail* and the *Cardiff Evening Echo* but no names were ever mentioned although it often hinted that those taking part were highly regarded local citizens.

Although they indulged in high-spirited fun they always seemed to manage to keep within the law and if Sarah's parents ever suspected that she was one of the flappers being described they never mentioned it.

Occasionally, dressed in his dark pinstripe suit and crisp, white shirt and sombre tie, Stefan came to her home for Sunday tea and behaved impeccably. Sarah marvelled at the serious way he discussed financial matters and politics. Lloyd seemed very impressed and always remarked afterwards what a knowledgeable man he was. Often he even went as far as to say how lucky Sarah was to have found such an intelligent friend.

She sometimes felt quite guilty about agreeing with him and wondered what they would think if they knew about his debauched parties and the drinking and drugs they both indulged in, not to mention the wild, passionate sessions of love-making that followed.

As these became more and more intense she arrived home later and later. Creeping indoors in the early hours of the morning, often high or light-headed, it took every ounce of care not to stumble over anything or cause any sort of noise that might disturb her sleeping parents.

When she went out on New Year's Eve she warned them not to expect her home until next day.

'Stefan has invited several of his friends to stay over at his flat to welcome in the new year, so he has asked me to do the same because it will mean breaking up the party if he has to bring me home,' she explained.

'Very thoughtful of him; a very sensible arrangement as long as you are not staying there on your own,' her father agreed. 'The streets will be full of crazy revellers for a couple of hours around midnight.'

It was the beginning of a new order; from then on her parents accepted that along with other friends she would be staying over at Stefan's on a Saturday night.

Her mother kept telling her that she was

burning the candle at both ends. She knew this and was aware that she couldn't go on for ever living the high life, drinking to excess and indulging in wild parties like Stefan did, but she'd become addicted to his lifestyle. She revelled in it all and was shocked to the core when she discovered she was pregnant.

Stefan was equally upset and tried to persuade her to have the pregnancy terminated.

'If you do that then no one needs to know. Tell your family that you are taking a week's holiday, arrange to have the time off and say nothing to anyone. I'll make all the arrangements; go to some place in Newport or Bristol perhaps, or even go down to London.'

At first she was in complete agreement with him, and then memories of Cladylliss began to surface and the longing to hold a baby in her arms again proved to be far too great for her to go through with his suggestion.

'I want this baby,' she told Stefan. 'I want us to get married so that we can be a proper family.'

They argued for weeks. He said he didn't want to settle down or have the responsibility of a family. He said they couldn't tell anyone at work because it might jeopardise his job when they found out that he was marrying someone who worked there.

'Surely', he argued, 'the fact that we love each other and want to be together is commitment enough and that's all that matters.'

When he took her in his arms and made love

to her she was persuaded that he was right and that it would be so much more romantic if they were married in a register office and no one at all except her parents knew anything about it. The way Stefan explained it all seemed so grown-up and exciting that Sarah was won over.

It was the modern way of doing things, she told herself; the only other person he'd said they'd tell was his long-standing friend and landlord, Ifan Hughes, who could be relied on to guard their secret.

Her only concern was that her parents would be disappointed. She was sure her mother had dreams of a white wedding and thought that perhaps even her father was looking forward to walking her down the aisle on his arm.

When she finally plucked up the courage to tell them that she and Stefan were getting married she emphasised that they intended it to be a very quiet wedding because then she wouldn't run the risk of losing her job.

'Very sensible. I take it that was Stefan's idea,' her father pronounced. 'He's quite right: the City Fathers are against married women working. I agree the woman's place is in the home but if they have the brains and the qualifications I see no reason why they shouldn't continue with their careers until they have a family. It's something you should fight for, Sarah. You women have the vote now so it's up to you to make sure it is put to good use.'

Their civil wedding was exceptionally quiet; only her parents and Ifan Hughes, who was there as a witness, attended. Occasionally in the days that followed Sarah wondered if it had actually happened and if she really was Mrs Stefan Vaughan.

She'd thought that since Stefan loved partying, and even though he had insisted on a quiet wedding ceremony, he would have wanted a big party afterwards. As it was, the meal at the Brecknock Hotel for the five of them seemed to be purely perfunctory. The moment they'd finished eating they went their own separate ways.

When before the wedding she'd said they must look for somewhere to live he'd looked astonished and said he had no intention of moving from Tydfil Place. The first-floor flat in a Victorian house close to Roath Park was quite spacious and he could see no reason at all for moving from such a desirable residence. Not only was the owner of the house a long-standing friend but also a great many of his friends lived nearby and he enjoyed all the parties that went on. If they moved, a new landlord mightn't like the idea of crowds of people, loud jazz music and dancing until late at night, whereas Ifan was always happy to join in.

When Sarah mentioned to her parents that they were staying on at Tydfil Place her father thought it was very prudent; but then, much to her surprise, he'd not objected to their quiet wedding.

'No sense in squandering money on non-essentials. Stefan is a very sensible man to be so thrifty,' he'd pointed out. She suspected that there was a sense of relief behind his remark and he was pleased he'd not been asked to foot a large bill that a full-scale white wedding would have entailed.

Once again Sarah found that her new life was different in every way from what she'd known in Cyfartha Street. Everything was to Stefan's taste, even the furnishings in the flat, and now that she was making her home there a great many of them seemed to be almost alien because they were so starkly different from what she'd been used to.

When she'd been merely a visitor she'd admired the fact that Stefan liked the bare minimum. Now she considered his black leather chairs and sofa far too masculine. He abhorred cushions, antimacassars, and all the other feminine trimmings that her mother had loved, and which had adorned her own home.

There were no photographs anywhere, only pieces of modern art which, like the furniture, were stark in outline. His kitchen had only the very minimal of utensils because Stefan didn't waste his time cooking; he preferred to eat out.

The only thing on which he did seem to lavish both time and money were his clothes. Finding room for her own things caused several arguments until in the end he compromised and bought a second wardrobe. It was a handsome affair in white which was fully fitted and had drawers underneath so that she no longer had any excuse for encroaching on his space.

Adjusting to living with each other caused a degree of friction. Stefan was so used to his own space that he resented having to take second place over anything. The few meals they did eat at home had to be when he wanted them.

He was never happier than when he was entertaining friends; with a house full of people, drinks flowing and jazz blaring, he was a completely different person: affable, caring and entertaining.

When they were at home on their own he often became moody and sullen. It wasn't the sort of companionship that Sarah had envisaged. Remembering the warmth between her own parents she felt uneasy; cheated almost. Sitting cosily in front of the fire enjoying each other's company on a wet evening, or as the days grew longer, had been something she'd been looking forward to once she and Stefan were married.

She would have been willing to cook for him every night but it wasn't what he wanted. He needed people around him who would make witty conversation and stimulate him; when that happened he was happy; the life and soul of the party.

Because of this he was considered to be good company. The invitations came thick and fast and he rarely turned any of them down. He'd told no one that they were married but one or two assumed that since Sarah was always there she'd moved in with him. They grinned knowingly and secretly admired his audacity.

Stefan never asked her to pay anything towards the running of the flat or towards the rent so she began to spend more and more on clothes and make-up. He liked to see her looking good, she told herself; she wanted him to feel proud of her when they went out together.

When he encouraged her to drink cocktails, to smoke and to continue taking drugs, she did just that even though she suspected that now she was pregnant she should be more circumspect. After all, she told herself, she wanted to have a good time, so why not join in and enjoy herself for as long as she could?

Soon she was throwing caution to the wind and matching him drink for drink and if she felt hung-over the next morning then she took a drink at breakfast time and that set her up for the day.

Even though she was now almost four months pregnant she'd not put on any weight. She put that down to all the mad dancing especially when it was Jazz, and Stefan was such a splendid dancer that they rarely sat down for a minute.

By the end of the evening she was usually so exhausted that she was asleep almost the moment her head touched the pillow.

Her own work began to suffer, but he seemed to be able to maintain the pace and when he dressed for the office each morning he looked a sombre, efficient businessman and no one would ever believe that he had danced half the night away.

Gradually, though, her body took over. She'd not suffered from morning sickness in the early part of her pregnancy but now she felt ill and uncomfortable most of the time. Within the next few weeks she seemed to balloon; so much so that she could no longer disguise the fact that she was pregnant and was forced to explain the situation to the head of her department and ask for extended leave. Stefan warned her that on no account was she to say that he was her husband in case it jeopardised his career when it was discovered he'd kept the matter secret.

'You really should have notified us that you were intending to get married,' her boss fumed. 'It is quite pointless taking leave because the rules are such that you won't be able to work here now that you are married,' she was told dismissively.

In some ways Sarah was relieved because these days she constantly felt tired. Stefan was always understanding when she said she didn't want to go out and said that she would prefer a quiet night at home. He never tried to persuade her to change her mind; he merely shrugged his expressive shoulders and went on his own.

At first she felt hurt and despondent; he was socialising so much and, although he constantly said how much her loved her, they had very little time together. When she realised he had no intention of changing, she began to spend more and more time with her mother. Together they shopped for baby clothes and either knitted or sewed items for the baby.

Sarah was alone in the flat in Tydfil Place when her labour started. Stefan had gone to a party but fortunately Ifan was still in the house. In desperation Sarah called out to him to help her.

When she told him that the baby was coming and she needed help he gaped at her in horror.

'Do you know where Stefan has gone? If you do, then I'll go and let him know and ask him to come back,' he offered.

'I've no idea; a party somewhere,' Sarah gasped as she began to writhe in pain. 'Can you go along to Cyfartha Road, then, Ifan and fetch my mother?'

'Surely it would be much better if I got an ambulance,' he protested, retreating hastily towards the door when she groaned again.

He refused to go in the ambulance with her but he did promise to let her mother know that she'd gone into the Royal Infirmary in Newport Road.

By the time her mother reached the infirmary the baby had already been born and she was both shocked and heartbroken to learn that it had been stillborn.

In the weeks that followed Sarah was consumed by guilt and bitterly regretted that she'd continued to live such a wild life while she'd been expecting. She was quite sure that the many excesses she'd indulged in were to blame for what had happened.

She was also aware of the obvious relief that Stefan felt because there was no baby and he'd been saved from the responsibility of having to bring up a child.

When Stefan found that she no longer had any interest in parties or even in their love-making, he began to spend more and more time going off out on his own, ignoring how lonely and depressed she was feeling. She tried to reason with him but to no avail.

One evening, determined to pull herself together after he'd gone off to a party on his own, Sarah forced herself to try and overcome her lethargy. She styled her hair with curling tongs, applied make-up to conceal her pallor, and put on one of her prettiest dresses. She'd expected Stefan to be overjoyed to find she had made so much effort but to her dismay, she found he was furious because she'd followed him to the party.

Even before she could explain that she'd done it to please him she found his attention being claimed by a petite blonde in a revealingly short dress. She took hold of Stefan's arm possessively, smiling up into his face as she dragged him on to the dance floor.

'Make a good pair, old Stefan and Florrie, don't they?' a man standing close by remarked. 'That's his latest floozy and they're crazy about each other.'

Blinded by tears Sarah stumbled off, the words 'his latest floozy' repeating themselves over and over in her head. Once again her life had fallen apart. How could she have been so blind, so besotted by the glamour of Stefan's lifestyle, that she'd been unable to realise what he was really like?

She felt heart-broken and ashamed that she'd been so gullible; what would her parents say? Looking back she suspected that since she'd returned home her mother had persuaded her father to be supportive and not to interfere; perhaps it would have been better if he had interfered, she thought dolefully.

Chapter Twenty

Sarah felt desolate and humiliated. She had lost not only her job, but also the baby she'd been looking forward to so much was dead and now, or so it seemed, her marriage was on the rocks.

She should have realised from the way Stefan conducted his life that he was a flirt. He'd convinced her that he was very much in love with her and to find him cavorting with a brassy blonde while she'd been confined was more than she could bear.

From the possessive way the woman had taken his arm and his compliance when she'd requested him to dance with her it had been obvious that they knew each other extremely well. That was bad enough but the fact that he had done so and left her standing there without a word of explanation had been humiliating.

Whether it was to prove that he still regarded himself as free as the wind, or because he didn't want to face her, he hadn't come home after the party. Sarah assumed that he was spending it with his new-found lover and with every passing minute her anger increased. She felt mortified as she realised she was no judge of character when it came to men. Stefan had turned out to be every bit as fickle as Gwyn.

When her mother called to see her early in the afternoon the next day she was appalled when, in a flood of tears, Sarah related what had happened the night before.

'The man's a monster,' Lorna stated furiously, 'but there's no point in upsetting yourself because you're not to blame. I was charmed by him and even your father was taken in by him and thought he was a gentleman because he was so knowledgeable and well mannered. The best thing you can do is to come home with me right now,' she advised as she held Sarah in her arms, trying to comfort her.

'I'll come later. Before I leave here for the last time I intend to tell Stefan exactly what I think about his behaviour and to inform him that I intend to divorce him.'

By the time Stefan arrived home after work that evening she had rehearsed what she was going to say to him a dozen or more times. The enormous bouquet of red roses that he brought for her did nothing to mollify her.

When she told him how repugnant she found his behaviour and how hurt she felt he tried to bluster and reassure her that things would be different in the future.

'I've suffered as well, you know,' he told her. 'I was worried out of my mind while you were having the baby and you'd been so cold and distant. I needed to take my mind off things. Perhaps I went too far, but blame the drink for that. Come on, Sarah, let me take you out for a quiet meal at your favourite restaurant and try and make it up to you.'

'It's too late for any reconciliation, I'll never be able to trust you again,' she told him. 'I intend to put things in the hands of a solicitor and to ask him to arrange for a divorce.'

Stefan looked very uncomfortable. 'There's no need to do that,' he protested.

'Oh yes there is. When I leave here I don't want anything more to do with you,' she told him sharply.

'If that's the way you want it then go ahead and pack your things. There's no need to go to the trouble of divorcing me because it's not necessary; you see, we were never properly married.'

She stared at him in disbelief. 'What do you mean by that? Of course we're married! Surely you remember our wedding ceremony . . .'

'Of course I do, but it meant nothing at all,' he told her in a mocking voice. 'It was a farce; something I arranged to keep you happy. You see, I already have a wife.'

Sarah looked at him in dismay, the colour draining from her face. 'You . . . you're saying that you're a bigamist?' she gasped.

He shrugged disparagingly and gave a sardonic smile.

'Call it that if you like, but it's not strictly

true because the chap who married us wasn't a real registrar.'

Sarah was mesmerised. 'Are you saying that it was all an act?' she asked in a shocked voice. 'Why?'

'You kept making such a fuss about being married when you discovered that you were pregnant that I arranged the whole thing in order to keep you happy.'

'So our marriage certificate is as worthless as you are,' Sarah retorted bitterly.

'Well, it's certainly not worth the paper it's written on.'

'That means that if our baby had lived the poor little thing would have been a bastard.'

He shrugged again. 'Not something we have to worry about, is it?' he said callously.

Sarah took a deep breath as she tried to control her shaking. 'You are an utter swine and I loathe you,' she told him, her voice harsh with contempt.

'Then you won't want to come for a meal with me,' he said with a deprecating laugh.

'I never want to see you again or even breathe the same air as you. Go for your meal on your own or take the brassy hussy you were with last night. By the time you come back I will have packed up and left.'

Although she was reeling with shock at what Stefan had told her Sarah went round the flat collecting up every item of her possessions and ramming them haphazardly into her suitcase.

She was determined not to spend another night at Tydfil Place or leave a single trace of herself behind.

Lloyd and Lorna were both utterly astonished when Sarah told them what Stefan had said. Their shock turned to anger and both of them were absolutely incensed that he could have done such a thing.

Lorna's first concern was about what would have happened if Sarah's baby had survived.

'Perhaps under the circumstances things have turned out for the best,' Lloyd sighed as he put his arms round Sarah's shoulders and stroked her hair in a comforting gesture.

'Oh, Dad, it's all so hopeless,' she said tearfully. Then as all the fury and bitterness that had overwhelmed her from the moment Stefan had told her reached its peak she gave way to her grief and broke down and sobbed as though her heart would break.

Lorna was incensed. Although her hysterically voiced opinions reflected precisely what Sarah was feeling Lloyd frowned and shushed her to silence.

'He was an evil man, a very clever and convincing rogue, but upsetting ourselves will do no good at all,' he warned. 'The important thing now is to extricate Sarah from this terrible mess with the minimum of scandal.'

'I'd like to shout it from the housetops and let everyone in Cardiff know what a swine he is,' Lorna declared heatedly. 'And believe me,

I would do if it wasn't that it would mean dragging Sarah's name through the mud.'

'I know, I know, cariad.' Lloyd reached out and patted her shoulder. 'What about making us a cup of tea and then we'll all sit down and try and work out what is to be done for the best.'

'I'm not going back to Tydfil Place ever again,' Sarah declared vehemently, pulling herself free of her father's embrace and angrily scrubbing away her tears.

'Of course not; we wouldn't expect you to do so; there's no question of that,' her father told her.

'It's going to be lovely having you back here again,' Lorna affirmed. 'We'll be able to go shopping together like old times.'

'As soon as you feel capable of doing so I think you should look for another job and try and pick up the pieces of your life again,' Lloyd said gravely. 'It's important to plan your future, not brood about what has happened.'

'Perhaps, you're right, Lloyd, but there's no rush; all in good time. It's easier said than done,' Lorna commented.

'I know that, but being positive and looking forward will be for the best,' Lloyd insisted.

'I wish I could go back to my old job at the City Hall,' Sarah said wistfully.

'I'm sure you do, but that's completely out of the question. For a start, they don't employ married women—'

'I'm not a married woman, remember?' Sarah interrupted bitterly.

'No, cariad, I am well aware of that, but if you try to explain the situation then you will have to incriminate Stefan.'

'Surely that's the best thing that can happen. He deserves to be shown up for what he is,' Lorna said heatedly.

'I agree but it will not only blacken his name but also Sarah's as well and I very much doubt if they would give her back her job once they found out the truth.'

'I'll go and make that tea,' Lorna said a trifle huffily. 'I can see that you're determined that she does things your way.'

'I want things to be handled as judicially as possible so that Sarah isn't implicated in any way,' Lloyd said firmly.

'Sarah, you do want me to take care of things for you, don't you?' he asked quietly the moment they were alone.

'No, Dad, I don't expect you to do that. I think that with all my training I ought to do it myself, but not yet. I'd prefer to leave it for a while; I need to come to terms with everything. Somehow I can't believe that I could let anyone take me in like this.'

'I know, I know. He fooled us all, not just you. He'd convinced me that he was an honourable, upright sort of chap. I admired his integrity and his breadth of knowledge, but he's obviously a blackguard. In some ways it's as well that you know the truth and things have turned out as they have, because you are better off without him. It all could have been a lot worse, you know,' he added awkwardly.

'Well, have you two sorted everything out and planned what you are going to do?' Lorna asked as she brought in the tray of tea things and placed them down on the table.

'Sarah must concentrate on getting her life back to normal again and that means the very first thing she must do is find a new job,' Lloyd emphasised.

'I don't think she's in any fit state to do that,' Lorna argued as she poured out the tea and passed a cup across to him. 'She's had some terrible shocks, remember.'

'I know, I know, cariad, but what useful purpose will it fulfil if she simply mopes around the house brooding about what has happened and working herself up into a state about what she'd like to do to Stefan Vaughan?'

'I think Dad is right,' Sarah told her mother. 'It's probably much better for me to put the past behind me and try and forget what has happened. I'm not even sure if the sort of bigamy he has committed can be considered a criminal offence.'

'Oh, Sarah, it must be,' her mother protested. 'The wretch should be tarred and feathered and paraded from the City Hall all the way down to St Mary's Street.'

'I know how you feel, Mam, but I think if it

went to court it would make me into a laughing stock. Also what else would come out if we tried to expose him? Everyone would know all about my past as well as his and some people might feel I only got what I deserved.'

Lorna stirred her tea angrily. 'Don't talk such nonsense, why should they think that?'

'For quite a few reasons. Before I married him I was well aware that Stefan not only drinks like a fish but also likes to party and live it up in all sorts of ways; some of which would shock both of you if I told you about them.'

'All the more reason why everyone should know what a terrible sort of man he is.'

'I would be shown up as well and when people heard that at one time I was living in Tiger Bay, think what conclusions they would draw from that. There's bound to be some who would say that I was no better than I should be.'

'That's all water under the bridge and has nothing to do with what happened between you and Stefan Vaughan.'

'Maybe not, but other people might see it differently to you. Let's face it, Mam, the whole episode might end up with people actually feeling that Stefan was the one who deserved sympathy, not me.'

'You're talking absolute rubbish,' Lorna declared as she collected up the empty teacups.

'Not really, Mam. You see, I never told Stefan that I'd been living with Gwyn or anything about poor little Cladylliss,' she added with a catch in her voice.

'Does anyone need to know those things?' Lorna argued.

'Once I make it known about Stefan all the rest of it is bound to come out,' Sarah warned.

'Quite; so forget all that has happened and concentrate on building a new life for yourself,' her father stated sombrely.

'This false wedding business . . . surely you need to do something about that, cariad?' Lorna persisted. 'Supposing you ever want to get married one day, properly married, I mean, wouldn't you have to say you are already married?'

'Don't worry about it, Mam. The ceremony wasn't legal and in time I'll find out what I need to do to sort it out. From now on I shall be calling myself Sarah Lewis and hope that no one questions it.'

'Well, you probably know the law better than we do, so let's hope you're right, but do look into it and make quite sure so that there are no complications later on,' her father warned.

Chapter Twenty-One

Although Sarah was determined to make a new life for herself, she found it increasingly difficult to clear her mind of all that had happened. Memories of how she'd been deceived by Stefan and let down by Gwyn Roberts haunted her.

Her heart ached whenever she thought about poor little Cladylliss and she wondered if her death and that of the baby that had been stillborn was some sort of punishment for her waywardness.

She knew that the sooner her mind was occupied by other matters the better, but so far she'd not been able to decide what sort of job she wanted to do from now on.

She'd thoroughly enjoyed working in the Housing Department at the City Hall and there were times when she felt she'd give anything to be able to turn the clock back to those days.

It was so much on her mind that one afternoon she took the risk of going back there. She felt it might break the spell the place seemed to have over her if she could simply walk through the main hall visualising what it would be like to be working there again.

She knew she was taking a risk going there

because there was the possibility that she might be seen by someone she'd worked alongside or who knew her. She was pretty sure she wouldn't bump into Stefan, however, because he worked in a separate part of the building. Thinking back she could never remember him coming into the main public area where the Housing Department was sited all the time she'd worked there.

As she strolled in through the door and made her way towards the far end of the main hall she was startled to hear someone call out her name. For one awful moment she froze, afraid that it might be Stefan, but as she turned round she saw to her relief that it was Bryn Morgan, the owner of a large building contractors with whom she'd dealt on several occasions in the past.

'It's good to see you again, Miss Lewis,' he greeted her, holding out a podgy hand, a warm, friendly smile lighting up his plump face. 'I heard you'd left?'

'Yes, about three months ago,' she murmured and felt the hot colour rush to her cheeks as they shook hands.

He frowned in disbelief. 'It seems longer. I've missed you because you were always so helpful and you seemed to understand my problems whenever I had any. Nowadays . . .' He shrugged and left the sentence unfinished.

'Look,' he pulled out a watch from his waist-coat pocket and consulted it, 'I was about to go for a cup of coffee, would you care to join me? I would enjoy talking about old times.'

Sarah hesitated. The very last thing she wanted to do was go to the canteen where there was the possibility that she might bump into Stefan.

'I know a very nice coffee shop not too far away in Queen Street,' Bryn Morgan went on, replacing his watch and tugging the points of his waistcoat back into place over his rotund stomach. 'So will you come along with me?'

'Thank you, that would be very nice,' Sarah agreed.

She found him an easy companion to talk to but it was not until they were sitting drinking their coffee that he touched on anything to do with the City Hall.

'Incredible old carry on, wasn't it?' he remarked. 'You must have heard about it,' he went on as he saw her frown in bewilderment. 'One of the top men, a chap called Stefan Thomas.'

'Stefan Thomas? No, I don't know anyone by that name, only a Stefan Vaughan from the education department,' she said, her colour deepening.

'That's the fellow. It seems his real name was Thomas; Stefan Vaughan Thomas.'

Sarah felt her heart racing. 'What happened?'

'Well, it appears he was a lively sort of chap, very good-looking, enjoyed partying and living it up; something of a rascal, though, by all accounts. It turns out that he had a wife and children who are living up in the Valleys but he was more or less separated from them and had his own flat here in Cardiff. Apparently, or so the story goes, he went on a wild drinking spree and afterwards took a lady he'd met up with during the course of the evening back to his flat, presumably intending for her to stay the night there.

'They'd only been back about half an hour or so when some chap burst in and accused him of seducing his girlfriend. The upshot of it was that there was a terrible argument that ended in a fight and this Stefan fellow was knifed by this other man. Dead as a doornail before the police even got there.'

'That's really terrible,' Sarah gasped, the colour draining from her face.

He stared at her in concern. 'Oh dear, I didn't mean to upset you. I take it you knew him, then?' Bryn Morgan commented.

'Yes, I did,' she murmured non-committally. 'I knew him as Stefan Vaughan, of course.'

'So did everyone else at the City Hall by all accounts. It was only when the police needed details and started looking into his background that all these revelations came to light. As I've said, he was quite a wild character by all accounts; mad on dancing, indulged in drugs and drank like a fish. Seems he'd had another woman living with him for the past few months but no one was sure who she was. In fact, some people said they'd thought she was his wife, but she'd disappeared and it seems that this blonde he'd picked up with was intended to be her replacement. Apparently, from the account I read in the papers, she was no saint either. In fact, from what the police implied, they'd already had dealings with her in the past.'

Sarah sensed that Bryn Morgan was prepared to go on talking about it for ever so she said quickly, 'I'm sure it will all be in the paper again when the case comes to court.'

'Bound to be,' he agreed and, much to her relief, changed the conversation to enquiring about her. 'So where are you working now?' he asked.

'I'm not working anywhere at the moment; in fact, I'm looking for a new job.'

'I see!' He frowned. 'What about coming to work for me? At the moment I use a local solicitor to deal with our legal problems but we are expanding so rapidly that we could do with someone of your calibre actually working for the company.'

Sarah stared at him in astonishment. 'Do you really mean that?'

'Of course I do; I think it would be a very good arrangement. When would you be able to start?'

'I'm free now so I could start at any time that suited you; immediately, in fact.'

Bryn Morgan stood up. 'Look, if you have the time, why not come back to the office with me now. I can show you around and explain what sort of work you would be doing and then you can let me know if you are interested.'

Sarah felt she was walking on air as she accompanied Bryn Morgan back to his office. She could hardly believe that he was actually offering her a job.

She knew he was the managing director of a prosperous building company but she was surprised to learn that he had over a hundred employees.

'I take an active part in the running of the company,' he told her, 'but I also rely a great deal on my general manager. He's been with me ever since he was invalided out of the army with a damaged leg and he really is my right-hand man now. You'd be working closely with him but I think you'd get along fine together.'

Owen Phillips looked as though he was in his mid- to late twenties and Sarah liked him as soon as they were introduced. He was tall and broad with thick fair hair and light blue eyes. Although he had the firm, square jaw of a prize-fighter he also had an air of gentle calmness and when he spoke his voice was soft and rather studied.

'You two would be working in close co-operation a great deal of the time,' Bryn Morgan told them, 'so it's important that you see eye to eye over things.'

'I don't think there will be any problem over that,' Owen said with a reassuring smile. 'However, if Miss Lewis would like to come along for a day and see exactly what goes on here, it might give her a better insight into what is involved. I'd be more than pleased to show her around and tell her how we run things.'

Sarah agreed that it was a good idea. 'It will also give you the opportunity to see if you are confident that we can work together,' she pointed out.

There was only one problem, she thought as she said goodbye to them both after agreeing to be there at eight o'clock the next morning; how much should she tell Bryn Morgan about her association with Stefan Vaughan?

She was still trying to make her mind up when she sat down with her parents for their evening meal.

'You're very quiet tonight,' he father commented. 'Worn out with all this job hunting, cariad?'

'No, not really. As a matter of fact, I think I've found the ideal situation.'

Her father listened in silence as she told him about Bryn Morgan's business and how he had offered her a job.

'I've heard of Morgan Builders, of course,' he stated when she had finished. 'They have a very high reputation but I had no idea it was quite as large a concern as you say it is.'

'Apparently it is growing all the time. The general manager has promised to show me around tomorrow and give me some idea of what my job would entail.'

'So you haven't exactly got it yet?' Her father queried.

'No, but as far as I can tell it is mine if I want it. The idea of spending a day with the general manager is to see if we get on all right as I would be working very closely with him. He seems to be an extremely nice person, though, so I don't think that is going to present any problem at all.'

'Well, don't rush it, cariad. I can see you have doubts of some kind because you seem to be brooding about something.'

'Yes, it's to do with Stefan, as a matter of fact,' Sarah told him worriedly.

'That scoundrel! I thought we'd agreed never to mention his name again,' Lloyd said angrily.

'I know, but I was told something today that I think you both should hear.'

They listened in silence as she repeated what Bryn Morgan had said.

'I did read something about it a few days ago,' her father commented when she finished, 'but because the name was Thomas I didn't mention it; I hoped it wasn't the same chap,' he added lamely.

'Well, like I've just told you, it seems his real name was Stefan Vaughan Thomas but here in Cardiff he dropped the Thomas.'

'So the fact that he was calling himself Vaughan when he married you meant that he wasn't legally married to you anyway,' Lorna said, shaking her head in disbelief.

'I've already told you that we weren't legally married, Mam. That wedding ceremony was all a sham; just something he arranged to keep me happy, as he put it,' Sarah reminded her bitterly.

'Yes, yes, I know you did, my lovely. I was just running through what was in my mind. Terrible old fraud, wasn't he? Thank heavens you're free of him. Do you reckon they'll send him to gaol over this?'

'Mam, he's dead,' Sarah reminded her.

'Oh yes, so he is. Well, it's only what he deserved. Will the man who did it be sent to gaol?'

'Probably,' Lloyd said gravely. 'Let's hope that nothing more about Stefan Vaughan's background comes out and you're not involved in any way, Sarah.'

'That's the problem. I'm afraid it might, and I'm wondering whether or not I ought to tell Mr Phillips that I was involved with him for a time and that was one of the reasons I left the City Hall.'

'Duw anwyl, why do a thing like that?' her mother exclaimed. 'Let sleeping dogs lie. Tell him that and he won't give you the job, and you've already said how much you want it.'

'Better for her to tell him now than for it to come out later on,' Lloyd protested.

'Why tell him at all that's what I say,' Lorna insisted stubbornly. 'It wasn't as though she was properly married to him, now was it?

Anyway,' she went on even more firmly, 'he already has a wife and family so think what it will do to that poor woman if she discovers that her husband was an even bigger scoundrel than she's already been told.'

'You certainly have a point there,' Lloyd agreed sombrely. 'It just shows what a quagmire your life becomes when you start to lie. I understand you were taken in, cariad,' he said more kindly. 'Even though he was a highly intelligent man he was greatly lacking in honesty and integrity.'

'Yes, cariad, it's time to try and put it all behind you. You say this man Bryn Morgan is ready to give you a job, so the best thing you can do is take it and get on with your life and, whatever you do, don't go falling for him.'

'I'm hardly likely to do that, Mam,' Sarah told her with a smile, 'he's going bald, has a pot belly and is nearly sixty.'

'He's also an outstanding businessman and, in addition, he's a city councillor and he'll probably be made an alderman in the very near future,' Lloyd added.

'That doesn't mean he's any different to Stefan Vaughan. We all thought he was a clever businessman and look . . .'

'Don't give it another thought, Mam.' Sarah smiled cynically as she reached out and took her mother's hand. 'I won't be falling again for any man.'

Chapter Twenty-Two

Sarah found her job at Morgan Builders far more challenging than she'd anticipated it would be.

After the smooth, slow-moving, almost pedantic pace of life she'd known at the City Hall it took her some time to adjust to the cut and thrust and fast-moving action of the commercial world.

At the end of the first month, however, she felt she'd adapted well but she was also aware that it would have been impossible for her to do so without the help of Owen Phillips.

He didn't intrude on what she was doing but he often enabled her to make acceptable short-cuts. Also, because he'd worked there for several years he was able to give her valuable inside information about the companies and people she had to deal with and was always ready to give advice if she asked for it.

When she had been working there for six months and it was time for a review of the situation as they'd agreed, Bryn Morgan seemed to be more than happy with her progress. He also expressed his relief that she and Owen Phillips got along so well.

She felt such a debt of gratitude to Owen Phillips that on the anniversary of her starting work there she wanted to show it in some way but she wasn't quite sure how to go about it.

If it had been a woman colleague, then a bouquet of flowers or even a box of chocolates would have been ideal. Under the circumstances, though, she felt that she could hardly give either of those sorts of presents to a man. She enjoyed working with him and this had helped to bond the friendship during the year they'd now known each other and this was something she greatly valued.

Sarah pondered the problem for several days then, summoning up her nerve, she asked him if he would allow her to take him out to dinner as a way of saying thank you for all he'd done for her since she'd joined the company.

For a moment he looked startled, then, with a twinkle in his blue eyes, he said, 'That's the first time a lady has ever invited me out. I'm very flattered but—'

'You are going to say no,' Sarah interceded quickly, colour rushing to her cheeks.

'On the contrary, I was going to say that I'd love to have dinner with you but that I would like to be the one to take you out. You've brought a new dimension to the office. In fact, I've never enjoyed working with anyone as much as I have with you.'

For a moment they stared at each other in silence as they weighed up the problem. Then

Sarah laughed. 'This is beginning to sound like a mutual admiration society. I suppose we could compromise and go Dutch?' she added tentatively.

He gave a deep sigh. 'If you insist, but I really do want to take you out. I was afraid to suggest it in case you felt uncomfortable about accepting.'

Sarah spent a lot of time deciding what to wear. She wanted to look smart, but not dressed to the nines in case he thought she was making more of the occasion than it deserved.

In the end, after trying on three or four of her dresses, she settled for a pleated dark blue skirt that reached below her knees and a long-sleeved draped blouson top that reached to her hips. This was trimmed at the bottom with a wide band of light blue.

With her hair, which she now wore in a neat bob, parted to one side, and light stockings and shoes, she felt smart but rather subdued so she added a long rope of white beads.

Finally, she very carefully outlined her mouth with a pale pink lipstick and picked up her bottle of California Poppy scent to put a dab behind her ears. Then she hesitated, studying herself critically and wondering if she hadn't already done enough. She wasn't sure how Owen might react to scent. She never wore it to work because she didn't think it was appropriate to do so and she knew some men found such pungent perfume rather distasteful.

Owen was smartly dressed in a light grey

suit, a crisp white shirt and a dark blue and grey striped tie. His face lit up in admiration when she arrived and he handed her a spray of sweet-smelling Lily of the Valley to wear as a corsage.

After the first few minutes which they spent choosing which dishes they would like from the rather long menu they slowly took stock of each other. Even though they saw each other most days they still found they had plenty to talk about.

'I haven't a very active social life these days,' Owen confided. 'I can't play any sports because of my leg. Before it was damaged I played rugby regularly every Saturday, unless there was a big match on at Cardiff Arms Park when, of course, I went to watch. I still do so occasionally, but it's not the same being a spectator, when you don't ever take part in the game itself.'

'I've never really had any interest in sport,' Sarah confessed. 'As I was growing up I was always being made to study. My dad was very keen that I should go to university and get a degree.'

'Well, that has certainly paid dividends,' he told her, a look of admiration in his blue eyes. 'There aren't many women who could handle legal matters as efficiently as you do.'

'You've been a great help; without you I don't think I would have managed to learn the ropes so speedily.'

'Yes, we seem to make the ideal team. Bryn Morgan was remarking on it only the other day.'

Getting to know Owen socially meant that they exchanged background details. Like her he was an only child which, he agreed, was probably the reason why they had such a close affinity. Unlike her he no longer had anything to do with his parents.

'My father died while I was quite young,' he explained, 'and when my mother married again I'm afraid I didn't get on too well with my stepfather.'

'Why? Were you jealous of him?'

'Yes, I suppose I was in a way. I was too young to understand that my mam was lonely and needed someone other than me in her life,' he said sadly. 'He's a good man, pillar of the chapel and all that sort of thing, but he was inclined to be rather strict and I resented him telling me what I could or could not do. It was one of the reasons why I volunteered for the army the moment I was old enough to do so.'

She expressed surprise when Owen went on to say that he had volunteered for military service in 1918 when he was only seventeen.

'It was a daft thing to do but I did it in order to get away from home and my stepfather. It also meant that I missed out in a number of ways. If my own father had still been alive he would probably have encouraged me to take an apprenticeship in engineering or something like that.

'You can imagine what a shock the army was.' He smiled, as he speared the last piece of potato on his plate. 'I'd jumped out of the frying pan into the fire. I'd exchanged a strict stepfather for an even stricter drill sergeant. It was 1918 and men at the Front were dying so fast that the moment I'd finished my initial training and knew how to handle a gun I was sent over to France.'

'So did you see much action?' Sarah asked as she laid her knife and fork down on her plate and lightly dabbed the corner of her mouth with her napkin before taking a sip of wine.

'Not really. The very first week I was over there I had the misfortune to be the victim of a sniper's bullet.'

'How terrible,' Sarah exclaimed.

Owen paused as a waiter came to clear away their plates and proffer the pudding menu. He waited until they had ordered before he went on.

'The bullet hit me in the top of my leg and shattered the bone. I didn't reach a military hospital until several days later and because I wasn't considered to be one of the more seriously injured I wasn't treated immediately. By the time they came to attend to my leg there'd been shrinkage or something. The outcome of it is that one leg is slightly shorter than the other one and of course I've walked with a limp ever since.'

'It's hardly noticeable,' Sarah told him.

'I'm conscious of it, though, and worst of all it has meant I can't play rugby.'

They continued reminiscing for the rest of their meal and Sarah found herself enjoying herself more and more. In fact, in her estimation their evening was a tremendous success.

When they finally parted Owen confirmed this when he said he hoped that this was going to be the first of many such outings because he'd found her such a delightful companion. He added that he'd enjoyed the occasion immensely and found it had been a pleasant form of relaxation.

Going out for a meal together, although not on a regular basis, became quite frequent. Occasionally they also went to the pictures if there was anything on that they both wanted to see. Sarah was surprised at how similar their tastes were and found that their trips to the cinema were all the more enjoyable because of this.

The only thing that worried Sarah was the fact that although Owen had told her a great deal about his childhood and what had happened while he had been growing up, so far she'd said very little to him about her own background apart from details about her parents.

She hesitated for quite a while before she told him the entire truth about her past and when she did summon up the courage to do so she wondered if it would be the death knell of their friendship.

She probably wouldn't have told him at all except that she realised that their friendship seemed to be gradually developing into something closer and she decided she had to clear the air. She'd already told her parents about him and she was anxious for them to meet him so that they could understand how different he was and why she considered him to be such a good friend.

Sarah and Owen were in their favourite restaurant having a meal when she broached the subject.

'I thought you might like to come and meet my parents; perhaps on Sunday for tea?' she suggested.

His face lit up. 'That would be very nice. You've talked so much about them that I feel I already know them.' He smiled. 'Don't worry, cariad, I'll be on my best behaviour and I won't tell them any of your dark secrets, like how you invited me out before I had a chance to ask you,' he teased.

She didn't smile. 'There are several things I think you should know before you accept,' she said slowly.

He looked puzzled but remained silent and took a long, slow sip of wine as he waited for her to continue.

'It's about my past,' she said and her voice dropped to almost a whisper so that he had to lean across the table to hear what she was saying.

He stretched out a hand and took hers, holding it tightly. 'You don't have to tell me anything you'd rather keep to yourself, you know, Sarah. I judge you on what you are today not on what you may have done in the past.'

Sarah smiled weakly, took a sip of her wine and nervously cleared her throat. Then in a low voice, and watching his face for his reactions, she told him all about her affair with Gwyn Roberts and how she'd had to drop out of university before she could take her final exams because she'd been pregnant.

'So what happened after that?' he asked quietly.

'We never married but we lived together in a squalid room in Tiger Bay.' Her voice was shaking as she began telling him about what happened and how her parents had refused to have anything at all to do with her.

When she reached the part where little Cladylliss had taken ill and died, she was so overcome with emotion that she had to stop speaking.

Owen refilled her glass and waited while she took one or two sips then looked at her expectantly. 'Go on,' he said gently. 'Tell me what you did after the child died.'

'After that I made my peace with my parents and went back home. The university agreed to let me take my exams and so I eventually completed my studies. After I got my degree I went to work at the City Hall.'

'So everything turned out well. That's where you first met Bryn Morgan, wasn't it?'

She nodded. 'Yes, I was working in the Housing Department, as you probably know, and of course he often came in to discuss building plans and so on.'

'I remember him saying something about it at the time. He seemed to be impressed by your efficiency even in those days,' he told her with a warm smile. 'So why did you leave?'

Sarah took another sip of her wine. 'That is something else I feel you should know about,' she said as she put her glass down.

He took a sip of his own wine and waited for her to go on.

'I worked there for about two years and during that time I got to know a man called Stefan Vaughan,' she said bitterly. 'After my previous experience I was so determined to live life to the full that when I discovered that away from the office he shed the mask of respectability and lived the high life I thought he was exactly the sort of companion I wanted.

'Stefan loved dancing, especially jazz, he enjoyed drinking, and he was into drugs and everything else. To me it was an exciting new world and one I wanted to take part in.'

Owen listened quietly, nodding from time to time as Sarah told him how she'd become more and more friendly with Stefan. 'When he suggested that I should move into his flat I agreed to do so, but only if we were married.'

Owen's face registered incredulity when she told him all about the bogus marriage that Stefan arranged.

'So was that why you eventually left the City Hall, because you found out what an utter cad he was?'

'Not exactly. I had already left because I was pregnant again. I was looking forward to having the baby although Stefan wasn't too keen on the idea. He still wanted to live the high life and stupidly I tried to keep up with him. I didn't take enough care of myself, I'm afraid, and the baby was stillborn,' she said forlornly.

He leaned forward and took her hand again, shaking his head sadly. 'I'm so sorry.'

'I was terribly upset but, even worse, I discovered that while I had been in hospital Stefan had been cheating on me. That was when I went back home again. My parents were shocked but very understanding.

'It took me a while to come to terms with what had happened. The day I met Bryn Morgan I'd gone to the City Hall to convince myself that I could never work there again. He told me the whole story about Stefan Vaughan.' She shivered. 'I expect you read all about it in the papers.'

'Was this the woman who was with him on the night he was attacked?' Owen asked.

'I can't be sure but I'm pretty certain it was the same woman.'

Owen smiled gently, his pressure on her hand increasing. 'That meeting with Bryn Morgan was fate; you were destined to come and work at Morgan's,' he assured her.

'Now that you know everything will you still be coming to tea on Sunday?' Sarah asked tentatively.

'Of course! All that is in the past, but I'm glad you've told me.'

She gave a smile of relief; he was the first person apart from her parents who knew all there was to know about her and it felt as though a great weight had been lifted from her shoulders.

Chapter Twenty-Three

Sarah found that both her parents were very concerned when she told them that she'd invited Owen Phillips to tea on Sunday.

'Do you think that is a good idea, cariad?' Lorna asked in a slightly puzzled voice.

'Isn't he the chap you work alongside at Morgan's?' Lloyd frowned.

'Yes, he is, but he's become quite a good friend and I'd like you to meet him.'

'When you go off out in the evenings are you telling us that's who you've been with, Sarah?' her mother asked sharply.

'Yes. There's nothing wrong with that, is there?' Sarah asked, looking from one to the other in surprise.

'I thought you said that you weren't going to get involved with any of the men you worked with ever again after what happened last time,' Lorna said in a disapproving voice.

'Your mam's right,' Lloyd agreed. 'After what happened with that Stefan Vaughan we'd hoped you'd learned your lesson. That other chap, Gwyn Roberts, wasn't much better either. This may be 1927, and you younger women seem to think you can do as you like now that you've got the vote, but I would have thought that it would have made you more responsible for your actions,' he said sternly.

'Look, I know I made some bad mistakes in the past, but Owen Phillips is quite different from either of them,' Sarah said defiantly.

'That's what you said the last time,' her father reminded her. 'I grant you I was taken in by that Stefan fellow as much as you were, he seemed to be a very intelligent sort of chap, but look what a rogue he turned out to be.'

Sarah didn't bother arguing with him because she knew there was no point in doing so. She did wish, though, that she hadn't asked Owen to come to tea on Sunday but it was far too late to back out now.

Her mother made a great fuss about it all, claiming that she liked plenty of warning when she was expected to entertain people so that she could plan ahead.

'The very last thing I want you to do is start making any special arrangements,' Sarah told her quickly. 'Owen would hate to think he had inconvenienced you in any way so don't go making a fuss or doing anything special.'

She knew it was pointless saying this and wasn't at all surprised when her mother busied herself making a Victoria Sponge cake and worrying about whether there was enough cold ham left to make sandwiches.

As she changed into one of her prettiest dresses ready to greet her visitor Sarah herself began to have qualms about what she was doing and wondered if she was on the verge of ruining a friendship she valued very much.

Owen arrived promptly at four o'clock and as he presented her mother with a bouquet of flowers she saw the look of pleasure on her mother's face and smiled to herself that at least he'd found favour in her eyes.

When she introduced him to her father she noticed that as they shook hands the two men studied each other carefully, as though they were two sparring partners weighing each other up.

Lorna had laid the table with her best china all carefully arranged on a lace tablecloth. As they took their places and she brought in the teapot, Sarah took a deep breath, determined to make the best of what looked as though it was going to be a disastrous occasion.

At first the conversation was very stilted. Owen was polite but withdrawn, and her mother nervous and on edge. She kept fussing over whether they wanted more to eat or their cups refilled instead of enjoying the meal herself.

Sarah realised that her parents were both concerned about meeting him because of all that had happened in the past but she found herself wishing it was all over and wondering how soon she could suggest that she and Owen went for a walk without her parents looking affronted.

They were drinking their second cup of tea when Owen seemed to be aware that things weren't going well at all. He made a special effort to talk to Sarah's father, asking him about his job.

Slowly, very slowly indeed, Lloyd started to relax. By the time the meal ended and Sarah started to clear the table they'd moved away into more comfortable chairs, still deep in conversation.

'He seems a nice solid sort of chap,' her mother commented as they did the washing-up together.

'He's certainly been a very good friend to me,' Sarah said quietly, 'both at work and outside.'

He mother looked at her sharply. 'You are sure you know what you're doing by getting involved again?'

'I'm not getting involved, Mam. I simply asked Owen to come to tea because I wanted you both to meet him; there's nothing more to it than that.'

'Are you quite certain about that?' her mother pressed. 'It doesn't look like mere friendship to me. I suppose it could be worse,' she added with a sigh. 'He's a fine-looking chap and he has a responsible job, but then so did that Stefan Vaughan.'

'He's nothing at all like Stefan, Mam. Stefan was all out for a good time. At work he was head of a department and highly respected but when he was out enjoying himself he was quite wild. Owen is nothing at all like that. He is always very quiet and reserved.'

'Well, he and your dad seem to have plenty to say to each other,' she agreed.

Although Lloyd acknowledged that Owen was a quiet, industrious sort of chap, he did rather hold it against him that he wouldn't discuss trade unions or say whether or not he was a supporter of them.

'Do you or do you not agree that they are justified in holding the bosses to ransom in order to be paid the sort of wages they think they're entitled to receive?' Lloyd probed.

'It's a question that never arises at Morgan's even though we have a large number of men working there, because we make certain that they are all quite happy with their terms of employment,' Owen explained to Lloyd with a bland smile.

'I'm not very interested in politics,' Sarah told her father when he mentioned the matter later that evening.

'Then you should be. With the education you've had you could make your opinion heard. I shouldn't have to keep reminding you that women have the vote,' he told her frowning, 'and therefore it is their duty to interest themselves in such matters.'

'It's part of Morgan's policy that as a company they don't support or even recognise trade unions,' Sarah told him. 'If any new employee belongs to a union, they prefer him to keep his views to himself and not try to persuade his fellow workers to join.'

Although Lloyd seemed to approve of this he was curious as to what Owen thought about such matters.

'Owen may advise them because that's what he's expected to do but I have no idea what his personal views are,' she told her father.

'From the way he spoke when we were discussing the miners' strike he sides with his boss over such matters. He blames the miners for striking instead of negotiating and says that the root cause of the depression we're entering into now is the result of their disruption.'

'Well, then, as General Manager and as Mr Morgan's right-hand man, it's no wonder he doesn't want to have anything to do with trade unions,' Sarah pointed out.

'Yet he agreed with me that many of the improvements that have been made in the work-place or in the wages people are paid has come about through union intervention,' her father argued. 'As someone who knows the law as well as you do you should also be aware of that.'

From then on Sarah avoided talking about Owen or getting involved in any conversation with her father that touched on trade unions or political matters of any kind. She noticed her mother had said nothing when they were talking about it and she wondered whether her mother was disinterested or whether she knew from experience that it was one of her father's hobby-horses.

Her mother certainly seemed to have been impressed by Owen and seemed to have taken to him. She was constantly saying what a nice chap he was and frequently asked her how he was and seemed to be interested in anything she cared to tell her.

It was only a few months later when Lloyd came home from work, ashen-faced and shaking so much that they both thought he had been taken ill.

Lorna made him a cup of tea and insisted he sat down in front of the fire, but he pushed her aside.

'Tea won't solve my problem,' he told her harshly. 'In future we may not even be able to afford to drink tea,' he added gloomily.

'What on earth are you on about? Don't tell me that there's going to be another General Strike; we're only just recovering and getting back on our feet from the last one.'

'It's worse than that. I've been given the sack.'

They stared at him in disbelief. He'd never worked anywhere else except the few years when he'd been in the army. The moment he'd been demobbed he'd gone straight back there. His work record was exemplary; he was never late and never took a day off.

'Thirty years of loyal service and they give me my cards without a word of warning,' he said bitterly.

'There must be a reason,' Lorna protested.

'They're cutting back. They said the older men in top jobs were too expensive to keep on. They got rid of three of us older ones and kept on the young lads we've trained up, who only earn half of what we do.'

'Didn't any of the others have anything to say about it?' Lorna asked.

'Plenty, but it did no good. We were all told that if someone had to go then this was the best way. Our families were all grown up so we weren't still struggling to make ends meet.'

'Surely the younger men stood a better chance of getting taken on somewhere else, though?' Sarah frowned.

'Watching their own backs, aren't they?' her father said bitterly. 'Make too much of a fuss about us being sacked and their own jobs might be on the line. All these years I've done my best, ever since I joined the company, and this is how they treat me.'

'So what are you going to do now?' Lorna asked in a bewildered voice. 'You're not yet fifty, Lloyd, so you can't simply sit back and do nothing. You're far too young to retire so you'll have to try and find another job.'

'I'll certainly do my best but the chances of finding one at my age is going to be difficult. I don't suppose for one minute I'll get another one as a manager. To think I kept everything in shipshape order all these years and now some half-trained youngster is stepping into my shoes. Give him three months and without my guidance everything will be in utter chaos. It takes years of experience to run things there as efficiently as I did,' he said morosely.

'Well, if you can't get a managerial position then you'll have to compromise and be prepared to take something else, I suppose,' Lorna sympathised.

'All because of the damned miners coming out on strike,' Lloyd muttered gloomily.

'If they'd treated them right in the first place, paid them a living wage and provided them with decent homes, then none of this would have happened,' Sarah opined.

'Maybe with your education it would have been better if you'd put up for Parliament and helped to run the country instead of working where you are,' her father told her sourly.

Sarah felt stung by his words and was about to start arguing with him but her mother gave her a warning look.

Afterwards, Lorna said gently, 'Don't start riling him, Sarah. He's depressed enough as it is. He's never been out of work in his life before and this is a terrible blow for him having to go on the dole. It's going to take a lot of persuading to get him to go and sign on because he'll feel it is such a disgrace having to do so.'

'There's no disgrace at all about it. He's been paying in for it ever since he started work so it's his due.'

'You know that and so do I but to him it

seems like a handout, a form of charity, and it will go against the grain for him to have to queue up to sign on each week, I can tell you.'

As the weeks passed and Lloyd had still not managed to find work, he grew more and more depressed. Even though she was handing over almost all of her wages Sarah knew that her mother was having a hard time keeping things going on these and her father's dole money.

At the end of twenty-six weeks they all knew that even this would stop and then things would be more difficult than ever. For a start they would be means tested and the very thought of that sent shudders through all of them.

'We may as well not bother because they'll tell us that we have a daughter living at home who is working and, what's more, they'll tell us that we have plenty of furniture and other stuff that we can sell,' her father pointed out.

It made him all the more determined to find work. He'd long since given up looking for anything managerial, having faced so many rejections because of his age. By now he was ready to do almost anything rather than have to submit himself and his family to suffering the indignity of the Means Test.

From the very first he'd asked Sarah not to mention his dilemma to Owen because he felt so ashamed of their plight. Now, however, she was so worried that Owen sensed something was wrong.

When he asked her a direct question about why she was so quiet and evasive she had no alternative but to tell him the truth.

'I'm sorry to hear that,' he said shaking his head in dismay. 'As a matter of fact, I wondered if you were having trouble at home because of me. The fact that I've never been invited back again made me think that perhaps your parents disapproved of me.'

'No, nothing at all like that. My mam thought you were lovely, in fact.' She smiled.

'Well, that's good to hear.' He grinned. 'What about your dad, does he think the same?'

She shrugged. 'I have made a point of not mentioning your name lately because he is so indignant that he is out of work and blames the miners' strike for the fact that he is on the dole.'

'How long has he been looking for work? You've never said a word and I thought we were friends,' he commented reprovingly.

'His twenty-six weeks are almost up and that means the Means Test, if he is to get any more money and he and my mam are absolutely sick with worry at the thought of that.'

'I'm sure they are,' Owen agreed quietly. 'It must be terrible for a proud hard-working man like your father who has had a highly responsible job to be subjected to that sort of thing.'

Two days later, Owen handed her a form.

'What's this?' Sarah asked, her voice tinged with alarm. 'You're not giving me the sack I hope,' she added with a weak smile.

'No, it's an application form for your father to fill out. I'm sure we can find him some sort of work here.'

'Thank you.' Sarah bit her lip, not knowing quite what else to say because she wasn't at all sure how her father would react.

Chapter Twenty-Four

Sarah took the application form that Owen had given her home but she gave it to her mother, not her father.

'I'm not at all sure how your dad will react over this, cariad,' Lorna said uneasily. 'The mood he's in these days he might think you're interfering.'

'That's utter rubbish. Surely he can't afford to turn down any help he gets.'

Her mother read the form through again, running her finger down the page to make sure she missed nothing out as she did so.

'Who would he have to see if he completed this application form?' she asked frowning.

'The general manager, of course,' Sarah told her.

'Isn't that what that Owen Phillips is?' her mother asked in a puzzled voice.

'Yes, Owen is the general manager.'

'I don't think your dad would feel comfortable about having to do that at all. What's more to the point, he might regard it as charity if he was actually offered a job at Morgan's, and he would hate that,' her mother said worriedly.

'Believe me, it wouldn't be charity; he'd have

to have the necessary qualifications,' Sarah told her quickly. 'It was Owen's idea that he should fill in an application form.'

'What on earth were you thinking of, telling Owen about our problems?' her mother exclaimed.

'I hadn't told him about Dad losing his job, not until today,' Sarah defended herself.

'Why tell him at all?' Lorna said indignantly.

'I wouldn't have done so but he questioned me because he said I seemed to be troubled and he thought it might be because you two disapproved of me going out with him.'

'What utter nonsense! I thought he was an extremely nice chap. You must invite him to come again soon; that is, once your dad is fixed up in a job,' she added hurriedly.

'Well, what are we going to do about this application form? Are we going to give it to Dad to fill in or not?' Sarah challenged.

Neither of them was at all sure about what his reaction would be so they decided it might be best to leave it for another couple of days and see what developed. Lloyd was in a grim mood as it was and was constantly carping about the injustice of it all.

'The miners have already taken pay cuts so why couldn't the bosses be satisfied with that? The men have to live, they have to feed their kids, and a chunk of their money goes back to the pit owners in the form of rent anyway.'

'It's no good blaming the miners for the fact

that you've lost your job,' Lorna told him. 'It's the company you worked for that's to blame. Mind you, most firms are penny pinching these days.'

'Yes, so that the bosses can line their own pockets,' Lloyd retorted bitterly.

He constantly nagged Sarah that she should take these matters more seriously and that with her legal training she ought to be trying to do something about it.

'If I start getting involved in politics then I might lose my job and that would mean we were both out of work and on the dole,' she pointed out. 'Furthermore, as a woman with no dependants I probably wouldn't get any dole and even if I applied I would be told that I didn't have enough stamps on my card to be entitled to any.'

'You've got an answer for everything,' he told her. 'Wait until you're given your cards for no reason at all and see how you feel about things then.'

Sarah was on the point of telling him about the application form but her mother shook her head, warning her to say nothing.

They probably wouldn't have told him about it at all except that a couple of days later he came home from the dole office after going to sign on to say that they had told him that his dole money would cease forthwith.

'The next step is that I have to appear before a tribunal and be means tested,' Lloyd told them bitterly. 'I suppose you know all about that,' he added sourly.

'I should do, you've told us often enough,' Lorna sighed. 'They will want to know all your personal details, like how much rent we pay and what our outgoings are and so on, I suppose,' she added worriedly.

'We've been through the details all before and I don't want to talk about it again,' Lloyd said huffily. 'Duw anwyl, how the devil do you think I will feel when I have to sit here watching you turn sheets to middle because we can't afford new ones and patching and darning my socks over and over again.'

'As long as we have enough to eat and some coal to put on the fire to keep us warm and enable us to cook then we shouldn't grumble, I suppose,' Lorna said philosophically. 'Think of those who have a young family to feed; how do you explain to kiddies that are crying with hunger that there's nothing in the cupboard for them?'

As far as Lloyd was concerned the fact that he was the one undergoing the indignity of being subjected to the Means Test was the last straw. He kept repeating that he was too young to be on the scrap heap, that he was fit and willing to work, and that he had years of valuable experience.

'I'd sooner throw myself in front of a train than have to face this,' he declared angrily as he polished his shoes and smartened himself up ready for the interview.

'There's no need for you to do either,' Sarah told him, ignoring her mother's warning look. 'I've got a job application form here for you to fill in. Do that and I'm sure you'll get work of some sort, even if it is not quite the sort of job you want.'

Lloyd took the piece of paper from her, his face lighting up with relief; then he scowled darkly as soon as he saw the heading. Morgan Builders.

'Have you been bleating about me being out of work to that fellow you brought here for tea?' he asked belligerently. 'I don't want anyone making a job for me because they feel sorry for me, let me tell you. I'm not a charity case.'

'Believe me, no one is going to give you a job at Morgan's unless there is a vacancy and you have the right qualifications or experience to fill it,' she told him crisply.

'So even if I fill in the answers to all these damn questions it still won't mean that I've got a job?'

'Not unless there is a vacancy for a man with your talents,' she agreed.

He studied the form more closely. 'Probably a complete waste of time filling it in,' he said morosely.

'If you don't try you'll never know,' Sarah told him as she turned and walked away. 'If you're right and nothing comes of it, then at least you'll be able to tell me what a complete waste of time it was,' she added as she reached the door.

'I'm not at all sure you've done the right thing,' her mother whispered worriedly as she followed Sarah into the kitchen. 'I saw the look on his face when he read through that form.'

'It's too late to worry about it now and it is up to him whether he fills it in or not,' Sarah replied.

The next morning the completed form was alongside her plate on the breakfast table. She said nothing but slipped it inside her handbag to take in to work with her.

'I thought he might not respond,' Owen said as he took it from her.

'He swallowed his pride when it was a case of either this or the Means Test. I'm sure that deep down he is very grateful but he's a proud man and in some ways the fact that you have held out a helping hand is a bit like charity in his eyes.'

'Yes.' Owen sighed and shook his head. 'I suppose it does seem like that; I know I would hate to be in his position. Anyway,' he gave her a warm smile, 'I'll see what I can do and I'll be sure to make it quite clear when he comes for his interview that I'm employing him on his abilities, not because I know him.'

'Oh dear,' Sarah looked discomfited, 'I haven't told him that it will be you interviewing him.'

Owen frowned. 'No, I suppose that might be

embarrassing for him. I'll explain the situation to Mr Morgan – in confidence of course,' he added hastily, 'and ask him if he will sit in on the interview with me. That might make it easier for your father.'

It was two days before Lloyd received a letter in the post asking him to come for an interview.

'He's as nervous as a schoolboy going after his first job,' Lorna told Sarah. He's been fussing around all day over what to wear and polishing his shoes and telling me which shirt and tie he wants to wear and to see that they're well pressed.'

'Don't worry, I'm sure it will all work out all right,' Sarah reassured her.

'I do hope so. It says in the letter that he has to ask for Mr Morgan himself so I suppose that's a good omen. I think he was loathe to be interviewed by Owen, much as he likes him.'

'Owen will be there, I'm afraid. He's only asking Mr Morgan to sit in on the interview because I explained Dad might think he was being offered charity if he was given a job by Owen.'

Lloyd never told them what transpired at the interview and Sarah thought it best not to ask Owen. The great thing was that her dad was offered a job as an assistant in the stores.

He regarded it as something of a come-down after his previous position and the responsibilities that had entailed, but he took it nevertheless.

'It's better than nothing and preferable to having to be means tested,' he told them both when he announced that he would be starting work the following Monday morning,

Sarah was relieved that he was back at work because she knew her mother had been desperately worried about him. Even so, she felt slightly apprehensive because it meant that they were working for the same company so they were bound to come into contact with each other from time to time and she was afraid that he might feel uncomfortable because of her senior status. The other was that she hoped he would not create a fuss about the fact that those men who worked at Morgan's were not allowed to belong to a union.

When she spoke to her mother about it Lorna said that as long as Sarah wasn't embarrassed about them both being at Morgan's then she didn't see why he should be.

With regard to the other matter she decided the best thing would be for Sarah to have a quiet word with him and warn him that it would be best if he kept his political opinions to himself.

Sarah picked her moment carefully. She'd been afraid he might flare up, tell her it was none of her business. Either that or lecture her on how he realised that it was essential for working men to form a united body in order to have the strength to confront the bosses. To her surprise he did none of these things.

'You've no need to feel any concern about me doing anything like that,' he told her. 'The unions did damn all for me when I was given the sack. Not one of the men I'd worked alongside for countless years spoke up in my defence or was even willing to say anything on my behalf when I asked them to do so. From now on I look out for myself. The only battle I shall be fighting is the one for my own survival.'

When later in the week she asked him how he liked working at Morgan's, Lloyd looked at her thoughtfully. 'If this is a roundabout way of asking if I get on with that Owen Phillips then the answer is that I think he does a good job. He's a hard taskmaster and expects the men to do their job well but he's fair in his dealings. I like the way he handles things and the way he speaks to the men. I'm very grateful to him for giving me the chance to work again.'

Her friendship with Owen had remained unbroken, though slightly strained, and she was anxious for things to return to what they had been.

'Maybe then it's safe for me to bring him to tea next Sunday,' Sarah probed in a light, teasing voice.

Her father nodded. 'Maybe that's not such a bad idea,' he said approvingly. 'It's reassuring to know you have such a staunch friend.'

With her father once again in work her mother was no longer stressed and their problems seemed to be over. Sarah knew that it had been a struggle for her mother to make ends meet and so she'd dipped into her own savings, pleased to be able to help after all they'd done for her.

Sarah felt that her life was improving in every respect. Owen was now taking her out at least twice a week and enjoying his visits to her home again for tea on Sunday afternoons, after they'd been for a walk in the park, or had been listening to the band.

On these occasions they never mentioned Morgan's or discussed anything that went on there and Sarah was relieved to find that her father and Owen were always extremely affable towards each other.

'He's such a nice chap, it's a pleasure having him here,' her mother frequently said after Owen had gone home and her father usually nodded in silent agreement.

Her own friendship with Owen had now developed into a regular pattern and Sarah felt happy and comfortable in his company. He certainly had a more mature outlook and led a much quieter, more predictable life than either Gwyn or Stefan had done.

There were no wild excesses, no parties or jazz sessions that went on until the early hours of the morning. She'd done all those things and now, she realised, she was content to accept this new pace.

Although she enjoyed her work, from time to time she hoped that one day she would have a home and even children of her own. She knew there was no one else in Owen's life and she often wondered if he felt the same way.

Their friendship was as close and enjoyable as ever but Sarah hungered for more than the occasional cuddle and the sweet, but rather chaste, kisses.

She sometimes wondered if perhaps telling Owen so much about her background had been a mistake and was the reason why he was so restrained. Was her slightly sordid past deterring him from taking their relationship any further, she wondered?

Chapter Twenty-Five

Sarah was almost as surprised as her parents were when, on the first Sunday of the new year, Owen joined them for afternoon tea and asked her father in a very formal way if he would give his permission for them to be married.

She'd wanted to invite Owen for Christmas dinner but her mother had been against it.

'We're having a very quiet Christmas this year, cariad. There are outstanding bills still to be cleared so I am only buying a chicken big enough for the three of us, and I'm not bothering with all the usual trimmings.'

'Surely there will be enough on it for one more, and you always cook so many vegetables that there are always leftovers that we have to use up next day,' Sarah said in surprise.

'Not this year I won't be; I've made only a very small Christmas pudding and a few mince pies to have later on in the day. I'm not making a Christmas cake. Waste of money when you are struggling to make ends meet.'

'You're not though, are you?' Lloyd argued. 'It's true I'm not able to give you quite as much money as I did before but it's not all that much less.'

'I know all about that, Lloyd, and I'm not grumbling,' Lorna assured him.

'I'm giving you more money each week as well,' Sarah pointed out, 'so you shouldn't be any worse off than you were before Dad lost his original job.'

'Give it time and things will be straight again, cariad,' Lorna told her. 'While your dad was out of work I had to put off paying for some of the things we needed and now I have to clear off all those back debts. I want to start the year with a clean slate and squandering money on unnecessary luxuries isn't going to help me to do that, now is it?'

'I still don't see why we can't ask Owen to join us on Christmas Day,' Lloyd said in a perplexed voice. 'He's been damn good to us getting me fixed up at Morgan's and he's never said a word to make me feel uncomfortable about it.'

'Why should he? He's done well getting a conscientious worker with all your experience for less than what he's worth.'

'Oh, so this is what it's all about, is it?' Lloyd said angrily. 'You don't think I'm being paid enough and you're holding it against him.'

'No, I don't think that at all,' Lorna insisted.

'Then why not invite him to come and share Christmas with us? Poor devil, he'll be all on his own in that bedsitter; not much of a holiday for him, now is it?'

'His landlady will probably give him a

dinner; she feeds him all the rest of the year,' Lorna answered tartly.

'That's not the point,' Lloyd protested. 'I'm damn sure that Owen would sooner sit down and share the scraps on our table than stay in his lodgings even if he has half a turkey all to himself there.'

Lorna had refused to give way so their Christmas had been quiet and there had been a strained atmosphere between the three of them.

What worried Sarah was why her mother was being so parsimonious. Normally she was one of the most generous people imaginable and furthermore she usually enjoyed cooking and putting on a good spread.

Sarah kept wondering what debts there were outstanding that still had to be paid off. Although they'd needed to be careful about what they spent when her dad had been out of work they'd been a long way from being on the bread line. She'd had two pay rises since she'd been working for Morgan's and each time that had happened she'd increased the amount she gave to her mother each week.

When she mentioned the matter to her father when they were on their own she discovered that he was as mystified as she was.

'I know you've pulled your weight, cariad,' he agreed. 'As you say, your mam's had almost as much housekeeping money as she ever had so I can't understand why she's so worried or why she has got behind with payments and isn't able to manage.'

'Have you tried asking her about the bills she still hasn't paid? If we knew exactly how much money was involved, then perhaps between us we could do something about clearing them off and set her mind at rest.'

'I did ask her, cariad, but she avoided the issue; she simply wouldn't talk about it. I don't know what's going on. The only thing I can think of is that she's borrowed from a tally man and, knowing what I think about them, she doesn't want to tell me.'

'Either that or she's saving up for something that needs replacing in the home.'

'Maybe, but for the life of me I can't think what that can be. Whenever we need anything of that sort she usually talks about it and even asks me what I think.'

Although she was delighted by Owen's surprise proposal, Sarah felt rather concerned when he started talking about an Easter wedding. Even a quiet wedding cost money so if her mother was worried now about debts what was she going to be like when it came to paying out for that? Offering to pay for everything herself was one solution, but would her mother agree to such an arrangement?

To her surprise her mother seemed to be delighted by the idea of a wedding and suddenly much happier than she'd been for weeks.

Lloyd was a little more restrained, but as he shook hands with Owen he said he would be more than pleased to have him as a son-in-law.

For several Sundays after that they seemed to talk of nothing else. Easter that year would not be until mid-April so they had plenty of time for all the planning. Even so, Sarah wondered if her mother realised all that was entailed. In addition to the cost of all their new clothes and everything else, once she was married and had a home of her own she would no longer be handing over money each week like she did now.

'Unless you move in here with us,' her father suggested when she mentioned the matter to him.

'I don't think that would work, Dad,' she told him doubtfully.

'It wouldn't bother me,' he told her. 'You and your mam get on well enough. I've always said that it's impossible for two women to share the same kitchen, but it's not quite the same in your case as you've managed to do so all your life.'

'What about Owen, though? We've no idea what he would think about such an arrangement.'

'There's only one way to find out,' her father told her, 'and that's to ask him. It's something that you and Owen will have to talk about anyway because if you are not coming to live here then you'll have to start looking for a place right away or it won't be ready for you to move into at Easter.'

When Sarah brought up the subject and said that they could live with her parents Owen looked doubtful.

'Do you think it is a feasible idea?' he asked doubtfully. 'It will mean that the three of us will be working together as well as living together.'

'We'd have the front parlour as our own living room and a bedroom and only have to share the kitchen so we needn't see all that much of them if we don't want to,' Sarah said thoughtfully. 'I wouldn't go along with the idea if it meant us all being in together.'

'No, I agree with that, but I still think that we would be better off if we moved right away into a place that really was our own. That way we'd feel free to do exactly as we liked,' Owen insisted.

In many ways Sarah agreed with him and once again she turned to her father to discuss it with him.

'If only we knew what debts it is your mam's talking about,' he said worriedly. 'There's something on her mind. She doesn't look at all well these days. In fact, there are times when she looks quite drawn and she's certainly very touchy and short-tempered and that's not like your mam. Something is worrying her, there's no doubt about that.'

The truth came out quite by accident. It was in the middle of March, on a cold wet blustery day and Sarah had such a heavy cold that around midday she decided she would take the rest of the day off.

When she reached home she found her mother getting dressed ready to go out.

'You don't want to go out in this terrible weather,' she told her. 'What is it you need? I'll pop out and get it before I take my coat off.'

'No, I need to go myself,' her mother told her. 'Anyway, what are you doing home at this time of day?'

'My cold is making it difficult to concentrate on what I'm doing so I thought I'd be better off coming home.'

'I can't stop to make you a hot drink so make one for yourself then fill a hot water bottle and get to bed,' her mother told her.

'You really shouldn't go out in this weather, Mam. It's blowing a gale, you'll get soaked through,' Sarah warned her.

'I need to go so I'll wrap up and take an umbrella,' her mother insisted.

'You won't be able to hold on to it for more than five minutes. It will blow inside out before you reach the end of the street.'

'Well, in that case I won't bother taking one at all,' her mother snapped. She looked at the clock anxiously as she fastened the collar of her coat. 'I must go or I shall be late.'

'Late? How can you possibly be late when you're only going to the shops for food? For heaven's sake let me go and get whatever it is you need.'

'You can't do it, I have to go myself, so stop interfering,' her mother said furiously.

Sarah gasped, shocked by her outburst. Her mother had never spoken to her like this in her life before. Without a word she stood to one side and let her pass.

As the front door slammed behind her Sarah couldn't help feeling guilty in case her mother was finding the arrangements for the wedding were getting too much for her.

She was still wondering where her mother was going in such a hurry as she went into the kitchen to put the kettle on. As she did so she noticed that her mother had forgotten the strong canvas bag that she always took with her when she went shopping.

With a sigh of resignation Sarah picked it up, pulled her wet coat back on, and went after her. She could see her hurrying down the street ahead of her but thought that rather than call out to her she would catch her up. Perhaps she even ought to go with her because the wind was so strong and gusty it was enough to blow her over.

To her surprise, her mother stopped at the tram stop and before she could reach her she'd already boarded a tram going towards the city centre.

Puzzled, Sarah decided to follow on the next tram. The trouble was that she had no idea where her mother could possibly be going or where she would get off. Since she would only be about five minutes behind her there was a remote chance that she might spot her walking along the street after she left the tram.

Sarah sat with her face glued to the window as the tram she was on headed in the same direction and, to her relief, as it went along the High Street, towards St Mary's Street, she saw her mother walking along the pavement. Quickly she reached out and pulled the bell strap to request a stop and was on the platform ready to jump off the minute the tram slowed down.

She looked back up St Mary's Street in time to see her mother turning into one of the arcades and she hurried after her. She'd almost caught up with her when she saw her enter a building about halfway down the Arcade.

When she reached it she studied the window in bewilderment. It was draped with net curtains but in the centre was an ornate urn filled with very tall dried leaves and flowers and in front of it a parchment scroll. On it, in large gold lettering, was inscribed: 'Artus Gribbling, Faith Healer'.

She read the sign twice more then shook her head in bewilderment. Her mother didn't believe in that sort of thing, so what on earth was she doing here? she wondered.

The first thought that came into her mind was that her mother was trying to earn some extra money and had come to clean the offices. Then she remembered that her mother had been wearing her best coat and hat and so that couldn't be the answer. Anyway, it was the middle of the day so that was out of the question.

So if it wasn't for that purpose then what was it for? she wondered. She wasn't sure whether to go home and say nothing, to wait until her mother emerged and then ask her why she was there, or to march in and see what was going on.

None of these things seemed to be the right sort of action to take. There was a small café opposite so she decided to go in there and have a hot drink. She'd sit by the window and wait until she saw her mother come out again.

The moment she emerged Sarah followed her, taking care to keep out of sight until the tram came along and then she boarded it after her mother and went and sat next to her.

'So are you going to tell me what all that was about?' she asked quietly.

Her mother looked both startled and a little shamefaced as she turned and found Sarah alongside her, but she remained silent as Sarah held out the money to the conductor for the two of them.

'I wish you hadn't followed me, Sarah; I didn't want you or your dad to know what I was doing,' Lorna said quietly.

'No, you made that pretty obvious from the way you said you were going out shopping and then scuttled off as if the devil himself was on your heels.'

'I was late for my appointment,' Lorna said, her mouth tightening into a grim line.

'What appointment? What on earth are you doing making an appointment to see a faith healer? I thought you were dead against such things.'

Again a stubborn look came over her mother's face and she didn't answer.

'You'd better tell me,' Sarah insisted. 'I won't let it rest until you do. If you don't tell me right now what it is all about then I shall tell Dad and ask him to talk to you and find out.'

'No, no, you mustn't do that,' her mother begged. She laid her hand beseechingly on Sarah's arm. 'Don't go saying a word to him, promise me now?'

'It depends on what you tell me,' Sarah told her. 'Am I right in thinking this has something to do with all the worrying you've been doing over paying bills?'

'Yes, it has in a way,' her mother admitted, staring out of the window and refusing to look at Sarah.

'Please, Mam, I need to know what's going on,' Sarah persisted.

'Yes, I know you do,' her mother sighed. 'Look, I'll explain everything when we get home; not here on the tram,' she promised.

Chapter Twenty-Six

Sarah and her mother were both drenched by the time they reached home and Lorna insisted that the first thing they did was to change into dry clothes.

'I'll just put the kettle on,' she told Sarah, 'and then it will be boiling by the time we've got out of our wet things.'

'Yes, and while we sit down and have a cup of tea together, you can tell me what's going on and why you were visiting a faith healer today,' Sarah told her.

Sarah was changed first and had made the tea by the time her mother came downstairs.

'Well?' she asked as she poured it out and handed her mother a cup.

Lorna concentrated on putting two spoonfuls of sugar into her tea and stirring it very slowly, staring down into the cup all the time she was doing so.

'I'm waiting,' Sarah said impatiently. 'Come on, you did promise, Mam.'

'Yes, I know I did,' her mother sighed. 'I'm wondering if I ought to wait until your dad comes home and then tell you both or whether it would be best to keep it between ourselves.'

'If you told me what it's all about then I might be able to give you an answer to that,' Sarah commented solemnly.

Her mother took a sip of her tea then put the cup down quickly and dabbed at her mouth. 'That was far too hot,' she said, reaching for the milk jug.

'Mam,' Sarah leaned across the table and took one of her hands, 'I need to know why you were visiting a faith healer; a man who is known to be a quack.'

'You shouldn't say that, Sarah, he's done me far more good than our own doctor has. He's offered me hope.'

'I think you'd better tell me more, don't you?' she told her mother.

Sarah felt panic rising inside her as she waited for her mother to continue. What on earth was she talking about? She knew that her mother hadn't been looking too well but what was it she had she been to see the doctor about in the first place? she wondered. It obviously had something to do with why she was short of money.

'Go on, then, tell me what's wrong,' she pressed as her mother remained silent.

'I've had a lump in my side and this terrible pain,' her mother confessed. 'I put up with it for a couple of months and then it became so bad that I went to see the doctor.'

'What did he say it was?' Again, Sarah had to press her to speak because it was almost as if her mother didn't want to tell her.

'He said it was a growth that was pressing on some of my internal organs and that was why I had this terrible pain. He said it was cancer and that I had left it too late to do anything about it.'

'Oh, Mam! This is dreadful! Why on earth didn't you tell me, and not go through all that on your own?' Sarah gasped. 'So this is why you went to see a faith healer?'

'Yes,' her mother nodded her head, sniffing back her tears.

With tears in her own eyes Sarah got up and put her arms round her mother, hugging her close. 'What did he tell you?' she asked in a shaky voice.

'He confirmed what the doctor had said about it being a growth but he said not to worry because he could cure it. He gave me some red ointment that I had to apply every morning and a bottle of some sort of herbal concoction to take twice a day.'

'And has either of them done you any good?' Sarah asked in a cynical voice.

'I thought at first they were making me feel better but lately I'm not so sure. The lump feels bigger and the skin where I have to rub the ointment in is all puckered and blistered and very tender, almost as if it has been scalded.'

'What about the medicine? Is that doing you any good at all?'

Lorna sighed unhappily. 'It makes me feel so dizzy that sometimes I'm not sure what I'm doing or where I am and that makes me so miserable that I want to scream.'

'Is this one of the reasons why you're finding it hard to make ends meet, because you are spending so much money on these treatments?' Sarah probed.

'Yes, cariad. I was doing it for the best, though,' her mother added hurriedly. 'I was so frightened when the doctor said it couldn't be cured and then this man gave me hope.'

'Who told you about him? Not the doctor, I'm sure.'

'I saw a piece in the newspaper telling what he'd done. He was a miner and he developed a growth on his arm from some infection he picked up down the pit. Well, his dad had been a farmer and had taught him a lot about herbs and what they could do, so he treated his own arm and it cleared up in next to no time. After that all his fellow miners were asking for lotions and potions to cure all their ailments and he was so successful that he decided to leave the mine and set up a practice here in Cardiff.'

'Well, he may know how to cure some things when they are on the outside but curing internal illnesses is quite different, now isn't it?' Sarah pointed out.

'Yes, but that's what this herbal concoction was for and herbs are something a lot of country folk are knowledgeable about. There's nothing new about it; people have been using herbs to cure their ailments for centuries. Every wild flower and plant has some medicinal property if you know what it is and how to apply it.'

'Yes, I know, Mam, but I've heard of such people as the one you went to see and they are regarded as quacks and very expensive ones at that. They latch on to sick people with all sorts of promises of a cure. They tell them they must go on taking the concoctions they've made up for them and keep them coming back again and again.'

'These herbal people do know what they're on about,' her mother insisted. 'There was a chap called Nicholas Culpepper who lived on the outskirts of London way back in the Middle Ages and who had a special garden given over entirely to herbs. He was known everywhere for his skill in prescribing the right herbs and curing whatever illness people had.'

'Has this man told you what is in the concoction he's prescribing for you?'

Lorna chewed on her lower lip. 'He did tell me what was in the bottle but it meant nothing; something about the extracts from the roots of Burdock, Berberis and several other herbs. I'd never heard of them and I can't remember what the others were.'

'What about the ointment? Was that supposed to be made from herbs as well?'

'Yes, that has bloodroot, zinc, hemlock and saffron in it. He also gave me a carbolic smoke ball to use.'

'What on earth were you supposed to do with that?' Sarah asked in alarm.

'I'm not sure because I didn't use it. The smell was horrible and I threw it out as soon as I got home,' her mother admitted. 'I was afraid that if you or your dad got a whiff of it you'd want to know what it was.'

'Are you going to tell Dad all this?' Sarah asked as she poured out another cup of tea for her mother.

'Not quite all of it. I suppose I ought to tell him why I've been so short of money.'

'Yes, I think you should, because he's been very concerned. In the past you've always been able to manage with the housekeeping money perfectly well. How much has it been costing you to go and see this man every week?'

'I don't go every week; only about once a month. He does charge a lot, though,' she admitted reluctantly.

'I bet he does and I'm afraid Dad is bound to tell you that he's a complete charlatan.'

'He may be right,' her mother admitted sadly. 'I certainly don't feel any better; in fact, if the truth be told I seem to feel worse as time goes by.'

'Then you must go and see the doctor again.'

'It's pointless doing that, cariad. He's already told me that I've left it too late and there's nothing he can do for me.'

Lloyd was most distressed when he heard about what had been going on. Like Sarah he was anxious that Lorna should go back to the doctor.

'You've not been looking well for a long time and I suspected there must be something wrong with you. In fact, I said to Sarah that you look very drawn sometimes. What's more, you've lost weight. I put it down to the fact that you've been economising and not eating as much as you should be.'

'Well, now you know all there is to know you can stop worrying.'

'Oh no,' Lloyd told her firmly. 'You're going back to see the doctor and this time I'm going with you. I want to hear what he has to say with my own ears. You may not have understood him correctly. I'm sure there is some sort of medical treatment you can have.'

'Oh I heard him correctly,' Lorna assured him.

'Well, perhaps he thought you couldn't afford to pay for special medicine or whatever it is that is necessary and that is why he didn't hold out any hope.'

Two days later they went to see the doctor together and when they returned home Sarah knew from the look on her father's face that the news had been far more serious than he'd expected.

'It's not good, not good at all,' he told Sarah when they were on their own.

'What did the doctor tell you?'

He shook his head. 'Nothing that was helpful. He said the growth had gone too far when she first went to see him and that it was still growing and there was nothing he could do for her.'

'Did you tell him that she'd been seeing a faith healer?'

'Yes, I did and, like me, he considered the man to be a quack and said he shouldn't be allowed to build up people's hopes like he does.'

'Or take their money.'

'Well, yes, there's that as well but you can't blame him if people are gullible, now can you?'

'I suppose if you are told something is incurable and then you are offered what seems to be a miracle cure you are going to want to try it, no matter what it costs,' Sarah said thoughtfully.

'That's what he plays on; I wouldn't grudge him the money if there was any hope of a cure but to string folks along like he does is all wrong.'

'So what happens now? Is there anything at all that we can do?'

'Absolutely nothing, apparently, so we must do all we can to look after your mother and make things as easy as possible for as long as we can,' Lloyd said gloomily.

Sarah looked shocked. She knew her mother was desperately ill but it sounded so final and the thought of losing her was heart-breaking. They'd all had problems recently but her mother had been their rock and even though at times she must have felt desperately ill she'd never said a word and her main concern had been supporting them.

'Is that what the doctor said? I can't believe he told you that in front of her?'

'She asked him outright how long she'd got so the poor man had no alternative but to tell her the truth. He did it as kindly as he possibly could.'

'Does she know that you are telling me?'

Lloyd nodded. 'She thought it might be best if I was the one to tell you because she thought you might be upset and she didn't want you making a fuss. She wants us to treat her as normal and she doesn't want either of us to worry about her.'

'Maybe not, but things will change. For a start we must cancel the wedding.'

'You'd better talk to her about that. I think she will probably insist that you go ahead. She says it will give her peace of mind to know you are married and settled.'

'I think all the worry about getting everything done is going to be too much for her and will make her worse,' Sarah protested. 'She needs peace and quiet, not all the fuss associated with a wedding.'

Owen understood Sarah's concern when she told him the news and he suggested that if her mother insisted they went ahead then it should be a very quiet wedding with just a meal for the four of them afterwards.

'Who's going to be best man?' Sarah asked. 'We'd have to invite him to the meal as well.'

'I have no family and no really close friends so I thought of asking Bryn Morgan. He knows both of us and he knows your dad. I'm not sure if he would want to stay on afterwards but if he did then that would be no problem, would it?'

When she talked to her mother about it and told her what they were planning Lorna was adamant that things should go ahead as already arranged and wouldn't hear of them cancelling or even cutting back on what they'd planned to do afterwards.

'I've been looking forward to seeing you married more than anything in the world. It's what's been keeping me going. You two need to concentrate on more important matters, like deciding where you are going to live,' she scolded.

'That's all very well, Mam, but we don't want you to be stressed out, it won't help you, you know.'

'Your wedding is less than a month away so nothing is going to happen to me between now and then, is it, so I want the three of you to stop making such a fuss.'

In that Lorna was wrong. A week later she started coughing up blood and when the doctor was called in he instructed her to go into hospital right away.

She struggled feebly against his decision. 'If

I'm that ill and it means that I'm near the end then I'd rather stay here and die in my own bed,' she protested.

Two days later she was in a coma. The doctor visited twice a day but there was very little he could do for her except administer morphine to help control the pain she was in.

Owen was in complete agreement when Sarah said they must call off the wedding. He also arranged for both Sarah and Lloyd to take time off from work so that they could be with Lorna.

'Bryn Morgan agrees with me,' he told them when they protested. 'You can't possibly concentrate on what you should be doing here, so it is far better that you have the time off.'

Chapter Twenty-Seven

Lorna died three days later. Lloyd and Sarah were with her at the end; one on each side of the bed holding her hands, devastated to be losing her but thankful that it was very peaceful.

At Easter they found themselves arranging a funeral instead of a wedding. Lloyd was beside himself with grief because he hadn't realised how ill she was. There had been so many times when she'd been quiet and withdrawn and probably in pain but he had been so wrapped up in his own troubles that he had said nothing. Now, he was certain that if she'd gone into hospital earlier they could have done something for her.

Both Sarah and Owen tried to explain to Lloyd that there was as yet no treatment or known cure for the sort of illness she'd been suffering from and that they should all be grateful that her life had ended so peacefully.

Several of the neighbours they were on speaking terms with came to pay their last respects. As they were about to leave the churchyard Sarah felt a hand on her arm and gasped in surprise as she turned and found herself face to face with Gwyn Roberts.

'What are you doing here?' she asked. It was six years since she'd last seen him and she was shocked to see him there.

'I spotted your mother's name at the office on a list of bereavements that we receive to alert us about current happenings and I thought it would be an opportunity to see you again. I wish it could have been under better circumstances. I am so sorry for your loss. I know how close you were.'

Sarah nodded. She felt awkward and wished he hadn't intruded at such a time.

'You remember my dad, of course,' she said hesitantly, remembering how much her father disliked Gwyn.

'Of course I do.' Gwyn turned and held out a hand to Lloyd. 'As I have just said to Sarah I am very sorry about your loss; your wife was a wonderful lady.'

Lloyd shook Gwyn's hand and nodded but from the dark look on his face Sarah wasn't too sure that he wanted to remember him.

'This is Owen, Owen Phillips, my fiancé,' she said, introducing the two men to each other. 'Owen, this is Gwyn Roberts. I have mentioned him to you.'

The two men shook hands, weighing each other up and saying nothing.

'Well, I must get back to the office,' Gwyn stated, replacing his black Homburg. 'Perhaps we could meet sometime; I'd like to have the chance to catch up.'

'Well, I'm not sure about that,' Sarah said hesitantly, looking at Owen.

'If you can spare the time, the three of us were going for a meal, perhaps you'd like to join us,' Owen invited.

'I'm sure Gwyn is far too busy to do that,' Sarah said quickly. 'Perhaps some other time.'

'No, I would very much like to join you,' Gwyn affirmed as he fell into step alongside them.

Sarah felt sick with embarrassment. What on earth would they talk about, she thought anxiously. With the mood her father was in at the moment, if he did recall everything that had gone on between her and Gwyn there might well be ructions. It wouldn't be so bad if Owen wasn't there but things she had skimmed over might well be discussed in detail and that could be very disturbing for all of them.

As the meal progressed Sarah began to relax. She quickly discovered that Gwyn hadn't changed all that much. He was still adventurous and kept them all entertained with stories about his trips as a foreign correspondent. It appeared that he'd been to most parts of the world and as she listened to his lively dissertation Sarah couldn't help feeling that Owen seemed very reserved in comparison.

Owen was curious to know why Gwyn was back in Cardiff covering what must be such a very minor occasion.

'I've come back to take up my new appointment as Assistant Editor on the *Western Mail*,'

Gwyn explained. 'I happened to see the name Lorna Lewis and recognised the address and, of course, it immediately brought back memories of the past and I thought it would be rather nice to pay my respects.'

'So does that mean that from now on you will be based in Cardiff?' Owen questioned.

'For the present. My next step will be an editor's chair. There probably won't be a vacancy where I am for a long time to come so I will have to move somewhere else. It will all be good experience, though, and one day I'll be back again as Editor of the *Western Mail*. That's always been my ambition, hasn't it, Sarah?'

'Yes, I think you did mention it when we were at university,' Sarah said non-committally. 'Things have changed since those days,' she added pointedly.

'Some things never change,' Gwyn countered.

Sarah felt a prickle of fear tingle down her back as he raised his thick eyebrows and stared back at her speculatively. She was aware that Owen was listening and watching the interchange between them and she felt uneasy, wondering what he was thinking.

Sarah found that with the funeral over and both of them returning to work it was difficult to establish a routine that suited her father and herself.

In the past Lloyd had never had to lift a finger around the house when it involved anything to do with domestic matters because Lorna had taken care of everything.

He was used to being waited on and his meals being on the table when he arrived home from work. He expected his shirts to be washed and ironed ready for when he needed them, and having his buttons sewn on and his socks darned.

He handed over the housekeeping money on a Friday night and everything was taken care of from then on. He never asked how Lorna spent it.

Now, he was expecting Sarah to do the same. On the first Friday when he sat down to his meal he placed the housekeeping money on the table.

'I think we've got to talk about sharing the responsibility of running the home,' she told him as she pushed it back towards him. 'Perhaps you should be the one to pay the bills for a start.'

'You'll be doing the shopping so you'll be the one needing the money,' he pointed out.

'You are much better placed to do it than I am,' she told him. 'I don't finish work until six o'clock, whereas you finish at five. The shops are still open then so you can buy what we need on your way home.'

'Are you asking me to shop for groceries?' Lloyd exclaimed in a startled voice.

'I'm not only expecting you to shop for them

303

but I'm also hoping you'll learn to cook them as well. You are home an hour before me so there's nothing to stop you starting the dinner before I come in.'

'Don't talk rubbish, cariad; I've never cooked a thing in my life. That's been your mother's job.'

'Yes, but Mam's not here now and I can't do everything. I work just as hard as you do and I'm tired, too, when I get home. As well as the shopping and cooking there's all the housework and the washing and ironing to be done. Either we share the load or we pay someone else to come in and do it for us.'

Neither suggestion appealed to Lloyd. He simply wanted things to go on as they'd always been, but Sarah knew that wasn't possible; there simply weren't enough hours in the day.

She'd worked hard to justify Bryn Morgan's faith in giving her a job in his firm and she still needed to be alert to keep on top of things there.

Instead of being willing to discuss it and trying to find a solution, Lloyd pushed the money back across the table towards her. 'You do whatever you think best,' he told her. 'I don't know anything about these sorts of things.'

Sarah hadn't the heart to argue with him. She suspected that even thinking about domestic matters only brought back memories of her mother and that was why he couldn't do it.

For a while she struggled to do everything

herself, not only because it was easier but also so that the home her mother had loved so much stayed pristine. She got up an hour earlier, usually so that she could prepare their evening meal before she went out in the morning. That way it took very little time to cook in the evening. If she was able to cook it the night before so that all she would have to do would be to heat it up when she got in, then she'd spend the extra hour in the morning cleaning and doing other domestic chores.

The one task she couldn't do in the morning was the washing because it took too long to heat up the copper, boil the clothes and then rinse them and hang them out to dry. Occasionally she did wash them the night before and then hang them out before she went off to work.

Eventually she began doing the bulk of the household chores at the weekends. Although she knew her father hated her doing the washing on a Sunday, it was really the only day when there was enough time to do so.

It also meant that after shopping and cleaning on a Saturday she was far too exhausted to want to go out with Owen in the evening and although he was very understanding she could see that he was beginning to get very perturbed by her constant claim that she was too tired to even go to the pictures.

Lloyd spent his evenings and weekends slumped in his armchair and although the newspaper was on his lap more often than not his eyes were closed, and he completely ignored what was going on around him.

'You really should get him to help you,' Owen told her. 'There're quite a lot of jobs he could be doing around the house to give you a bit more time for yourself.'

To prove his point he drew up a list, dividing up everything that had to be done each week between what Sarah should be responsible for and what Lloyd should be doing.

When Sarah studied the list she started laughing. 'Can you see my dad peeling potatoes and scraping carrots? Or cleaning the windows,' she gasped.

'I don't see why not. There are men who make their living cleaning windows so surely there's nothing wrong with him doing them on the inside?'

'Some of the neighbours might spot him.'

'I really don't see how that would matter. They'd admire him for pulling his weight.'

'I don't think that either of us could convince him of that.' Sarah smiled.

'Well, he could lay the fires and clean out the grate every day; he used to do that for your mother. He could also do quite a lot of the preparatory things in the kitchen as well as help with the washing-up. Anything is better than for him to be sitting there brooding.'

'I know,' Sarah agreed. 'It worries me to see him looking so depressed and unhappy.'

'Then why not encourage him to do some cooking. You never know, he might discover that he has hidden talents and that he actually likes doing it.'

Although all Owen's suggestions were good ones they simply didn't work. Lloyd had been brought up to consider running a home as women's work. Nevertheless, he did agree to light the fire and clean out the grate. When it came to the other tasks in the kitchen that Owen had listed he did them so badly, and had so many accidents, that Sarah was glad to take over again.

She decided to stop trying to do all the washing and ironing at home and to send everything except her own personal items out to the laundry.

At first her father strongly disapproved of this but when he found that it meant he always had clean clothes and well-ironed shirts he stopped objecting and accepted that there had to be changes in the way the household was being run.

Sarah also arranged for one of the neighbours to come in two mornings a week and do most of the cleaning. She decided not to tell her father and if he noticed that things were being organised better he made no comment at all.

Gradually she was able to resume her nights out with Owen. Sometimes she felt quite guilty about going out and enjoying herself, especially when she went out on a Saturday night and left her father slumped morosely in front of the fire, listlessly turning the pages of the newspaper on his lap.

Owen still came to tea on Sundays and occasionally her father would join in their conversation. For brief spells as he engaged in an argument about something the old Lloyd would shine out and Sarah would feel hopeful that perhaps at last he was pulling himself out of the doldrums and would soon be his old self again.

One Sunday they had an unexpected visitor. As her father went to answer the door Sarah thought it was Owen arriving a little early and rushed upstairs to finish getting ready. As she came back down again a few minutes later she realised that although it was a man's voice talking to her father, it wasn't Owen's.

'Surprised to see me again?'

Sarah stopped in the living-room doorway in surprise. 'Gwyn, what are you doing here?'

'I came to say goodbye; I'm going to America. I've landed myself another new job, this time as Editor on the *New Hampshire Echo*.'

'So you've made it; you're going to be an editor at last,' Sarah said with a beaming smile. 'Congratulations!' Impulsively she walked over and kissed him on the cheek. She felt she could be magnanimous now she knew he would be leaving the country.

'It's an important stepping stone but don't worry, I'll still be back here in Cardiff the moment the top job becomes vacant on the *Western Mail*,' he said, grinning.

A second knock heralded Owen's arrival so Sarah went to let him in, leaving Gwyn talking to her father about his new job.

Owen seemed rather taken aback to see him there and barely congratulated him on his achievement. His mood became even darker when, to their great surprise, Lloyd invited Gwyn to stay and have tea with them.

Even Owen's brusque, withdrawn attitude couldn't stem Gwyn's garrulousness. He was absolutely bubbling over with enthusiasm about how much he wanted this job in America and what tremendous opportunities it would provide for his journalistic skills. He even regaled them with all the changes he was planning to make on the paper once he took over.

'So you've more or less reached the pinnacle of your ambitions,' Owen commented dryly.

'Oh no, I'm not quite there yet.' Gwyn smiled. 'There are one or two more important things that I still intend to do,' he said, looking directly at Sarah.

'And those are?' Owen challenged, eyeing him grimly.

'Well, for a start, I am determined that one day I'll come back here to Cardiff and be Editor of the *Western Mail*.'

Chapter Twenty-Eight

Gwyn stayed the entire evening, making it quite obvious that he was waiting for Owen to go home. Eventually, since Gwyn was in deep conversation with Lloyd, he decided to do so. Sarah went to the door with him and after he'd kissed her goodnight, he muttered, 'I don't like that fellow. I was hoping he'd leave before now.'

Sarah's inward smile at his obvious jealousy quickly vanished when she came back into the room and found Gwyn and her father discussing her. Sarah had been amazed that her father had invited Gwyn to stay let alone converse with him so amicably. He had definitely mellowed in his old age. However, she didn't like the fact that the conversation had turned to her. It was one thing for them to have been discussing Gwyn's career prospects but she didn't want things to get too personal.

'I was just telling your dad all about what I've been doing since we last met and how this job in America is a stepping stone to even greater things,' Gwyn said, turning to her.

'I rather gathered that from what you'd been telling us all evening,' Sarah commented.

'Yes, but there's a lot more to it than what I

said in front of that Owen chap. We don't want him to know too much about our private business, now do we?'

Sarah struggled to keep back the sharp retort she wanted to make and before she could think of an appropriate answer Gwyn was already in full stream.

'I've been telling your dad that the time has come for us to get together again – only properly this time. I want us to be married and for you to move to New Hampshire with me.'

Sarah stared at him in astonishment. 'Are you out of your mind, Gwyn? I haven't seen or heard of you for years and now suddenly you come storming back into our lives and expect everything to be as if nothing has changed. Can I remind you that I am engaged to be married – to Owen.'

'I know all about that, but I've been travelling, all over the world, see, so how could I have time for writing letters and such like?' he blustered. 'The only writing I've done is what I've been obliged to do and damned hard work it has been, I can tell you. Well, it's paid off, cariad, and now I'm not only back home again but I have fine prospects and I'm in a position to offer you marriage.'

'And you think I am going to change all my plans and accept, just like that? You spring up from nowhere and expect me to fall at your feet again as if nothing has ever gone wrong between us?'

'Come on, Sarah, it's not like you to hold a grudge. The pair of us were just kids and we rushed into things because we were too young to know what we were doing.'

'We're older now, though, and have a great deal more sense,' she said coldly.

'Of course we are, that's what I'm trying to say. We're old enough to know we are right for each other. We'll have a good life together, I can promise you. I'll be earning good money and I'll be able to provide you with a fine home and everything you want from life.'

'Everything?'

'You have only to name it. I'm leaving from Liverpool in three weeks' time. That gives you plenty of time to work out your notice and to pack your bags. From now on the world will be your oyster, my lovely. Isn't that right, Mr Lewis?'

Lloyd looked from one to the other of them, shaking his head in bewilderment.

'The choice is hers, of course, but from what you've been telling me you're certainly a very enterprising fellow. You seem to have your future well mapped out.'

'I always have had, Mr Lewis. It's just that I was so eager to get started that I rushed things at the very beginning. I admit I made a bit of a mess of our lives when we were at university, but it's different now. I won't be letting Sarah down this time.'

'No, you certainly won't,' Sarah told him firmly. 'You won't be letting me down because I won't be going with you. I'm not interested in your proposal and I think it is high time you left.'

'Sarah!'

The hurt in Gwyn's voice and the look of surprise on his face almost made her smile as she stood up and opened the door into the hall indicating she wanted him to leave immediately.

'You cleared off and left me to grieve on my own after I lost our baby,' she reminded him as her father pushed past them and walked up the stairs saying that he was off to bed. 'I had no one except my family and even though I'd broken their hearts by going off with you, and living down in the slums of Tiger Bay, they took me back and forgave me. Now you want me to desert my dad and leave him on his own.'

'No, of course I don't. He can move with us, I'm sure we can find him a place nearby.'

Sarah shook her head. 'I've no intention of coming with you or of leaving him on his own. I'm marrying Owen and I'm pleased to hear that you are moving so far away from Cardiff because that way I shan't have to worry that someday I might bump into you again.'

'Sarah!' There was rasping anger in his voice and a look of fury on his face.

Before she knew what was happening he had grabbed hold of her and was holding her in such a tight grip that she couldn't even struggle. As his mouth came down hard on hers she was left so breathless that she couldn't even scream or protest.

His embrace was savage and possessive. It was as if he intended to force her into submission and it revived vivid memories she'd thought she'd managed to forget about the turbulent life she had endured in the squalid rooms in Tiger Bay. Now it came rushing back in such frightening clarity that she couldn't stop shaking.

Owen's warning words before he'd left drummed inside her head. Not that she needed them; never would she contemplate going back to Gwyn. All she wanted now was to get free from the stranglehold he had on her and to see him out of the door.

Gwyn had no intention of letting her do any such thing. Roughly he backed her up against the wall and, oblivious of the fact that her father was upstairs, he began fondling her intimately, all the time keeping his mouth glued down on hers so tightly that she was unable to make a sound.

Sarah fought wildly, struggling and kicking at his legs but they were like solid rock and her feeble attempts to hurt him made no impact whatsoever.

She felt terrified about what the eventual outcome was going to be. She knew from the past that Gwyn had no compassion or tenderness. As he struggled to get her down on to the floor he stumbled against the chiffonier. The impact dislodged all the glasses, vases and ornaments displayed on it causing everything to crash to the ground with such a horrendous noise that it roused her father.

'Duw anwyl! What is going on down there?' he demanded in a startled voice.

Sarah was unable to answer; she was pinned down on the floor by Gwyn's bulk and she felt terrified. Memories of his brutish ways came flooding back into her mind; horrendous experiences that she'd tried so hard to forget since they'd parted.

She tried desperately to call out to her father, to ask him to make Gwyn release her, but her face was pressed so hard against Gwyn's chest that her words were muffled.

Gwyn seemed to ignore him completely, intent on one thing and one thing only. As his hand slid up under her skirt and she felt his fingers kneading her bare flesh she struggled even more frantically.

She knew Gwyn was far too caught up in his own desires to even notice her struggles or resistance and panic built up inside her until she felt a black mist forming in her mind.

The last time he had acted like this when she'd been pregnant she'd closed her mind to what was happening because she'd been so afraid that her unborn child might suffer if she struggled too violently.

Now she did not have anything like that to consider so she fought against the enveloping mist, kicking and screaming. Far away she could hear someone hammering on their door and she prayed that her father would answer it. He was obviously too bewildered by what was going on to help her but if someone else came into the room then surely they would come to her assistance and do something to stop Gwyn.

The waves were getting darker now and she was afraid she would lose consciousness.

When it seemed impossible to stop that happening or to free herself from Gwyn's assault, the pressure on her body lifted.

Her breath caught in her throat as she tried to scream, then strong hands were on her arms again, only this time they were gently lifting her to her feet. Someone was holding her close, comforting her, reassuring her that she was safe and that all was well.

She tried to focus, to thank them, but she felt so disorientated that it was impossible to do so. Everything was spinning and then it went blank and even the voice that was murmuring words of comfort faded as she felt every scrap of energy drain from her body.

When she next opened her eyes she was lying on the sofa, a rug over her, and someone was sitting close by. The moment she stirred they were at her side.

'What happened, what are you doing here?' she whispered weakly as Owen gently pushed her hair back from her face and bent and kissed her on the brow.

'Thank heaven's you're all right,' he breathed. He held a glass to her lips. 'Have a sip of this; it will make you feel better.'

She took a mouthful and then gagged as she

swallowed it. She'd been expecting it to be water, not brandy, and the fire as it hit the back of her throat almost choked her.

Even so, it restored her and she struggled to sit upright, glancing around the room bewildered.

'Where is he? Where's Gwyn Roberts?' She shuddered.

'Gone and he won't be coming back if he knows what's good for him,' Owen told her grimly.

'How is it you are here?' Sarah frowned. 'I thought you went home ages ago?'

'I did, but I didn't like the way that fellow was behaving before I left and I felt uneasy so I came back again to see if everything was all right. I must have arrived outside just as that crashed over,' he went on, pointing to the chiffonier that lay on its side, with all the ornaments that had been displayed on it strewn everywhere.

'Thank heavens Dad let you in.'

'Only after I'd almost banged the door down,' Owen said grimly. 'If he hadn't answered when he did, then I'd have put my shoulder to it and forced my way in because I was so sure that there was something wrong. As I've already said, I had my suspicions about that fellow and felt that I shouldn't have gone home and left you.'

As she attempted to stand up Owen gently, but firmly, pressed her back on to the sofa again.

'Stay where you are, Cariad. Your dad's gone back upstairs to bed so I'll make you a hot drink before I leave.'

Sarah felt so shaky that she did as she was told without any argument. When he brought in their drinks she patted the sofa for him to sit there beside her.

'Do you have to go home tonight? Couldn't you stay here in the spare room? I don't want to be in the house alone.'

'Well,' Owen hesitated, 'you won't be on your own; your dad will be here with you.'

Sarah shook her head. 'You saw how he reacted.' Tears trickled down her face. 'If you hadn't come back when you did then I don't know what would have happened.'

'Of course I'll stay if that is what you want,' Owen assured her. 'Will your dad mind, though?'

'No, I'm sure he won't.'

Owen nodded; then he pulled Sarah into his arms, holding her protectively. 'I don't want you to be in a situation like that ever again,' he murmured. 'Don't you think it's time we were married so that I can be with you all the time?'

'I want that more than anything but surely it's too soon after my mam's death? Shouldn't we wait at least a year?'

'Sarah, you're talking nonsense. Your mother wouldn't want you to do that. She was looking forward to our wedding.'

'Yes, I know she was.' Sarah nodded, her eyes

filling with tears at the memory of all the preparations they'd made together and how excited Lorna had been. 'I'd like to talk to my dad about it first, though, before we go ahead.'

Lloyd didn't like the idea at all. 'Who is going to look after me if I'm left here on my own?' he grumbled. 'I need you, Sarah, far more than he does. He's still a young man; he can afford to wait awhile before he takes you away from me.'

'We've already postponed our wedding once,' Sarah reminded him gently. 'What about if we move in here with you?' she suggested hopefully. 'If you remember, that was what we were planning to do before Mam died.'

'Oh, I don't know, cariad, I don't know anything any more,' Lloyd said wearily, running his hands through his hair. 'Do whatever you think best but let's hope it turns out all right this time.'

Sarah bit her lip, then with a deep sigh she admitted contritely, 'Yes, Dad, I know that up until now I seem to have made a mess of things but this time it is quite different. You like Owen and you know what a good, reliable man he is. I want to marry him and we both love each other and want to settle down and have children and enjoy a happy home life like you and Mam always had.'

Chapter Twenty-Nine

As she prepared for her wedding Sarah was constantly reminded of how her mother had wanted things to be done. She knew how excited her mother had been about it all, and how she had longed to see her married to Owen, so although there had to be some compromises she did her best to carry out as many of Lorna's wishes as possible.

All the talk of the wedding seemed to bring Lloyd out of the inertia that had gripped him ever since Lorna had died and he assured both Sarah and Owen that they had nothing to worry about as he was feeling more than ready to play his part.

'It will be the proudest day of my life walking down the aisle with Sarah on my arm because I know I will be handing her over into the care of a man who will look after her as well as I have tried to do all my life,' he told Owen.

As well as having to make all the wedding arrangements, they also had to make plans for her father's future and they did this together.

They discussed the matter at great length and they both agreed that perhaps it was better if they found a place of their own.

'We can always move back in with your father later on if we find he can't manage living on his own,' Owen promised. 'We'll find somewhere close by, of course, so that you will be able to see each other every day as well as at work.'

Even so, Sarah wanted to be sure that he was properly cared for so she made arrangements with two of the neighbours to help look after him. Marie was coming in to do the cleaning and the weekly washing and Alvia was going to prepare his evening meal and take it along for him as soon as he came home from work each evening.

Sarah herself was going to take in sandwiches for his midday meal at work. Alvia said she'd be happy to come in every morning and cook breakfast for him if that was what he wanted but Lloyd assured her that he was quite capable of getting his own breakfast.

Sarah was not so sure about this and she and Alvia agreed that they would let him try doing so for a few weeks and then perhaps ask him again.

'I think he will soon change his mind with winter almost here,' Alvia said. 'He needs a good hot breakfast inside him if he is only having sandwiches at lunchtime,' she pointed out.

Alvia and Marie were also going to help Sarah in any way they could with the preparations leading up to the wedding.

'It's years since my own girl got married and

I feel almost as excited about your wedding as I did about hers,' Alvia told her.

It was a glorious September day, so warm that even though she was wearing the low-necked, short-sleeved cream satin dress her mother had chosen for her to wear when they'd been planning for the wedding at Easter, she still felt comfortable in it.

Her father looked so upright and proud in his new three-piece charcoal-grey suit: his gold watch chain looped across the waistcoat and gold links shone from the cuffs of his pristine white shirt which peeped out below his jacket. She had only the one regret and that was that her mother couldn't be there with them to see her and Owen married.

Owen, accompanied by Bryn Morgan who was acting as best man, would be at the church waiting for her, she thought happily. In her mind's eye she could see Owen looking so tall and solid, his thick fair hair shining in the light from the altar candles, and she felt an overwhelming love for him flood over her; a sensation of pure, unadulterated happiness.

She could imagine the warm smile of welcome that would light up his face, and felt an immense sense of optimism knowing that from this day on Owen would always be there for her no matter what lay ahead.

After the service was over they would go back to Cyfartha Street to enjoy the feast that had been organised by Alvia and Marie and her father would make his speech and then hold his glass of champagne aloft and drink a toast to them.

As the car that had brought them to the church slowed to a stop and she gathered up the full skirt of her dress, ready to alight and walk down the aisle on her father's arm, she felt that this was the happiest moment in her life.

Before the chauffeur could help her to step out on to the pavement someone came and whispered something in his ear. Sarah saw him hesitate and then get back into the driving seat and restart the engine. As they pulled away Lloyd leaned forward to ask what was wrong.

'The bridegroom and best man are running late so I've been asked to drive round for a few minutes,' he told them.

The next time they approached the church someone simply waved them on but as they circled for a third time Lloyd insisted that they should stop and find out what had gone wrong.

The driver offered to do so but Lloyd muttered something and got out of the car and went over to the lych gate, where a small crowd was gathered. Sarah watched in concern as he seemed to be engaged in some deep conversation with them. As he turned to come back to the car he was shaking his head as if he couldn't believe what he'd heard.

'Well, what's happened, Dad?' Sarah asked as he clambered back into the car and sat down beside her.

'Drive round once more,' he ordered the chauffeur.

'Why does he have to do that? What's the reason for all this delay?' Sarah persisted.

'Owen and Bryn Morgan haven't arrived yet. They're supposed to be coming in Bryn's car but so far there's no news of them. Someone's gone to find out if they've broken down,' he told her.

Once more they were driven slowly around the block. When they next reached the church there was a policeman standing by the lych gate and Sarah felt a ripple of unease as their car pulled up and he walked across to them and leaned in through the window as Lloyd opened it.

'I'm afraid I have some rather bad news,' he told them in a halting manner. 'Mr Owen Phillips will not be able to attend; I'm afraid he's been taken to hospital.'

'Hospital? Why, what has happened?'

'He's been injured but so far we're not able to give you the full details.'

'Injured?' The colour drained from Sarah's face. 'Do you mean he has been in an accident?'

'Not exactly an accident, Miss. He has certainly been involved in an incident of some kind,' the policeman told her, clearing his throat uncomfortably.

'Surely you can tell us more than that, officer,' Lloyd pressed. 'He is due to be married today.'

'I know, Sir. I'm very sorry about this but I

324

would like Miss Lewis to come with us to the hospital.'

Lloyd insisted on going with her and tried to get the policeman to explain what had happened.

'We haven't any details as yet, except that Mr Phillips appears to have been attacked from behind and has received some serious blows to his head and neck. He was found lying by the side of the road unconscious and was brought into hospital.'

'Has he regained consciousness yet?' Lloyd asked worriedly.

'Yes, about an hour ago. He was very agitated and kept repeating that he had to be at his wedding. He managed to tell us where it was being held; that's how we managed to trace you.'

'You have no idea who attacked him?' Lloyd persisted.

'None whatsoever.'

'Do you have any idea what time this attack happened?' Sarah whispered.

'Not really, Miss.' The policeman pulled his notebook out from his top pocket and checked an entry in it. 'As far as we can tell, it was probably shortly after midnight. He was found by a passer-by just before one o'clock this morning.'

'It was while he was on his way home, then,' Sarah exclaimed. 'He left our house in Cyfartha Street a few minutes after midnight.' She gave a shaky little laugh. 'I remember telling him that it was unlucky for the bridegroom to see the bride on her wedding day and he teased me about being superstitious.'

The policeman nodded rather grimly. 'I suppose you have no idea who might bear Owen Phillips a grudge?' he asked as they stopped outside the infirmary.

'No one I can think of,' Lloyd asserted. 'He was one of the nicest blokes you could ever meet. As well as the fact that he was about to become my son-in-law I worked alongside him.'

'Well, never mind, perhaps he will be able to tell us who was involved,' the policeman said non-committally as he guided them into the building. 'It doesn't appear to have been for money, as his wallet was untouched and so was the loose change in his pockets.

People turned and stared as Sarah, who was still in her wedding dress, and Lloyd, in his smart suit, sporting a flower in his buttonhole, were led through the hospital waiting room and into the lift.

When they reached Owen's bedside Sarah gasped in dismay. He was propped up in the bed, his head was swathed in bandages and his eyes were closed. There was considerable bruising and discoloration around them and also a deep gash down one side of his face which had several stitches in it.

'Oh Owen, whoever did this to you?' she

sobbed as she picked up one of his hands that was lying on top of the bedclothes and pressed it against her own face.

Owen stirred. His eyes opened a mere fraction, squinting painfully in the light, then he closed them again but not before he'd murmured her name.

Making a visible effort he struggled once again to open his eyes and this time they not only focussed on her but he also even managed to give her a weak smile.

The policeman who had been standing behind her gently moved her to one side and bent down to speak to Owen. 'Can you tell us anything about what happened to you, Sir?' he asked quietly.

'I really think you should come back again tomorrow, Constable. Mr Phillips is far too weak to be questioned at the moment,' the rather severe voice of the ward sister cut in as she came over to the bedside and laid a restraining hand on the policeman's arm.

'No . . . no, there is something I want to say,' Owen muttered weakly. 'I was attacked . . .' His voice drifted away as he sank back against the pillows, too weak to continue.

The moment the policeman decided that there was nothing further he could do and had left the ward the sister came back to Owen's bedside and suggested very firmly to Sarah and Lloyd that it might be better if they also left.

'If you come back in the morning after Mr Phillips has had a good night's sleep, I am quite sure he will not only be very much better but will also be able to talk to you,' she assured them.

When Sarah told Bryn Morgan about the state Owen was in and who she thought might have attacked him the previous night, and why he had done so Bryn looked very grave.

'You know you really ought to be giving the police all this information, Sarah, so that they can check it out,' he said as they all got into his car.

'You are probably right but I think it is best to wait until tomorrow and see what Owen can remember,' Sarah hedged.

'Well, let's hope they get to the bottom of it. That's if that's what took place,' Bryn said dubiously. 'I can't think that this Gwyn Roberts would go that far, but then again, I don't know the chap and you two do. Obviously the police are taking the attack seriously so we can only wait and see what transpires.'

'It was a dreadful thing to have happened,' Lloyd muttered morosely as he settled himself in the back of the car.

'Indeed it was,' Bryn agreed. 'Now, do you want me to take you straight back to your home or do you both want to go back to the church again?'

'It had better be to the church because probably everyone is still there waiting for information about what is happening and we'll have to break the news that there isn't going to be any wedding taking place today,' Lloyd sighed.

The moment they returned they were plied with questions and there were murmurs of consolation for Sarah. By now she was past tears but she looked so pale and drained that Bryn Morgan insisted that she must go home.

'Lloyd, you will let me know how Owen is after Sarah has been to see him tomorrow?' Bryn requested after he'd helped Sarah out of his car and had walked with them to their front door.

'Yes, I'll certainly do that and thank you for all your help today,' Lloyd said gratefully as he opened the front door and ushered Sarah inside.

Chapter Thirty

Sarah spent a sleepless night tossing and turning, her mind in turmoil as she went over and over again what had happened to Owen.

Somehow she was sure that Gwyn Roberts was responsible for the attack and that he'd done it because she'd turned down his proposal. She felt guilty that Owen had suffered because of her.

It was late morning before she went back to the hospital and she had to wait for over half an hour before they let her see Owen. He was propped up in bed again, his head still heavily bandaged, but he looked a great deal better than when she'd seen him the previous day.

Within minutes of her arrival a police officer appeared; not the one who had been there the previous day, but a sergeant who, after a brief greeting, began cross-questioning Owen in a crisp, rather brusque manner. It was obvious that he was determined to extract as much information as he could from Owen about the attack.

He made no comment when Sarah explained what her relationship with Gwyn Roberts had been, but he noted down that he was about to move to America.

'If that is so and he manages to leave the country before we can apprehend him, then there is probably very little we can do to interrogate him.'

After he'd left Sarah tried to tell Owen how upset she was that all this had happened. He was equally concerned that it had meant that their wedding had been called off.

'Never mind, we've still got it to look forward to and we'll fix a new date just as soon as you are out of hospital and well enough,' she reassured him.

When Sarah told him that she intended to go straight from the hospital to let Bryn Morgan know how he was getting on, Owen immediately became concerned about all the problems the absence of all three of them must be causing.

'Don't worry your head about that, concentrate on getting better so that you can come home,' she told him as she made to leave.

'With any luck it might be later today, after the doctor has done his rounds,' Owen said hopefully. 'Apart from a huge bump on the back of my head and a few scratches there's not much wrong with me. I was lucky in some ways as there are no bones broken and no internal injuries of any kind.'

Owen's hopes of being discharged later in the day came to nothing. Because of the blows on his head the doctor insisted that there was always the possibility of delayed concussion and insisted that he remain in hospital for another couple of days.

When he was finally discharged Owen was surprised at how weak he felt and agreed with Sarah that it would be another couple of days before he would be able to go back to work.

She insisted that he came back to Cyfartha Street where she could look after him and make sure he didn't exert himself by doing anything too strenuous.

'I don't think you want a semi-invalid on your hands,' he protested. 'I'll go back to my room; my landlady will make sure I have everything I need.'

'I very much doubt it,' Sarah told him dryly. 'You moved out of there over three weeks ago, remember? We should be living in our own place by now. In fact, I've been wondering if we ought to tell our new landlord that we are not going to need the rooms and that we'll be staying on at Cyfartha Street.'

Owen looked crestfallen at the idea of doing that so Sarah relented and said she'd see how things went. They'd definitely re-plan the date for their wedding as soon as Owen felt well enough to do so.

'In the meantime I'll see what arrangements Bryn Morgan wants to make. If you are at home with my dad then the two of you should be able to manage to take care of each other for a few days and I can help Bryn sort things out in the office,' she suggested.

'You could always bring home any files that I can deal with and I can work from home for a few days,' Owen suggested.

Within a week Owen was back in the office, Lloyd was also feeling much stronger. There had been no further action taken over finding Owen's assailant, however. Sarah and Owen both remained certain that it had been Gwyn Roberts but since according to the police he'd already left the country the matter was closed.

Bryn kept asking what was happening about their wedding and finally Owen was able to give him a firm date for when it would take place.

'It's going to be a very quiet affair in a register office this time,' Owen told him. 'I still want you to be my best man but the only other person there apart from Lloyd will be Alvia Peters, one of Sarah's neighbours, and she'll be the other witness.'

With Alvia's help, Sarah modified her original wedding dress by shortening the skirt so that it was at mid-calf. She dispensed with both the train and the veil and instead had a tiny cloche hat trimmed with a single flower.

The ceremony was simple and was over within half an hour. They all signed the register and then travelled back to Cyfartha Street in Bryn's car to enjoy the spread that Marie had stayed home to prepare for them.

Lloyd looked tired but happy, relieved that this time everything had gone according to plan. As he stood up to speak, to wish them well and say how happy he felt about what had taken place that day, the glass suddenly fell from his hand. He leaned forward, gasping, clutching at the nearest chair and missing it. He grabbed the starched white linen tablecloth, dragging it from the table and bringing dishes, glasses, food and wine as well as the two-tier wedding cake, all crashing to the ground.

Panic ensued. Owen tried to move him clear of the debris, Sarah tried desperately to help by trying to lift up her father's head and putting a cushion underneath it.

Alvia and Marie tried to collect up or move some of the food and broken dishes which were crunching underfoot as they all did their best to revive Lloyd.

'Fetch a towel, one of you,' Owen instructed. Taking it, he tried to gently wipe off the residue of food from Lloyd's face and the front of his clothes.

Blood was streaming from a multitude of cuts. None of them looked very deep but there were so many it was impossible to tell. Far more serious was the fact that his face was a dingy-grey hue and his breathing so shallow that several times Sarah thought he'd stopped breathing altogether.

They asked Alvia to fetch the doctor, but Bryn Morgan suggested that as his motor car was outside the door perhaps they should take Lloyd straight to the Royal Infirmary.

Before he and Owen could reach a decision

on how they were going to manage to lift Lloyd up from the floor and get him outside and into the car, the doctor arrived.

He gave a surprised look at all the mess on the floor, even though Alvia and Marie had managed to clear away a great deal of it so that it was possible for the doctor to kneel down and examine Lloyd. They all looked on anxiously as he folded up his stethoscope and shook his head.

'He's suffered a stroke and we need to get him into hospital as soon as possible,' he stated. 'Has anyone sent for an ambulance?'

The waiting seemed interminable. Sarah remained kneeling on the floor amidst the debris by her father's side, holding his hand and murmuring to him although she realised that he probably couldn't hear her.

'Why don't you go upstairs and get changed out of that dress, Sarah?' Alvia suggested. 'You'll want to go with him to the hospital and you can't go dressed like that.'

Sarah shook her head. 'No, I don't want to leave him, not even for a minute. I'll be all right.'

She was still in her wedding dress when the ambulance arrived; still holding on to her father's hand.

'I'll bring Owen in my car and we'll meet you there,' Bryn Morgan told her as Owen helped her into the ambulance.

It was almost midnight before Lloyd regained consciousness and Sarah sat by his bedside, watching him anxiously, oblivious to what was going on all around her.

'Look, cariad, there's nothing you can do here now,' Owen told her. 'He needs to sleep. The nurses will watch over him. You are completely exhausted, so let me take you home and we'll come back again first thing tomorrow morning.'

Sarah hesitated for so long that Owen thought she was going to refuse. Then at last, with a deep sigh of resignation, she nodded in agreement.

They went back to Cyfartha Street and not to their new home. Sarah refused to have anything to eat but Owen insisted she drank a glass of hot milk to which he added a small tot of brandy.

As he tucked her into her own single bed she put her arms round his neck and pulled his face down to hers. 'I'm so sorry about all this,' she whispered.

'Tomorrow is another day, cariad,' he said tenderly as he gently kissed her on the brow. 'Sleep well, my darling, all will turn out all right, you'll see.'

He waited for a few minutes to make sure that she was asleep then he went into Lloyd's bedroom, collected up a couple of blankets, and carried them back downstairs to the living room.

Alvia and Marie had cleared away the remains of the meal and all the debris from the floor. The room was so neat and tidy that it looked as though nothing untoward had happened there.

Owen tried not to think about what difference Lloyd's stroke was going to make to their future. He was so utterly exhausted and even though he'd been looking forward expectantly to his wedding night he was so tired that he was asleep in no time at all.

Sarah was still sound asleep when he woke next morning so he decided not to waken her. Instead, he went next door and asked Alvia if she could come in and stay until Sarah woke so that he could go into the office and let Bryn Morgan know what was happening.

'Surely he won't be expecting to see you?' Alvia said in surprise. 'By rights the pair of you should be off on your honeymoon. Going away, weren't you?'

'Yes, we were, but this changes everything doesn't it?' Owen pointed out. 'If things had gone according to plan then Lloyd would have been at work. Since he's not, I need to go in and make sure that someone will be doing his job.'

'Do you mean permanently?' Alvia said in alarm. 'Break his heart if he thought he was out of work again. You've no idea the state he was in when he lost his job before.'

'Don't worry, I hope it won't come to that,' Owen assured her. 'That's why I want to see that there are a few changes made to cover things until he's well enough to return to work.'

'What do I tell Sarah if she wakes up and wants to know where you are?'

'Tell her I've gone to change out of these

clothes and that I'll be back in next to no time and then I'll take her along to the infirmary to see her father.'

The curtains were drawn around Lloyd's bed when they arrived at the Infirmary and for one moment Sarah thought that perhaps he had died because he'd appeared to be so ill the night before. She clung tightly to Owen's hand.

Even when the nurse assured them that Lloyd was only sleeping they were both shocked when they moved inside the curtains and saw him.

Sarah knew he was only in his fifties but he looked like a man of seventy. His face was devoid of colour and his mouth was twisted grotesquely on one side.

'Dad.' Tentatively, she moved closer and bent to kiss him on the forehead.

He tried to smile but his lips refused to move and she noticed that he was drooling from one side of his mouth. Helpless, she looked towards Owen.

'How are you, Lloyd?' Owen asked, leaning down in case he was able to reply but apart from a slight movement of the head there was no response.

When the nurse reappeared they asked what was happening but she was non-committal and said they must speak to the sister in charge of the ward.

The sister took them to one side and in a low

voice confirmed their worst fears. The stroke had left Lloyd slightly paralysed down one side.

'How long is he going to be like this?' Sarah asked in a shocked voice.

The sister shook her head. 'We are unable to tell you that, my dear. With careful nursing and encouragement he should recover. He will probably never be the man he was, of course, but given time and the right exercises he should regain all his faculties.'

Sarah looked at Owen in despair. The news was such a blow that she couldn't think of what to do or say. It seemed unbelievable that yesterday he'd been a proud, upright man, about to celebrate her wedding, and that today he appeared to be merely a shell without the power of speech or movement.

'Do you think he knows us even though he can't talk to us?' Owen asked.

The sister smiled pityingly. 'None of us know for certain. We must treat him kindly and with respect in the hope that he does. The reason I moved away from the bed to explain all this to you is because if he does comprehend what we are saying then it could distress him if he heard us discussing his condition.'

'Do people recover?' Sarah pressed. 'Have you known anyone who has?'

Again the sister hesitated. 'I am sure he will improve, but it is impossible to tell at the moment how much he will do so. He appears to be a very strong, healthy man, so with the right rest and treatment I am confident that he will make some improvement. What happens over the next few days will be critical.'

'Does that mean that he will have to remain here in hospital?' Sarah asked.

'For the present. As soon as we are satisfied that there is nothing else we can do for him then we will discharge him and you can take him home. He will probably need careful nursing, though, for quite some time to come.'

They left the infirmary in a daze. Sarah couldn't put the memory of how ill he looked out of her mind. He seemed to be so old and frail that it made her heart ache.

Although she said nothing to Owen she couldn't help feeling that all her optimism about the future had been misplaced; their marriage was blighted before it had begun. First of all her mother had died, then Owen had been attacked, and now that her father was so terribly ill it meant that, once more, their married life was going to be on hold.

She felt she was burdening Owen with problems that were not really his responsibility. When, haltingly, she tried to say this to him he quickly shushed her to silence.

'Your family is my family now and I feel as responsible for your father as you do,' he told her firmly as he pulled her into his arms and held her close.

She felt so distressed by it all that she couldn't even cry. Her head was aching and the tears were there, preventing her from speaking, and she longed for some form of release.

She was too scared to think ahead, to even contemplate what sort of a future they were going to have. At the moment all she wanted was to go back to the hospital and find that it had all been a mistake; to find her father sitting up in bed, laughing with them as they told him about the trauma of his falling over, clutching at the tablecloth and pulling everything, including their wedding cake, on to the floor.

It all seemed such a fiasco, all so unreal, and the sight of his distorted mouth and face haunted her. The sister had said that he was paralysed all down one side so she supposed that meant he couldn't walk or perhaps even stand.

All they could hope for now was that it wasn't going to be a permanent disability. If he ever fully regained his senses then he would hate the disfigurement and he'd be terribly distressed if someone had to help him all the time with everything he wanted to do.

She wasn't at all sure that she was going to be capable of looking after him for the rest of his life, yet she was aware that it was her duty to do so. She wondered how Owen would react when he'd had time to think everything through and realise that possibly her father might be a permanent invalid, and that there would be an enormous responsibility involved in looking after him.

Chapter Thirty-One

It was almost the end of October before Lloyd was discharged from hospital. He looked frail and shaky and his face and mouth were still slightly twisted.

Although he could now speak and had regained almost full use of his limbs and he could now walk with two sticks, he still had trouble grasping things with his left hand and he had to use both hands when he was picking up a cup or a glass.

Eating was a slow struggle as he tried desperately hard to control any shaking so as not to spill anything. Even though Sarah made a point of cutting up his meat and vegetables into a manageable size he frequently found it difficult to lift the food from his plate to his mouth without dropping it.

Sarah and Owen had already given up the rooms they'd taken in Plasnewedd Place, even though it was only a few streets away. Instead they'd changed things around in Cyfartha Street so that Lloyd could have his bedroom downstairs because they thought it would be too great a strain for him to have to go up and down the stairs.

Sarah wasn't too sure how he was going to feel about this because she had redecorated the big bedroom that her parents had used all their lives, changed the curtains, and moved all her and Owen's belongings in there.

As it happened, Lloyd was so pleased to be out of hospital and back home that he made no comments whatsoever when he found that he now had a bedroom downstairs other than to say how sorry he was to be causing them so much trouble.

'You had your own place all set up and I know you were both looking forward to being there,' he said sadly. 'I've messed up every-thing for you one way or the other.'

'Nonsense, we're extremely comfortable living here and it is much better for us to be on the spot so that we can keep an eye on you than having to be dashing backwards and forwards to Plasnewedd Place,' Owen assured him.

'If Sarah has to look after me and isn't working, how on earth are we going to manage?' Lloyd asked worriedly.

'We will, don't you worry about it. I've got a good job and you'll have your sickness pay,' Owen reminded him.

'That's only ten shillings a week and it is only for twenty-six weeks,' Lloyd pointed out.

'Well, that's months away,' Owen reassured him. 'And by then you'll probably be as fit as a fiddle again,' he added cheerfully.

343

'Morgan's can't keep my job open until then,' Lloyd pointed out worriedly.

'Perhaps not, but I'm sure Bryn Morgan will be able to find some other work you can do.'

'You mean you will,' Lloyd said dryly. 'That's if we haven't all starved to death in the meantime,' he muttered gloomily. 'With all the special foods and medicines I seem to need these days it isn't going to be at all easy existing on your wage alone, Owen.'

When Sarah and Owen discussed the matter between themselves they both agreed that there was very little hope of Lloyd ever going back to work.

'In that case, it looks as though I will have to go on working for a while,' Sarah said firmly.

Owen shook his head. 'I'm inclined to agree with your father; it's not right for a married woman to be working.'

'Oh, why is that?' Sarah laughed. 'Is it because you don't like the idea that I can earn almost as much as you or because you feel people might think you can't afford to keep me?' she teased.

'It's no laughing matter, Sarah,' he told her sternly. 'A man should be the provider. You'll have enough to do nursing your father, there's no possibility of you working as well.'

Sarah was insistent. 'He's my responsibility, not yours, and although I am grateful that you are so willing to take care of him, it will not only make things so much easier for all of us

344

if I keep my job on, but I'll also feel better about it as well.'

'I'm not sure what Bryn Morgan will say about that. Morgan's have never employed married women before.'

'Well, there's a first time for everything and if you think it might worry him then I'll go and have a talk to him before we make any firm decision.'

Bryn was more than cooperative. He told Sarah that he'd been dreading the thought of having to replace her because she was such a valuable asset to his business.

'Sarah, take all the time you need off,' he told her. 'You might even find that you can do some of your work at home if it makes things easier for you,' he suggested.

'That's all very well, cariad, but I think you'll find it means you are going to be rushed off your feet all the time,' Owen warned her when she told him what Bryn Morgan had said and how she was determined to go on working.

'Not necessarily. Alvia and Marie can come in every day, like they started to do after Mam died. I'll fix it all up with them,' she promised.

'Your Dad might object and, if he does, then it will mean he's left on his own for a greater part of the day.'

Lloyd was divided in his reaction. He understood that with all her learning and experience Sarah wanted to go on working, but he was also afraid that it was all going to be too much for her.

'We don't want you cracking up, cariad,' Lloyd pointed out, his voice full of concern.

'Don't worry, I'm not going to let myself be overworked,' she promised.

'Duw anwyl, I hope not. We'd really be in a fix if you were ill now, wouldn't we?'

'I'm planning for Alvia and Maria to take it in turns to pop in during the day and make sure you're all right,' she assured him. 'They'll make you a cup of tea at mid-morning and again in the afternoon. What's more they'll bring in a midday meal for you and make up the fire. If there is anything else you want doing you have only to ask them while they're here.'

For the first few months everything went like clockwork. Even so Sarah knew that without Owen's wonderful support she would never have been able to manage to do so much and that things would not have run as smoothly as they did.

For the first time she felt that she really knew what being married was all about. Owen was so completely different from Gwyn or Stefan. He was not only tender and loving when they were alone but also so caring and considerate, always putting her needs first, and so understanding when it came to looking after her father.

Two or sometimes even three days a week

she worked from home and she had to rely on Owen to bring home all the documents and relevant papers she needed. Frequently he would also have to take them back in again the next day for Bryn Morgan's approval and signature.

Although they were not able to spend very much time on their own, Owen left her in no doubt about how much he loved her. He expressed his love in so many thoughtful little ways that sometimes she felt quite overwhelmed.

Fond though they both were of Lloyd, their bedroom became a haven of retreat as soon as they'd settled Lloyd for the night. It was the only time they could relax and feel comfortable about fully expressing their feelings for each other.

Lloyd could do very little for himself but in other ways he had adjusted well to his health problems. They now all accepted that there was very little chance of him making any further improvement so each of them, in their own way, did their utmost to help him to cope with his disability.

While Sarah and Owen were out at work, Alvia and Marie were his mainstay. Although both women had family responsibilities and homes of their own to run they arranged between them to take excellent care of Lloyd.

Sarah left them to arrange a rota between them, and it worked well. She had complete confidence that at all times one or the other would come in at regular intervals to make sure that her father was all right.

Sundays should have been a day of relaxation for Sarah and Owen but they were unable to do very much because they couldn't leave Lloyd on his own.

'I'll be all right if you two want to go for a walk,' he would insist whenever it was a fine Sunday.

'It's all right, Dad, we've plenty of odd jobs to do around the house,' Sarah reminded him. 'I'm going to do the ironing,' she told him as she spread an old blanket over the dining table and put a flatiron on the trivet in front of the fire to heat up.

'Rubbish, cariad! You shouldn't be ironing, not on a Sunday. It's enough to make your mam turn in her grave!'

'You're quite right, Lloyd,' Owen agreed, whisking the blanket away and folding it up. 'It's a lovely afternoon and I'm going to take your advice and take Sarah for a walk. She looks as though she could do with some fresh air.'

'Right you are, boyo. I promise that I'll stay right here in my chair and not move a muscle so you needn't worry about me falling over or coming to any harm.'

When they took him at his word and went for a short walk to Roath Park Sarah was on tenterhooks all the time and kept suggesting they should go home.

'Supposing he tries to go into the kitchen to fetch a glass of water or something and has a fall?' she said worriedly.

'Now why would he want to do that?' Owen laughed. 'We left him with a cup of tea on the table beside his chair and a plate of biscuits, so why on earth would he want a glass of water?'

Sarah had to admit that he was right but after Christmas they went out less and less on Sunday afternoon. This was not only because it was often very cold but because by Sunday Sarah found that all she wanted to do in the afternoon was curl up in front of the fire in Owen's arms and sleep.

She was always so tired that Owen became worried about her. He was convinced that trying to do her job and having all the worry of her father was proving to be too much for her. In the end he insisted that she went to see the doctor.

'What you really need, what we both need, is a holiday. I wonder if we could arrange with Alvia and Marie to take it in turns to sleep here overnight and look after your dad full time while we go away for a few days?' Owen pondered. 'A late honeymoon,' he added, his eyes twinkling.

'That's out of the question, they have their own commitments. It would be a waste of money, anyway. Why pay to sleep in a hotel at this time of year when we've got a perfectly good bed upstairs and all the things we need right here?'

'Think about it, cariad,' Owen urged. 'Wouldn't you like to be waited on, have someone bring you your breakfast in bed, and have your meals on the table all ready for you to enjoy without having to worry about shopping for groceries or having to do any cooking?'

'I'm waited on now most of the time. Alvia and Marie do all the housework, and a good deal of the shopping and cooking, so what more can I ask for?'

'More time to yourself? More time for me,' he added with a wide grin.

'Well, that probably would be nice, but Dad does go off to bed pretty early and once we've tucked him in we do have the rest of the evening to ourselves.'

'Yes, and by then you are usually too tired to do much more than crawl into bed. There must be some occasions when you long for more time to do other things? We never even find time go to the pictures these days.'

'Are you complaining?' Sarah teased.

'Far from it; that's the best part of the day as far as I am concerned,' he whispered. Possessively he pulled her into his arms, running his hands down her back and kissing her deeply as they started to make love.

'I think it's all to do with winter; it's cold and wet and dark in the mornings and dark again the evening. All I need is some warm weather and sunshine,' she murmured as she relaxed in his arms and gave herself up to his tender caresses.

More to please Owen and put his mind at rest than anything, Sarah finally agreed that she would go along to the doctor's and ask him if he could give her a tonic or something.

'Mind you, he must get countless people · asking him that at this time of the year,' she sighed. 'It's been a long hard winter for most people and at least we've not been struggling to make ends meet.'

'All the more reason why you shouldn't be feeling so tired all the time.'

'Stop worrying about me. I really am quite all right,' she protested smiling.

'Even so, cariad, promise me you will. Do you want me to come with you?'

'You mean to make sure I go?' Sarah asked a trifle irritably.

'Of course not,' he exclaimed, pulling her into his arms and stroking her hair. 'I'm concerned about you, cariad, that's all.'

'I've said I will and you needn't worry, I'll keep my word,' she told him pulling away.

A week later when she did go to see the doctor she came home in a daze and when Owen questioned her about what he'd said she merely shook her head. 'I'll tell you later, when we are on our own,' she said quietly.

Chapter Thirty-Two

The moment they went up to their bedroom that night Owen asked her again what it was that the doctor had said that she didn't want to tell him in front of her father.

'I think you'd better sit down,' she told him gravely as she sat down herself on the bed and patted the space beside her.

Looking very concerned he did as she asked. When she told him her news he was as startled as she had been.

'A baby? Are you quite sure about that?' he asked in a bewildered voice. He stared at her in disbelief for a moment then pulled her towards him and crushed her in his arms, holding her close and burying his face in her hair.

'Yes, I'm quite sure. I should have recognised the symptoms,' she added ruefully.

Owen pulled back, holding her by the arms and looking at her in awe. 'A baby! Our baby! I can hardly believe it, cariad. Do you know when it is due?'

'Not precisely, but somewhere around the beginning of July. I wasn't too sure about my dates but the doctor seemed to be pretty certain that was when it would be.'

'That's only about five months away! You must stop work at once, you need to rest up and take care of yourself. No wonder you've been so tired lately.'

'I don't need to stop work for ages yet. We will certainly have to start making some plans, though. There's my job to be considered as well as looking after Dad and—'

'I wonder what your father is going to say?' Owen interrupted, frowning slightly.

'I haven't said anything to him yet because I wanted to tell you first but I'm sure he'll be delighted.'

'It's going to make a tremendous difference to all our lives.' He smiled ruefully. 'It's come as quite a shock and certainly not something we'd planned.'

'I know, but you are pleased about it, Owen?' Sarah asked rather dubiously.

'Pleased? I'm over the moon! It's just such wonderful news that it has winded me.'

'I know, I felt taken aback, too, when the doctor told me.' She smiled. 'I must admit it was the last thing I expected to hear. In fact, his face was so grave, and he asked me so many questions when he examined me, that I was afraid he was going to tell me that I had something very seriously wrong with me.'

'A baby of our own; yours and mine.' Owen

pursed his lips in a silent whistle. 'I wonder if it will be a boy or a girl?'

'Which do you want it to be?' Sarah asked smiling at him indulgently.

Owen shook his head. 'I don't know; in fact, I don't mind. I shall love it whatever it is. I still can't believe this is happening. A family of our own. I'm so happy that I want to shout it to the whole world,' he added with a boyish grin.

'Well, I think we'd better tell my dad first before you do that,' Sarah teased.

'Tomorrow! We'll tell him tomorrow, the minute I get in from work. I'll buy a bottle of wine on the way home so that we can drink a toast,' Owen promised.

Lloyd seemed to be as delighted by the news as they were and agreed that it was certainly something to celebrate. 'It will be wonderful to have a grandchild running around here,' he told them. 'When I first got married I always hoped that we'd have three or four children, but there was only ever Sarah. Mind you, she's been the joy of my life and she still is,' he added as he reached out and took her hand and gave it an affectionate squeeze.

Sarah blinked back her tears, remembering poor little Cladylliss, the baby she'd had when she'd been only nineteen; the baby her father had never even seen. After that there had also been the baby who'd been stillborn and she felt a sudden fear in case anything went wrong with the baby she was carrying now.

Quickly she pushed such sad thoughts from her mind. This was a time for celebrating, not dwelling on the past, she told herself as she raised her glass and sipped at the wine in response to the toast Owen was making.

Alvia and Marie were equally delighted when Sarah told them the news. Both of them pointed out that from now on she really must take things easy. Alvia even went as far as to say she hoped that Sarah was going to give up work soon so that she could sit and put her feet up for part of the day.

'I'd grow fat and lazy if I did that,' Sarah laughed. 'No, I want to go on working for as long as I possibly can.'

Bryn Morgan warmly congratulated them but when he called her into his office afterwards Sarah found that he, too, was concerned about her working too long.

'You'll have to give up when the baby arrives so why not stop work a couple of months earlier,' he pointed out.

'I wasn't planning on giving up work,' Sarah told him quietly. 'We need the money; three of us can't manage on one pay packet, and when the baby arrives that will be four of us.'

'What does Owen think about you going on working?' Bryn asked frowning and fiddling with the pens on his desk.

'I haven't said very much to him about it as yet but I'm sure he'll understand.'

Bryn looked worried. 'I don't think that he will approve for one minute,' he told her bluntly.

Sarah shrugged uneasily. 'It really depends on you, though, doesn't it? If you say I have to leave then I suppose I'll have no option, but I am hoping you won't do that.'

'Look, perhaps we can have a compromise of some sort. I don't want to lose your expertise but I don't see that it will be feasible for you to come into the office every day.'

'Surely I can do a great deal of the work from home?' Sarah said hopefully. 'I've already proved that it's possible.'

'Yes, you can do quite a lot of it at home, I agree. There are always those occasions when you have to meet people either here in our office or in theirs and that's something we really do have to take into consideration.'

'That hasn't proved to be a stumbling block up until now,' Sarah pointed out, sitting bolt upright and squaring her shoulders as if to prove how alert and efficient she was.

'I know that over the past few months you have managed to do this,' Bryn agreed, fiddling again with the pens on his desk and avoiding her eyes as he added, 'but I'm sure it has not always been easy.'

'I can go on doing it, I can make arrangements,' Sarah told him confidently.

There was an ominous silence before Bryn spoke again. He continued rearranging things on his desk almost as if by doing so it would help him to reach a decision.

'What about if we take on a young lawyer, one who has just left university, to do the leg work,' he said at length, looking her straight in the eye.

Sarah frowned as if she didn't altogether approve of the idea, but she remained silent.

'You will still remain in charge of all our legal matters,' Bryn assured her. 'You can instruct him about what he has to do, but you will only have to come into the office very occasionally at times to suit yourself. In fact, if it makes things easier for you, he can always come and talk matters over with you at your home.'

Although it seemed an admirable arrangement neither Owen nor Lloyd were in full agreement with it.

'I think that once the baby arrives you'll find that caring for it takes up so much of your time that you won't have time to deal with all that,' Owen pointed out.

'Anyway, who is going to look after the baby when you do have to go into the office?' Lloyd demanded. 'You can't leave it with me, much as I'd like you to be able to do so,' he sighed. 'I blame myself for the obsession you have with work. I pushed you so hard when you were at school; I was always so anxious that you would make something of yourself. And you have. I'm very proud indeed of how you have turned out.'

'I can either take the baby along with me or I can ask Alvia or Marie to look after it. I'll only be away from the house for a couple of hours at the most.'

The two men looked at each other questioningly. Neither of them said anything and Sarah had an uneasy feeling that it was because they didn't approve of her idea.

'Perhaps we should wait and see what happens,' she told them. 'It's still several months off before we have to take any decision and in the meantime we can go on as we are.'

For Sarah, the spring and early summer of 1929 seemed to pass in a flash. There was so much to do both at work and at home that there were days when she felt so stressed out that she wondered if perhaps her father and Owen were right after all. How on earth was she ever going to manage to do her job and look after the baby when it arrived if she was constantly tired as she seemed to be these days, she pondered.

Marie and Alvia were both very helpful and took care of her father so well that she didn't know how she would have managed without them. Even so, with so many people organising everything she sometimes felt like a stranger in her own home.

Her only chance of escape from the gruelling routine was when her father was safely settled for the night and she and Owen could seek the solace of their bedroom.

She often wondered if he ever felt the same way as she did. Although he never mentioned it there were times when she felt sure that he must long for the peace and privacy they would have been able to enjoy if they had a place of their own, like the rooms he'd found for them in Plasnewedd Place and which they would have moved into if her father hadn't had his stroke.

At work, Bryn Morgan was as accommodating as he possibly could be. True to his word he'd hired an assistant to help her; a serious young man who had only recently obtained his law degree.

He was thin and dark haired, with horn-rimmed glasses. His name was Ion Quinn and he was exceedingly prim and proper. He always had a worried look on his face as if he was afraid he was going to do something wrong.

Ion was constantly asking questions and demanding detailed explanations about almost everything. At first Sarah found this very irritating, but he learned her system of working very quickly and he was extremely efficient.

He proved to be so dependable that Sarah found that as the time for her confinement drew ever closer she was quite happy to pass considerably more of her work over to him. She knew that she could trust him not only to do it well but also to do it in exactly the same way as she would have done it herself.

* * *

The month of June was hot and rather humid and Sarah found that her increasing bulk was something of a burden. The nights were warm and muggy and she often found it difficult to sleep, which added to her feeling of tiredness.

Both Bryn and Owen constantly pleaded with her to take things more easily and to spend more time at home resting but she took no notice of them at all.

'I'm quite all right and I feel better working than moping around the house waiting to go into labour,' she insisted.

'Surely there are things you still need to get ready for when the baby arrives?' Bryn suggested.

'No, I have everything ready and waiting and I even have a bag packed ready to take into hospital.'

She was stubbornly determined to work right up until the very last minute. The only thing she had relented over was agreeing with Owen that she would go into hospital for her confinement rather than having the baby at home.

'I'm thinking of your father as much as I am of you,' he told her. 'I think it might be rather an upheaval for him if it took place here. Alvia and Marie will take every care of him for a couple of days and it will give you the chance to have a really good rest.'

When she protested that they couldn't really afford it and that it would be much better to save the money for things they really needed,

Owen admitted that it was not simply his idea but Bryn's as well.

'Bryn is paying for it and it would be very discourteous to refuse,' he pointed out.

Sarah was still not completely happy about the arrangement but in the end she had no option. She went into labour early one afternoon at the end of June and there was no time to argue about where she was going.

Chapter Thirty-Three

Sarah's baby arrived on the first of July. She weighed seven pounds and had a mop of dark hair and a rosebud mouth and Sarah thought that she looked like a little angel.

The first time she held the baby in her arms Sarah wept as she remembered Cladylliss, her first baby, and the dreadful experience of her being so frail and weak and then eventually dying when she was only a few weeks old. She never wanted to go through something like that ever again.

This baby was plump and perfect in every way, though, with strong lungs, and Sarah resolved that she would watch over her every minute of the day to make sure that no harm came to her.

When Owen was allowed in to see them a few hours later he couldn't believe that a newborn baby could be quite so beautiful. He stared down at her in awe and seemed to be almost afraid to touch her, she looked so delicate and lovely.

'She won't break,' Sarah smiled when she asked him if he wanted to hold her and saw that he was nervous in case he held her too tightly and hurt her.

'She's so tiny, so fragile,' he protested as he took her from Sarah and cradled her in the crook of his arm, gently stroking her face with his forefinger.

'Not really,' Sarah assured him. 'She weighs over seven pounds and that is a very good start in life. Most newborn babies are a great deal smaller.'

'She's still like a little doll,' Owen murmured, looking down at her proudly.

'Give her a couple more years and she'll be a little tomboy, and will probably be climbing all over you and wanting you to toss her up into the air or give her rides on your knee.'

Lloyd was equally delighted and proud of the baby and eager to hold his granddaughter.

'I'll be able to help you for a change when you need someone to rock her off to sleep.' He smiled as Sarah placed her in his arms.

His one regret was that he would only be able to help look after her while she was in a pram and someone else was on hand in case she needed more attention because he knew that he probably wouldn't be capable of picking her up or doing anything for her.

'Tell me, have you and Owen decided what you are going to call this little angel?'

'We have talked about it but not really made up our minds yet. We did think of Rhoslyn if it was a girl because it's a name we both like,' Sarah told him thoughtfully.

'Rhoslyn! Well, that sounds a pretty name for a lovely baby who looks so much like you did that I know she will one day be a gorgeous little girl.' He beamed. 'Yes, I like the sound of Rhoslyn. I think we should have a little party so that you can tell everybody what her name is going to be.'

'Party!' Sarah stared at him in astonishment because it was so unlike her father to want something like that. 'I think that's a wonderful idea,' she agreed quickly before he could change his mind. 'I'll have a word with Owen first and see if he agrees with us. Is there anyone you'd like me to ask?'

'Well, Bryn Morgan for a start, and Marie and Alvia, of course, and anyone else you'd like to be there.'

'I think that's probably enough, don't you? We haven't room for too many people and I'm not used to entertaining. I can't really expect either Alvia or Marie to help with the preparations, not if they are going to be guests.'

'No, that's true enough,' Lloyd agreed. 'In fact, don't say anything to either of them until the last minute or else they will insist on taking over and it would be nice to give them a surprise.'

Sarah smiled and agreed but as she went to change Rhoslyn's nappy and feed her she did wonder what on earth had got into her dad because normally he wasn't all that keen on entertaining.

As she sat feeding the baby in the armchair that had been her mother's favourite, she wondered why a party, even a small one, was of such great importance to him and why he was so keen on the idea. He obviously didn't realise that she was still feeling extremely tired and also that she was finding it difficult to cope with the baby because Rhoslyn seemed to be very demanding.

Still, she reflected, her dad didn't have much fun in his life these days and if he'd set his heart on having a party so that they could show off little Rhoslyn, then she didn't mind going along with it.

She decided that Sunday would be the best day because Owen would be at home and would be able to help with the arrangements. When she mentioned it to him he seemed almost as keen on the idea as her dad had been.

'I'll buy some champagne so that we can celebrate in style,' he insisted. He also suggested that they should ask Bryn Morgan to bring his wife along.

The thought of what a grand house she probably had and the several full-time servants she must employ, made Sarah feel nervous about doing so, but she could see that it might be considered rude to invite Bryn without her so she kept her thoughts to herself.

As it turned out Celina Morgan was a motherly middle-aged woman with grey hair and a warm smile. Sarah felt comfortable in her company from the moment they shook hands. When Celina offered to sit and nurse the baby Sarah was more than happy to let her do so while she sorted things out.

After they'd all helped themselves to the variety of sandwiches and savouries that she'd laid out ready, Sarah cut the iced cake that Alvia had made in honour of the new baby. Owen poured out the champagne and made sure that everyone had a glass. He then announced that they were going to call the new baby Rhoslyn and asked them to drink a toast to her.

There were murmurs of delight and surprise at the name as they clinked glasses and sipped their wine.

In the weeks that followed, Sarah found that having a baby in the house certainly made a tremendous difference. As well as the daily routine of bathing and feeding Rhoslyn, which seemed to take up far more time than Sarah remembered from caring for Cladylliss, there was also all the additional washing and ironing.

They also had several sleepless nights and even after the baby had adjusted to her routine there was still night-time feeding to be undertaken. Sarah very soon found that having to feed the baby late at night and again in the early hours of the morning meant that she was not getting anywhere near enough sleep herself.

For a few weeks she struggled to undertake as much office work at home as she possibly could but in the end she was forced to admit that she wasn't able to cope any longer and that the time had come to hand everything over to Ion.

'Remember, I'm always here if you want to ask me about anything or check over anything you are not sure about, so don't hesitate to get in touch,' she told him.

'Thank you, Sarah, but I feel quite confident that I have most things under control now; you've been a splendid teacher but I'll certainly take advantage of your expertise if I need to do so.'

Bryn agreed that she'd made the right decision. He added that, like Owen, he felt that her main concern for the present should be concentrating on looking after Rhoslyn and her father and that was a full-time job.

He also suggested that she took the baby along to see his wife now and again if she could spare the time.

This suggestion surprised Sarah but, remembering how kind and helpful Celina had been, she fully intended to do so. To her delight, however, Celina took matters into her own hands and paid her a visit.

Sarah felt rather nervous as she invited her in, conscious that she was wearing an apron to protect her dress because she'd been changing Rhoslyn's nappy. Nevertheless, she asked her to sit down and offered her a cup of tea.

'That would be lovely but only if you let me nurse Rhoslyn while you make it,' Celina said smiling.

'Of course.' Sarah indicated a comfortable armchair and then settled the baby in her arms before she went through to the kitchen. When she returned a few minutes later she found Celina and her father chatting away as if they'd known each other all their lives.

After that, Celina became a regular visitor and both Sarah and Lloyd greatly enjoyed her company. Sarah found that she was extremely knowledgeable about young babies, but when she asked her if she had any grandchildren of her own, she saw the disappointment in the other woman's face and wished she'd said nothing.

'No, I haven't any grandchildren, I'm afraid,' Celina said in a sad voice. 'We only had one son and he was killed in an accident when he was twenty-four.'

'Oh, I'm so sorry, that must have been heart-breaking,' Sarah exclaimed.

'Yes, it left a great gap in our lives. Bryn never talks about it these days, but I find that never a day passes when I don't remember some small incident,' she admitted.

The baby had now become the centre of her life and Sarah was more than happy to concede that they were right and that she needed to be at home full time. As Rhoslyn began to develop a personality of her own Sarah delighted in her every look and gesture and didn't want to miss out on a single minute of Rhoslyn's babyhood.

Although she said nothing to either Owen or Lloyd she also watched anxiously to see if there were any signs that perhaps Rhoslyn was going to suffer any of the same effects that Cladylliss had developed when she was a small baby.

When Rhoslyn was four months old, she was not only alert and taking notice of everything that went on around her but also physically fit and well in every way. Sarah felt that her cup of happiness was overflowing. Owen had received a substantial pay rise so the fact that she wasn't working no longer mattered.

Even Lloyd seemed to have taken on a new lease of life since Rhoslyn had been born. He delighted in watching over her while she was asleep and Sarah was busy with household chores.

Together they noted when her first tooth came through, listened to her first words, and applauded the first time she managed to sit up on her own.

'You would have missed out on all this if you'd stayed on at work,' Lloyd reminded her the day Rhoslyn started crawling.

'Yes, you're quite right, I would have done, and that would have been a great pity.'

'Mind you,' he chuckled, 'she'll be into everything now so you won't have a moment's peace. There will probably be days when you wish you were back at work.'

'I doubt it.' Sarah smiled as she picked up some of the toys that Rhoslyn had discarded and put them back into the wooden toy box that Owen had made for the purpose.

By the following Easter, when Rhoslyn was nine months old, she was taking notice of all that was going on around her. She loved being taken out in her pram, sitting up so that she was able to see everything.

One of their favourite destinations was Roath Park. Usually they would meet Celina and after a walk in the park go back to her house in nearby Pen-y-lan Road.

At first Sarah had felt uncomfortable about this because everything from the carpets to the curtains and cushions were so pristine and expensive that she was afraid Rhoslyn might spill something or make a mess.

Celina soon put her mind at rest. 'They're only possessions,' she pointed out. 'Her enjoyment is far more important.'

Each time they visited it seemed that Celina brought out some new toy or something which had belonged to her son Twm and which she had treasured but now wanted Rhoslyn to play with and enjoy.

'You must remember that for me Rhoslyn is the grandchild I will never have,' she told Sarah. 'You can't possibly imagine how much happiness I get out of seeing her sitting here on the floor playing with them.'

Sarah accepted that this was true and marvelled how fortunate she was to have such a good friend. Her only worry was that with so many people dancing attendance on her Rhoslyn could become spoiled. When she mentioned this to Owen he pointed out that she had such a sweet, happy nature that he thought that was unlikely.

On sunny days, Lloyd liked nothing more than to sit outside on a chair with the pram alongside him and to talk to her, pointing out the birds and the flowers and telling her all about them.

When it was time for her to settle for her morning sleep then he would rock the pram until she dozed off.

A couple of months later when she'd started pulling herself up on to her feet and struggling to get out of her pram, this was no longer possible and he started to bemoan the fact, not only to Sarah and Owen but also to Celina Morgan who'd become such a regular visitor that she was almost one of the family.

'It makes me feel more useless than ever to know that now she's started getting around I won't be able to keep an eye on her any longer,' he sighed when Celina commented that Rhoslyn would soon be toddling and they'd all have to be running after her.

'Then we'll have to make sure she knows how to help look after you,' Sarah told him. 'She'll be able to fetch and carry for you so that will save me having to do it,' she said, smiling.

'The best thing you can do is put her in a playpen so that you don't have to chase after her all the time,' Celina suggested. 'If you'll let me, then I'd like to buy one for her.'

'That's a splendid idea,' Lloyd agreed. 'It's not right leaving her strapped into her high chair for too long.'

'And when you do start taking her out for little walks, then make sure you put reins on her,' Celina advised. 'I've seen little toddlers dash out into the road and get knocked down before today. They've no sense of danger, you see.'

'She'll be too busy looking after her Granpy to have time to do naughty things like that,' Sarah told them, smiling indulgently as she picked the little girl up and hugged her.

Chapter Thirty-Four

Bryn Morgan's death was sudden and completely unexpected. One minute he was sitting at his desk checking over a legal document that Ion had handed to him and the next he had slumped forward, scattering papers and sending a heavy mahogany desk stand that held his pens and glass inkwell crashing to the floor.

Ion jumped back thoroughly frightened. Nervously, he touched Bryn Morgan's arm and when there was no response he gingerly felt below his ear to see if there was a pulse. Unable to find one he went in search of Owen.

Owen also checked for a pulse and then, realising how serious the matter was, ordered Ion to send for an ambulance right away. Meanwhile, he did his best to loosen Bryn's tie and undo the collar of his shirt in the hope that it might help.

An hour later they knew the worst and Owen took it upon himself to personally go and tell Bryn's wife.

In the week leading up to Bryn Morgan's funeral, saddened though they were by his death, Owen and Sarah were also very concerned about what the future of Morgan Builders would be.

The chances were that Celina would not want to carry on trading, in which case the company would either be closed down or sold. In either instance there was a possibility that Owen would find himself out of work.

'There's absolutely nothing we can do about it except wait and see what happens,' Owen pointed out. 'Worrying our heads off about what will happen won't make one iota of difference.'

Knowing how devastated Celina must be and that she had no close relatives to support her, Sarah went to Pen-y-lan Road to see if there was anything she could do to help.

'I don't think there is, cariad,' Celina told her, 'Cledwyn Hughes, our solicitor, has everything in hand and he's organising the funeral. I would like it if you could be there but I don't suppose that will be possible because you wouldn't be able to bring little Rhoslyn to something like that,' she sighed.

'If you'd like me to be there then I could leave her with Alvia. She still sometimes comes in to keep an eye on my dad,' Sarah offered.

'Would you really do that for me? I would be so grateful. I feel I need someone to stand alongside me to give me the courage to see this through,' Celina admitted.

'Owen will be there as well,' Sarah reminded her.

'Oh, I know that, dear, and he'll be a power of strength but I would like to have you at my side as well.'

'Then I'll be there, and if you wish I'll come back to the house with you afterwards and so will Owen, so don't worry about it any more,' Sarah assured her.

It was a grey, damp, blustery day which added to the grimness of the occasion. The church was packed with employees of Morgan's and also a number of Bryn and Celina's neighbours and friends. Owen and Sarah stood either side of Celina, and Sarah held her hand throughout the service.

Afterwards, when Cledwyn Hughes read Bryn's will, there were gasps of astonishment, even from Celina. The solicitor revealed that Bryn had known for quite some time that he had a serious heart condition and accordingly he'd made careful provisions for his wife's future.

The business was left to Owen Phillips with the stipulation that a regular amount was paid each month to his wife for the rest of her life. His house in Pen-y-lan was left to Celina but his motor car, which belonged to the company, was left to Owen.

Owen was utterly flabbergasted. At first he didn't know what to say and then he protested both to the solicitor and to Celina that he was sure there must be some mistake.

Cledwyn Hughes suggested that the three of them should adjourn to a private room to discuss the matter more fully and Celina insisted that Sarah came as well.

'I had no idea exactly what my husband was planning to do,' she told them, 'but I am both pleased and relieved by his will. I could never have managed to continue with the business as I have no head for such matters but I'm sure that you will continue to run it as efficiently as he did.'

'I will certainly do my utmost,' Owen told her humbly, 'and I assure you that you will always be well provided for; I'll make quite certain of that,' he told her earnestly.

'My husband had always intended from the day he started on his own that our son would join him and that they would be partners but unfortunately, due to Twm's untimely death, this was not possible. Privately, he has always regarded you as the son he lost, Owen, and so it is a tribute to Twm's memory and I want you to accept it as that,' she told him, with tears in her eyes. 'You and Sarah and little Rhoslyn are as much family to me as if you were blood relations.'

Later, as everyone was taking their leave, Sarah suggested to Celina that she might like to come back and stay with them rather than be on her own.

'No, cariad, I would like to remain here. I need some time alone to come to terms with all that has happened. If you can spare the time tomorrow, then I would very much like to see you and, of course, little Rhoslyn.'

'In the afternoon perhaps?' Sarah suggested.

'Yes, that would be best. Perhaps you could bring your father as well. Lloyd has never been here and it would be such a pleasure to show him round.'

'He'd love it but I'm afraid it would be too far for him to walk,' Sarah said gently.

'Well, there will be no need for him to do so. Don't forget that you have a motor car now and I am sure Owen can spare a few minutes to bring you all round here and then collect you again at the end of the afternoon when he finishes work.'

The new routine soon became established. Two or sometimes three afternoons a week, Owen drove them to Pen-y-lan Road and left them there while he went back to the office before collecting them when he'd finished work.

Frequently Celina insisted that they should stay and have a meal with her because, she claimed, she didn't like eating on her own. Even so, they never stayed very late into the evening because Sarah felt that it upset Rhoslyn's routine too much as she liked to have her in bed by seven o'clock.

The change of management at Morgan's also had repercussions. Owen had been used to running things for a good number of years but he'd always known that Bryn was in the background. Bryn had always been on hand to discuss any problems that arose if Owen was uncertain about what action to take. Now that he had to make his own decisions he was often worried and unable to put the matter from his mind when he finished at night.

Bringing problems home was one thing but when it meant that he was irritable or even bad-tempered, Sarah became alarmed. She persuaded him to talk matters over with her but more often than not she found that he was too tired to discuss things rationally. Either that or she was distracted because Rhoslyn needed attention.

'Why don't you go into the office for an hour or so now and again and then you can help Owen to sort out these problems,' Celina suggested when she mentioned it to her.

'It's not really the answer though, is it?' Sarah sighed. 'It would be just as difficult to concentrate on things there because I'd still have Rhoslyn with me.'

Celina looked thoughtful. 'Do you think she would stay here with me while you went into the office?'

'She's quite a handful; do you think you could manage to look after her?' Sarah asked dubiously. 'She's full of life these days and into everything.'

'If she was in a playpen and Lloyd was here to sit and talk to her as well, then I think we'd be able to entertain her and keep her happy for a couple of hours.'

Sarah agreed to think about it and talk it over with Owen and see what he thought about it.

To Sarah's surprise Owen hugged her with relief when she put the idea to him.

'I think it would make all the difference,' he told her. 'There are so many semi-legal matters that I'm unsure about and yet I don't want to discuss them with Ion. For one thing, if I'm unsure then it rather undermines my authority and I find that Ion is inclined to be rather supercilious whenever I'm wrong and he's right,' he admitted uncomfortably.

'I'll have to see what Dad thinks about it because Celina says she would feel happier if he was there with her rather than Rhoslyn being left completely in her charge. What difference it will make having him there I really don't understand, since he can't move fast enough to catch Rhoslyn or even manage to pick her up if she falls over and hurts herself.'

'No, but Celina likes his company and trusts him and it will probably help boost her confidence if he's there. She also probably thinks that Rhoslyn will feel happier and more settled because she is used to having him around all the time.'

Although it worked quite well, and having Sarah in the office for a few hours several days a week certainly lightened Owen's workload, he occasionally grumbled about having to take time out to pick them all up and drive them to Celina's house in Pen-y-lan Road.

'Well, I suppose it wouldn't hurt to leave Dad for a few hours on his own; it's too far for him to walk. I could ask Alvia to look in on him and if I did that then I could take Rhoslyn round to Celina's in her pram and catch a bus from there to the office.'

'That might work, but wouldn't it be quite a trek for you, cariad?' Owen pointed out.

'Yes, you're right. It would probably be much simpler if I learned to drive the car,' Sarah said dryly.

'You drive!' Owen stared at her in astonishment.

'Why not? You learned to drive it, so why can't I?'

'You're a woman, that's why; you can't be expected to understand mechanical things.'

Sarah was not to be deterred. The idea festered in her mind for days and although Owen had not made any further comments about how long it took to collect her she was determined to broach the subject again.

To her surprise, delight and amusement, a few days later when she was sorting through the various documents Ion had left for her to deal with, she found a new driving licence issued in her name and it was obvious that Owen had sent for it.

She decided to wait for him to say something and to her relief he brought the matter up a few days later after they had safely delivered Lloyd and Rhoslyn into Celina's care.

'I've been thinking about what you said the other day about learning to drive and it does make a lot of sense,' he told her as they got back into the car.

'Yes, I thought you had. I found the driving licence you'd applied for.' Sarah smiled as she settled herself into her seat.

'Good. I was waiting for it to arrive. Now that it has, I'll show you what you have to do.'

'Is it very difficult?' she asked tentatively.

'Well, take notice as we drive to the office and then you can have a go yourself when we come back to collect your dad and Rhoslyn. How about that?'

Sarah had no problem in mastering the steering and braking but what she did find difficult was pulling away from standstill and double-declutching.

Her first attempts at pulling away resulted in them kangaroo-hopping for several yards until she managed to master the art of letting the clutch out. When it came to changing up or down, more often than not she caused the car to stall, or else there was a terrible grinding noise from the gearbox.

'I don't think I am any good at this,' she said dispiritedly after she'd stalled the car as she was pulling away, causing the traffic behind them to honk their horns and a waiting tram to sound its bell very loudly.

'Take no notice of them, they all had to learn at one time and they probably all made mistakes,' Owen told her.

Heartened, Sarah persisted and after the first couple of runs her confidence had been restored and she was almost enjoying it. For about a month Owen would only let her drive when they were in the car on their own. The first time she did so with her father and Rhoslyn on board Lloyd seemed very surprised.

'You never told us anything about Sarah learning to drive,' he commented, leaning forward in his seat. 'How long has this been going on, then?'

'For over a month now,' Sarah told him, keeping her eyes on the road ahead.

'I must say I never thought the day would come when I'd be driven around in a motor car by my own daughter,' Lloyd commented as he settled back again in his seat. 'You have a very clever Mummy, Rhoslyn,' he added proudly.

Now that Lloyd not only knew she could drive but felt quite safe when she was doing so, Sarah found life was more relaxed. It was so much easier to get Rhoslyn dressed and ready at her own speed instead of having to constantly chivvy the child to hurry.

Lloyd also found that it was less stressful when he could take his time and not be expected to rush.

Celina was delighted. 'I always intended to learn to drive but it always looked so complicated that I never plucked up the courage to do so,' she admitted. 'All those gears and levers and switches, I could never work out how to use them in the right order.'

'I'm sure you could,' Sarah told her. 'Why don't you give it another try?'

'No, I don't think so,' Celina protested with an affected shiver. 'Perhaps you should suggest it to Lloyd, though. I'm sure he'd enjoy driving and he is so much better these days that he might jump at the opportunity.'

At first Sarah felt quite startled by the idea. She thought about it and realised that Celina was right and that these days her dad's hands barely shook at all. She couldn't remember the last time he'd dropped or spilled anything and so she was inclined to agree with her.

For the next few days she didn't bother about cutting up Lloyd's food for him and she noticed that it didn't seem to bother him at all that he had to do it for himself.

'Perhaps you should learn to drive, Dad,' she said tentatively the next time she was collecting him and Rhoslyn from Celina's, 'then you could take Celina out sometimes. I'm sure she'd like a run out into the country or down to the seaside and we're always so busy that we never seem to get the time for any little jaunts like that.'

He dismissed the idea as nonsense. 'An old crock like me? What are you talking about, cariad? Duw anwyl! It takes me all my time to climb into this damn thing,' he grumbled as he settled himself in the back seat and waited while she put Rhoslyn in beside him.

Although she laughed with him it did put an idea into Sarah's head and she asked Owen what he thought.

'I don't see why not,' Owen agreed. 'There's nothing wrong with his eyesight or hearing. In fact, he's so much better these days that the only problem is that he can't walk very well.'

'So you think that once he is behind the wheel he could manage to drive all right?'

'Send off for a driving licence for him and when that comes through I'll suggest it to him and we'll see how he gets on.'

At first Lloyd didn't even want to give it a try. 'Damnio di, what are you trying to do, boyo, get me to make a fool of myself?'

'No, not at all. I simply thought it might give you a little more independence if you were able to drive.'

'Not likely to get much of that, not at my age and in my state of health, now am I?' Lloyd muttered gloomily.

'Of course you're not when all you do is sit in your armchair and wait for other people to ferry you around.'

'I'm past it, boyo, and the sooner I settle down and accept the fact the better.'

'If that's how you see things, then probably you're right,' Owen shrugged as he turned away.

'The sooner the lot of you accept that my life's more or less finished the more contented I'll be,' Lloyd muttered.

'You can't blame me for trying,' Owen said mildly as he started up the engine. 'I even thought that if you did learn to drive then it might be possible for you to have a job again at Morgan's. Even if it was only part time it would keep you occupied and prove to the rest of the world that you're not quite useless yet.'

Lloyd looked startled and so taken by surprise at his son-in-law's remark that he was speechless. He puffed out his cheeks and raised his eyebrows speculatively. 'Do you really think so?' he asked in disbelief.

Chapter Thirty-Five

'If I've managed to learn to drive then I'm sure you can as well,' Sarah told her father when he brought the subject up over the meal table the next day.

'It's not so easy learning new skills as you get older,' Celina said thoughtfully.

'Dad's not all that old, though,' Sarah argued as she helped herself to potatoes and passed the dish along to Owen.

'Well, he's middle-aged like me and I know I tried and I was absolutely hopeless.'

'Owen would probably say that was because you're a woman and therefore you find it more difficult to understand how mechanical things work,' Sarah laughed.

'Well, in that case, your dad shouldn't have any problem,' Celina murmured, her eyes twinkling as she looked across at Sarah.

Lloyd and Owen remained silent while listening to their banter.

The following day, however, Owen reported that Lloyd had said he was going to give it a try, that was if he was able to manage to climb in behind the wheel.

Three weeks later he had not only mastered

getting into the car, but was also driving as confidently and proficiently as if he'd done so all his life. Owen was pleased and Sarah was delighted. Celina was also full of praise about what he'd achieved although she declared that she'd known all along that he'd be able to do it.

'I shall expect you to fulfil your promise and find me a job back at Morgan's,' Lloyd reminded Owen.

'Well, you can start by chauffeuring Sarah and Rhoslyn around and taking Celina out,' Owen told him.

'Oh no, he's not doing that; I don't want him depriving me of driving,' Sarah told them promptly.

'She's right, boyo, it's not what I want to do. I'm hoping for a proper driving job, in either a van or a small lorry. I want one that will put me back on the payroll, in fact.'

'I'm still expecting you to take me out for a run now and again, Lloyd,' Celina reminded him. 'I'm looking forward to it, so don't let me down.'

'I can see we'll have to draw up a rota so that we know whose turn it is to use the car,' Owen laughed.

Although they never did anything quite like that they did arrange certain days when the car would be available for Lloyd to take Celina out and Sarah realised that these became the high-light of Lloyd's week.

Celina, too, seemed to enjoy their excursions which were extremely varied and depended to some extent on the weather. When it was bright and sunny they journeyed out into the surrounding countryside or to places like Penarth. Occasionally when they intended to go to Barry Island, Porthcawl or anywhere near the coast where they knew there was going to be a sandy beach, they took Rhoslyn with them.

Rhoslyn loved these outings and soon grew to know which days of the week Lloyd and Celina would be going out. She would have her little bucket and spade with her when she came down to breakfast in the hope that her grandfather would take her along as well.

Although they loved taking her with them they both admitted that they found it very tiring having to keep an eye on her. Celina was the one who had to run after Rhoslyn most of the time because she moved far too fast for Lloyd to keep up with her.

Sarah welcomed the opportunity to have a few hours on her own whenever they did take her. She found she was leading such a busy life that she had no time for personal things and welcomed these opportunities for shopping or a visit to the hairdresser's.

Although it was fairly hectic day to day, she wouldn't have changed things for a moment. Her father seemed to be so much happier and brighter now that he was working again, even though it was only for two or three days a week.

The other days while Sarah was at work he spent at Pen-y-lan Road with Rhoslyn and Celina.

As Lloyd's health improved over the next couple of years he spent more time at Pen-y-lan, and did more and more odd jobs for Celina while he was there; things which neither her daily woman nor her housekeeper could manage to do. It was a very big house with four bedrooms, a large drawing room and a spacious dining room as well as a huge kitchen and scullery.

There was also a greenhouse and potting shed in the big garden and Lloyd loved to potter around in there as well as in the well-equipped workshop that was built on to the side of the garage.

Sarah's initial envy that Celina's place was so much grander than their home in Cyfartha Street was tempered by the thought of how much maintenance it required, even though Celina had plenty of help. She found that cleaning their own small house took up most of her time when she wasn't at the office.

Owen kept telling her that she should never have stopped Marie coming in to help because they could afford to pay her now that their situation had improved so much.

'I couldn't bring myself to let someone do housework for me, not when I'm fit and well, because I always feel that my mother would have disapproved.'

'You are an idiot,' Owen laughed, pulling her

into his arms and kissing her. 'Lorna probably didn't have anyone to help out because she couldn't afford it; I keep telling you that nowadays we can. What's more, I want you to let someone else do it so that you can have an easier time.'

'It would make me feel guilty, though. The reason my mam couldn't afford it was probably because they were scrimping and scraping all the time to send me to university.'

'That's all water under the bridge, cariad. We have a new life now, we've moved on. Take your dad, for example: here he is, driving and having days out and enjoying his life, yet a couple of years ago he looked as though he was going to be a permanent invalid only capable of sitting in his armchair all day.'

'I know, and I'm very happy for him.'

'He'd be very happy for you if he thought your life was easier. He was saying only the other day that life seems to be rushing by and what with a home to run and putting in time at the office you didn't get much time to do anything else. In fact, he even suggested that this year we should arrange to take Rhoslyn away on holiday.'

Sarah's face lit up. 'That would be lovely!'

'She'll be four in July, old enough to appreciate a week by the sea. Next year she'll be off to school, remember.'

'It would mean leaving Ion in charge, would you be happy about that?' Sarah queried.

'Your dad would be there as well; he said he would go in every day to make sure everything was running smoothly.'

'What would he do if it wasn't?'

'Let me know, of course. I would arrange to telephone in at a set time each day and he'd be there to take the call and let me know if there were any problems.'

Sarah mulled the idea over for days before she reached a decision and agreed with Owen that it was a good idea.

'We'll go in the middle of June; before the schools break up for their summer holidays, so then it won't be too crowded. We won't talk about it in front of Rhoslyn in case anything goes wrong and we're prevented from going.'

There was so much preparatory work to be done that there were times when Sarah wondered if it was worth all the hassle it entailed. Then she thought of how excited Rhoslyn would be when they told her and all her doubts vanished.

At the beginning of the month they told her and made a special list of the days left before their holiday started. Each morning the minute she got up Rhoslyn crossed one off.

When Saturday 16 June arrived Rhoslyn crossed off the last day. She jumped up and down with excitement and could hardly eat her breakfast.

Owen had packed the motor car with everything they were taking the night before so the moment Sarah had finished washing-up the breakfast dishes and making the beds they were ready to leave.

Owen gave some last-minute instructions to Lloyd and then finally, to Rhoslyn's joy, they were in the motor car and heading out of Cardiff on their way to Swansea.

Their hotel was close to the sea front with a wonderful view of the sweeping bay as it curved towards Oystermouth. They could see the castle perched on the hill and, further along, even the gleaming white islets of Mumbles Head.

There was so much to do and they revelled in the feeling of freedom. The week passed all too quickly but Sarah found that it did give her and Owen an opportunity to recapture some of the romance that seemed to have been squeezed out of their busy schedule since he'd taken over at Morgan's.

Being out in the warm June sunshine all day was wonderful for all of them. Rhoslyn loved it when Owen rolled up his trousers as far as the knees and took her paddling in the sea. They built endless sandcastles and Rhoslyn had great fun exploring rock pools with her little shrimping net and turning over pebbles and stones to see what wildlife would scuttle from underneath them.

Every afternoon Rhoslyn had a donkey ride along the sand before they went back to the hotel for their evening meal. By the time they'd eaten she was ready for bed and once she was settled down they knew they wouldn't hear a peep from her until the next morning.

Although it meant they had to stay in the hotel themselves during the evening they soon discovered that this could be the best part of the day. Once Rhoslyn was asleep they pulled back the curtains, opened the French doors on to the balcony, and swivelled the sofa round so that they could sit there in comfort.

As dusk fell and the lights came on around the sweeping curve of the bay the whole scene was transformed. In such a romantic setting, with a bottle of wine on the table beside them, they were content to sit, talk, kiss and cuddle before eventually making their way to bed to complete a night of lovemaking.

Their feelings for each other were as strong as ever and as the end of the week approached Sarah felt reluctant to return to Cardiff; she wanted their holiday to go on for ever.

'Unfortunately that's impossible,' Owen sighed on their last evening there as they sat close together on the sofa, his arm round her and her head resting on his shoulder.

'I know, I was only daydreaming. We must try and do this again, though, and not keep putting it off. This is the first holiday we've had since we've been married.'

'Yes, but so many things have happened and in recent years our life has changed a great deal,' Owen reminded her.

'Yes,' Sarah sighed. 'I miss my mam and I was sorry that Bryn died when he did but in some ways we are so very much better off that we should be grateful that things have turned out so well.'

'Very true, cariad. What we have to do now is make sure that we plan things so that we don't get into the rut of putting work before our own interests. This break has done us good in more ways than one. It's shown us how much more there is to life than merely earning money.'

'If we weren't earning the money, though, we wouldn't have been able to afford to come on holiday,' Sarah laughed. 'We certainly wouldn't be sitting here drinking wine! I can't remember Mam and Dad ever having any wine in the house except at Christmas time and that was usually a bottle of home made parsnip wine or something like that. Mind you, it was pretty potent!'

She held up her glass and clinked it against his, 'I still like this better and we didn't have to go to all the trouble of making it, which can take weeks and weeks if I remember rightly.'

'Perhaps you should start making wine at home, it would be a nice little hobby for you,' Owen teased. 'You'll have quite a lot of spare time on your hands when Rhoslyn starts school.'

'Yes, and we should talk about it and decide which school would be best for her.'

Owen looked puzzled. 'What do you mean?

She'll go to whichever one is nearest to Cyfartha Street, surely.'

'That is certainly what I'd always intended,' Sarah agreed, 'but the other day Celina was talking about Rhoslyn starting school and she was saying that the schools in Roath are very much better than those in Cathays. She seemed to think that perhaps we ought to be sending her to one of them.'

'I see!' He looked perplexed. 'Perhaps we should make some enquiries after we get back and see what we can find out. We certainly want to give her the best start in life that we possibly can.'

'No harm in finding out whatever we can, I suppose,' Sarah agreed. 'I went to school near Cyfartha Street and I seemed to have got on all right, though.'

'You were probably one of the exceptions,' Owen teased.

'No, I was the one who was nagged silly by my father. I struggled hard in order to please him. I lost most of my friends and almost my way because I was so immersed in learning and education,' she said rather sadly.

'We certainly don't want that to happen to Rhoslyn,' he agreed seriously. 'Let's make some enquiries. There's plenty of time before we have to make up our minds. Has Rhoslyn said anything about going to school?'

'Not really; I must talk to her about it. She is going to find it a bit of a shock having to mix in with other children because she hardly knows any.'

Owen frowned. 'I hadn't thought about it until now but I suppose you're right. She is constantly in the company of grown-ups. While you are at work she is with Lloyd and Celina and when you are at home she's in the house or else out shopping with you.'

'That's right. We never let her go out in the street to play with other children and I haven't any friends who bring their children round. In fact, our only visitors seem to be Alvia and Marie and you can hardly count them because they're as old as my dad.'

Chapter Thirty-Six

Although it was quite a while before Rhoslyn would start school Sarah gave some serious thought to the fact that Rhoslyn didn't have any little friends. It worried her because she was well aware that her daughter would find it hard to adjust to the cut and thrust of school life unless she was used to mixing with other children.

'You ought to let her go out and play in the street; that's what all the other children around here do,' both Alvia and Marie advised when she mentioned it to them.

'Yes, I know that, but it's difficult because she's not here all the time. When I go to work I leave her with Celina.'

'What difference does that make? She can play out around there, can't she?' Alvia asked.

'I'm not sure. I don't think I have ever seen any children playing out in the street when I've been there,' Sarah admitted.

As she spoke she remembered the children she'd seen at all hours of the day and evening in Tiger Bay; most of them ragged and without shoes. There had been little tots who could barely walk sitting in the gutter playing with the debris that had accumulated there. Often these toddlers were knocked over if they got in the way of bigger children who were playing hopscotch, swinging from ropes tied to the lamp-posts, playing hide and seek or chasing after each other in a game of tag.

She knew quite well that that sort of thing didn't go on in the streets in Cathays. Little girls pushed their dolls in prams which had been handed down by their older siblings or cousins who no longer wanted them. Some of the boys played football, or bounced balls against the wall and caught them; the girls would have skipping ropes and both boys and girls played with a top or marbles from time to time.

It had never entered her head to let Rhoslyn go out and join in their games; in fact, she didn't even know the names of any of the children who lived nearby.

She could see now that she had been rather remiss; when they'd been talking about a party for Rhoslyn's fourth birthday she realised that there was no one of her age they could invite. Just as for Rhoslyn's previous birthdays, Marie and Alvia would plan a special tea for her and make her a birthday cake with candles on it. Apart from them, though, no one outside the family would be there to join in the celebrations.

Sarah knew that it was too late now to rectify matters – for this year, at any rate. But before Rhoslyn went to school in a year's time, she certainly intended to invite other children to their home so that Rhoslyn could get used to mixing and playing with them.

Even though it was rather a subdued affair Rhoslyn's fourth birthday was a tremendous milestone, not only for her but also for the rest of the family as well.

After they'd all sung 'Happy Birthday' Rhoslyn had blown out her four candles and they'd all clapped and cheered, Lloyd announced that he had something important he wanted to say.

'I've decided that next week I'm moving away from Cyfartha Street,' he announced as they all looked at him expectantly.

'You are doing what?' Sarah and Owen spoke in unison and stared at him in disbelief.

'I feel so much fitter these days, and I am capable of doing so much more that it's time I had a proper life. It's all right for you, Sarah; you've got a family of your own now. You've got Rhoslyn and before long there'll be another baby. Soon you won't have time for an old codger like me.'

'Oh, Dad. I think you've had too much excitement today,' Sarah told him with a little laugh, looking across at Owen to see if he was taking any notice of what her father had just said.

Owen looked at her with raised eyebrows and then shook his head in bewilderment. 'You seem to know more than I do, Lloyd.' He smiled.

'Rhoslyn's anything but a baby,' Sarah said

quickly. 'Another year and she'll be off to school.'

'I know what I know,' Lloyd told her sagely. 'There'll be a new baby before Easter, you mark my words.'

'This talk of another baby . . . we're not planning anything of the sort,' Owen protested mildly.

'I think Lloyd is right; you've left it too late to change your minds. Isn't that so, Sarah?' Celina said with a smile.

'How on earth did you know?' Sarah frowned. 'I've not said a word, not even to Owen, because I'm not sure myself yet. It's far too early to be certain.'

'Your dad's heard you being sick in the morning and he drew his own conclusions,' Celina said beaming.

'You old rogue,' Sarah laughed, shaking her head in mock despair at her father, as Owen came over and hugged her, looking down at her, a big grin on his face.

'It's impossible to keep any secrets when you're around, Dad. Even so, you don't need to move out,' she protested, pulling herself out of Owen's embrace and going over to her father's chair and kneeling down beside it. She took his hand in hers. 'This is your home, Dad, so we won't hear of you giving it up.'

'I've already decided,' he told her, patting her head. 'I can't change my mind now, Celina would never forgive me.'

'But, Dad—

'Shush! No arguing. Everything has been arranged. I've already moved most of my belongings over to Pen-y-lan Road while you were on holiday; we were just waiting for the right time to tell you.'

'Are you quite sure about this?' Owen asked as he looked across at Celina.

'Yes, we are. We've been thinking about it for quite some time but ever since we realised that another baby was on the way we decided this was the time to go ahead. Lloyd hasn't told you the whole story,' Celina continued. 'I told you to let me be the one to tell them,' she scolded, frowning at Lloyd. 'Now you've made a right hash of things.'

Lloyd gave a resigned shrug. 'Go on, then, tell them everything. I was trying to break it to them gradually, bit by bit, but it's probably better if they know the whole story and everything that you've planned.'

'Hold it, this sounds like a very important decision so I think we all ought to have a drink or a cup of strong tea,' Owen stated. 'Let's clear up the party first and then sit down and you can start afresh.'

While Sarah tucked a very tired Rhoslyn up in bed, Alvia and Marie cleared away and washed everything up. Tactfully, they declined to stay, saying that it seemed to be a family matter that was going to be discussed and they'd leave Sarah to tell them about it in the morning.

Sarah made some coffee and as the four of

them settled down in comfortable chairs Sarah and Owen looked at Celina enquiringly.

'There is a lot more to it than Lloyd has said so far,' she told them. 'We had plenty of time on our own while you were away on your holiday and we realised not only how greatly we enjoyed each other's company but how much we meant to each other.'

'Do you mean that Dad is going to move into your place and that you will be living together?' Sarah asked in astonishment.

'We will be, yes.' She held up her hand as Sarah was about to say something. 'We have reached what we hope you will consider to be a sensible arrangement,' she added rather primly. She paused and took a sip of her coffee. 'I want you to hear me out before you say anything,' she told them as she put her cup and saucer down.

Sarah and Owen looked at each other in bewilderment as they sat back to listen.

At first Celina seemed to be a little hesitant but once she got going she told them in a well-thought-out way exactly what she and Lloyd had in mind.

Halfway through Owen reached out and took Sarah's hand in his and squeezed it almost as if to signal his approval of what Celina was saying, but Sarah felt too astounded to respond.

'Are you saying that you and my dad are planning to get married?' she gasped when Celina had finished.

'Yes, that's right, that's exactly what Celina is saying, cariad.' Lloyd nodded.

'Don't you approve?' Celina asked, biting down on her lower lip that was trembling so much it looked as though she was going to burst into tears at any moment.

'And you want us all to move to Pen-y-lan Road and live with you?'

'Yes,' Celina said and waited anxiously for a reaction.

'I can hardly believe my ears, but I certainly approve of you and Dad getting married,' Sarah assured her warmly. 'I know that if anyone can make him happy it is you. It's so comforting to know that he has someone who cares so much about him.'

Pulling herself up out of her chair she went over and kissed them both.

'What about my other suggestion?' Celina asked.

'You mean us moving in with you?' Sarah said doubtfully. 'I'm not too sure that is such a good idea. If you are right and I am going to have another baby,' she said with a teasing smile, 'think of all the upheaval that would cause.'

'It wouldn't really cause any upheaval,' Celina assured her. 'My house is over twice the size of this one. There are four large bedrooms so if you should have a little boy this time he can have a room to himself.'

Sarah turned to look at Owen. 'What do you

think?' she asked. 'So far you haven't said a word.'

'It's a lot to take in,' Owen said sombrely. 'It certainly has some good points,' he added quickly. 'I agree with Sarah that I am very happy for you both but it's this business of us all living together that might prove to be a stumbling block.'

He stood up and placed his cup and saucer on the table. 'You know what they say, two women in the same kitchen . . .'

Celina didn't give him a chance to finish. 'That's all nonsense,' she said crisply. 'For one thing, neither Sarah nor I will be spending very much time in the kitchen because we have a housekeeper to look after all that sort of thing and to do the cooking. That alone will make life so much easier for Sarah and, furthermore, there will always be someone around to keep an eye on Rhoslyn when Sarah is at the office with you, Owen.'

'Rhoslyn will be off to school in a year's time,' Owen murmured.

'Yes, and by then there will be another baby who has to be looked after,' Celina told him promptly.

'You'll have to give us a while to talk all this over,' Owen said, stalling for time. 'It's all come as rather a shock.'

'Well, don't take too long about it. We need to start making plans and getting everything else organised for our wedding. It will be a very quiet affair, of course, but nevertheless there will still be quite a lot to do before the big day.'

There was so much going on in their lives over the next few months that Sarah found the time was flashing past. Fortunately her morning sickness was short-lived and from then on she felt extremely fit.

When she confirmed that the baby was due around Easter, Lloyd and Celina decided on an autumn wedding. Rhoslyn was to be bridesmaid and once they told her this she chattered about nothing else from the time she woke up in the morning until she went to bed at night.

They also told her that there would be a new baby but at the moment all she could envisage was being dressed up in a pretty white dress with a frilled skirt, rosebud trimming around the neck, and little puff sleeves.

She constantly rehearsed the part she would be playing either following Celina around the house pretending to be holding her train, or standing in front of the cheval mirror pretending to be taking the bouquet from Celina.

Even after she had agreed that they would move to Pen-y-lan Road, Sarah insisted that they went on living at Cyfartha Street until after the wedding. She planned that they would move whatever furniture they decided to keep and all their other possessions in while Lloyd and Celina were away on their honeymoon.

'When you come back it will be the start of

a new life for all of us. It will also give us plenty of time to get settled in before Christmas,' she said.

It was a beautiful warm, sunny September day when Lloyd and Celina got married. The church was packed with employees from Morgan's and several of Celina's own friends who lived nearby. Alvia and Marie were there, both of them wearing outstanding new hats that brought a smile from Owen.

Rhoslyn behaved perfectly and looked like a little angel in her dainty dress and with flowers in her hair. Her only disappointment was that although she'd been practising for ages how she would have to carry Celina's train she found that there wasn't one.

'I thought that a white wedding with all those sorts of things would be out of place at my age,' Celina said smiling.

Instead, she wore an oyster two-piece with cream shoes and a very ornate cream cloche hat which was tastefully trimmed with oyster-coloured silk roses.

Lloyd looked extremely smart in a new dark suit and a light cream-coloured shirt with a cream silk tie which had thin black stripes on it.

Sarah chose a navy blue loose coat in slubbed silk over a lighter blue dress and a dark blue cloche hat decorated with light blue silk flowers.

After the simple ceremony the family went

to a restaurant for a very special meal before Lloyd and Celina set off on a two-week tour of North Wales.

It was somewhere that neither of them had ever visited before. 'We're both looking forward to enjoying the scenery; seeing Snowdon and exploring all those great castles,' Lloyd told Sarah and Owen.

After Christmas, as the days to her confinement drew closer, Sarah sometimes wondered how she had ever managed to do all the mundane domestic jobs that had been her responsibility in the past. Now there was a daily woman to take care of all the scrubbing and general cleaning as well as a cook-housekeeper to make sure that meals were always served on time and there was no clearing away or washing-up to be done afterwards.

Donkey-stoning the steps, washing, mangling and ironing all their clothes and household linen, were no longer her responsibility either and although she still spent several days a week working at the office she felt nowhere near as tired as she'd done in the past.

Celina had made a good many changes in her house to ensure their comfort and welfare. Living together as one big family was proving far more enjoyable than Sarah had ever imagined it would be and so carefree and different from when she had been a child.

Later in the year Rhoslyn would be starting

school but she would be under no pressure from any of them to work hard or always be top of the class. Not only was Lloyd far more easygoing these days but he also readily admitted that he'd been wrong to pressurise Sarah so much when she'd been at school.

Lloyd and Celina were both so happy and contented that it was a delight to be in their company. They adored Rhoslyn but they were careful to make it clear to her that her Mummy and Daddy were the ones she was answerable to and they never interfered with any rules Sarah and Owen imposed.

Rhoslyn had also been encouraged to mix with other children. They occasionally played out in the street but more often than not Lloyd and Celina would take her and a little friend along to the park.

School seemed to hold no fears for Rhoslyn, but long before that eventful day there would be an even more momentous occasion when the new baby arrived. Sarah knew that Owen was hoping that it would be a boy who perhaps one day would take over the running of the business, but they were now such a happy, united family that the baby would be surrounded by love whether it was a boy or a girl.